TAMING FIRE

International Bestselling Author

ELIZABETH KNIGHT

Knight, Elizabeth
Taming Fire

Editing: Ms. K Editing & Leavens Editing
Cover artist: Ryn Katryn Book Covers

CHAPTER 1
LAILAH

The world was dark and the air smelt of ash, as the heat battered against my skin. I was, once again, back in hell, causing the symbols that had been carved into my skin to ache as they reminded me it was here I got them. There was a lime green glow flickering in the distance that had a scream crawling up my throat, but I couldn't make a sound. I was frozen, unable to move. Materializing in front of me, his fluorescent green flames flickering, gave me enough light to see him. I didn't need it though, the sight of him was burned into my mind, along with these scars on my body.

His razor sharp teeth grinned at me, and I felt his gaze on me even though he had no eyes, just black voids. A clawed hand reached out to me from his black exoskeletal humanoid body, that showed every bone that made up his form. The Dark Lord's face was a hybrid of a bat and human, sharp cheekbones and pointed ears. The top of his skull rose up, shaped like a crown of black bone flaring up with sharp points, making you think he was the ruler of hell —but he wasn't.

"You are mine, Synergy... you will host the Mother of All..."

Just when I thought he was going to reach me and torture me once again, the scene shifted and I was straddling a man. My hand was tightly gripped around the handle of my Sai that was plunged into his chest. He coughed up blood as his all too human eyes looked at me with judgement.

"My death is on your hands, Synergy. You might have killed me... but I'm not the only one..."

When I tried to let go of the Sai, I couldn't. Marvin wrapped his bloody hands around mine and laughed as if he heard the funniest joke in the whole world. No matter what I did, or how hard I tried to get away from him, his grip held me tight, his laughter echoing in my ears tormenting me with his death, until all I could do was sob...

"Angel, wake up. It's just a dream, you're okay we've got you," Brayden soothed as he pulled me into his arms and smoothed a hand over my wild curls. "Come on Angel, come back to me."

Another set of hands stroked softly down my back, placing gentle kisses on the exposed skin of my arms and shoulders. Gasping, I pulled in a deep breath of air, my eyes popping open at the same time to meet a pair of sky blue eyes.

"There you are Sunshine," Hudson murmured with the hint of a smile on his lips. "Take another deep breath for me, counting to five, like we've been practicing."

Hudson took my hand and placed it on his chest so I could breathe along with him. We stayed like that until I could breathe easily and I was no longer shaking. Each of them silently waiting for me to tell them when I was grounded again.

"I'm good now, thank you," I said as I sat up rubbing my face, trying to shake off the last of the nightmare.

That fateful day four months ago, on a day that typically represented starting a fresh new year, wasn't so much the case for me that New Year's Day. The Lailah that went into the catacombs didn't come out the same. It started in the form of nightmares, panic attacks, and scars littering my body, all in the name of saving mankind. The boys had been amazing, doing anything I needed, to help me deal with the repercussions of that day—but I worried I would never be the same.

The biggest, being that I couldn't sleep alone anymore, otherwise I would be trapped in one hellish nightmare after another with no one to pull me out of them. There was no outward sign that I was trapped spiraling from one terror to another, because nothing about this could be easy. All of them rotated the job, but since I was Bonded to Brayden and Hudson, our connection would wake them up when I fell into a nightmare. Jay was always a light sleeper, so he was quick to respond to my change in breathing, but Micah and Parker were struggling. In an effort to keep them included, we just made sure they were with me along with one of the others.

They had all brought up having me Bond with all of them right away, but I was in no shape to go through that level of emotional connection right now. It was bad enough that Brayden and Hudson had a front row seat to my emotions and nervous breakdowns over the stupidest things. Most of the time, it was someone touching me without realizing they were there, or when we had combat training and I was pinned down. My mind flashed back to the Dark Lord's ritual and him carving symbols into my skin.

The good news though, was that I made it through my first year of college and I was going home for the summer. Even better, was the boys were coming home with me for the whole summer. Cami also demanded to come, but Maggs couldn't leave for that long with the work she does for the Elementi. I didn't blame my best friend for being torn between coming with me and staying here with her girlfriend, who she was madly in love with. I'm not sure I could survive all summer without my boys with me, but thankfully, I didn't have to find out. Right now, the plan is for Cami to come with us, stay for a few weeks and fly back to be with Maggs. If it worked out they could both make a trip out, then we would send the plane for them.

"You managed to sleep longer tonight," Hudson mentioned as he made notes in his journal, ever my sexy scholar.

Seeing him sitting there in the dim light of the setting moon, his normally perfect blond hair tousled with sleep, with his black square framed glasses perched on his nose. He was my sounding board, the one I always wanted to talk to when I had a problem because he could always look at things logically. With everything that happened, it was all so overwhelming, and I was angry at how I was reacting to things. He would stop whatever he was doing, take my hands and walked me through what was overwhelming me, breaking it down to what I had to accomplish in that moment.

Hudson didn't handle the unknown well, so I understood why writing in his notebook had become an obsession. It was a way for him to have some control in a situation where he couldn't do much to help me otherwise.

I loved him even more for it, plus it did show me that I was making progress in some areas. Sleep was the hardest. I felt so vulnerable, and with whatever aftereffects the serum and the marks on my skin had on me, I was now connected to Hell whether I liked it or not. That being said, it was harder for me to leave the school grounds, where the wards kept us safe and the demons away. Every time I stepped out of their protective net, I could sense them all around me, lurking in the shadows. This would then trigger a panic attack but I was working on it, because I refused to be trapped here and unable to live my life. The demons would not win, and they certainly wouldn't be controlling my ability to end this war, thereby protecting everyone that's become important to me.

"What time is it?" I asked, half crawling over Brayden to get a look at the clock.

The bright red letters told me it was four in the morning-- it was later than most days, and I knew I couldn't go back to sleep. Groaning, I moved to get out of bed but Brayden had other ideas, wrapping me up tightly in his arms.

"Nope, you can't leave until you pay the toll," he demanded with an exaggerated frown on his handsome face.

I looked into his hazel eyes which shone with his love for me, causing me to smile. Sweeping his rich brown hair out of his face, I cupped his cheek and leaned in for a kiss, which lit up our Bond. The warmth and safety that I felt flowing into me, as our powers swirled around us, made me sigh, relaxing into him. With all the training we do, all my boys had fit bodies and now with the warmer weather, Brayden was not wearing a shirt. The feel of his skin against mine grounded me to this world, casting out all other thoughts of Hell or its inhabitants. This was the gift only my Earth Knight could give me, the peace of knowing I was loved and belonged right here beside him, on this earth.

Breaking the kiss, I leaned back with both my hands on his chest, grinning. "Was that fair payment?"

"I mean, I would have settled for a hug, but that was way better," Brayden teased wagging his brows at me.

Giving him another quick peck on the nose, he let me slide out of bed and I headed off to shower. The few times we'd tried to be intimate, I'd gotten too overwhelmed or accidentally trapped on my back when things got heated. Now, all the guys were too worried to do more than kiss and cuddle until they felt I was ready. Let's just say that I was more than ready to give it another try but convincing them was turning out to be harder than I thought. Especially because we were going to my home, where my parents and little brother were. The thought of being caught might excite Jay, but having it happen by my parents was not on my sexy time bucket that Cami had me making.

I wasn't surprised in the least to have Hudson join me in the shower, it had kind of become his thing in caring for me. With five of them all wanting to spend time with me, I had to find ways to get alone time with them throughout the day. Hudson seemed to love helping wash me in the shower, and being of service any way that he could to make my life easier. He'd become a master at shampooing my hair and I was glad that he was bound to me for life so I didn't ever have to go without that indulgence. I kept telling him he didn't need to be awake just because I was, but he wouldn't have it, ignoring my efforts to get him to sleep in. We'd created a routine so there was a comfortable silence that hung around us as steam filled the air.

"Are you excited to go home?" Hudson asked as he worked on my hair.

"To be honest, I have mixed emotions when it comes to this trip. I'm excited to be home and see my family but that also means I have a lot of explaining to do as well," I sighed, leaning back against Hudson's chest. "The ten hour flight we have to make is not something I'm looking forward to--something always seems to go wrong."

Hudson didn't answer me right away but I wasn't surprised, he wasn't one to speak just to fill the silence. "What if your parents know about the Elementi?"

Shocked by that idea, I turned to face him. "What makes you think they would have a clue about the Elementi?"

"The Elementi might be founded here in Europe, but they have facilities all over the world. There are two large bases in Washington DC and in Los Angeles, where the most activity happens with the demons. Personally, I think they need a bigger presence with how large America is and the swiftly changing status of power, not only in government but in businesses as well," Hudson informed me. "All that to say, there could be a chance that your family might have, at one point, had a connection to the Elementi and that is how you were able to have the same gene we do as Elemental Warriors."

When he put it that way, it was hard not to see how that made perfect sense. If my family did have a connection, even distantly, it would make it so much easier to explain all of this to them. "Let's hope that's the case because I don't want to hurt my family when they find out who and what we are," I murmured, dropping my head to stare at my feet.

Hudson framed my face with his hands, drawing my

head upwards to meet his gaze. "Sunshine, they are your family and they raised you to be the woman you are today, who has more than enough love in her to share it with five men who don't always deserve it. How could they not look past this and see that you are still their daughter, just with a bigger purpose in life than they expected?"

He leaned down to kiss my forehead, then my nose, and finally landed on my lips, causing me to wrap my arms around his neck so he wouldn't stop. I started to push him backwards till he bumped into the tiled wall of the shower. I hitched a leg over his hip, making it clear what my intentions were. Instead, he twirled us around, pushing me to sit on the bench that was built into the shower, and sank to his knees. Giving me a heated look, he spread me wide giving him enough space to work with, as he buried his face in my vagina. Gasping, I tossed my head back, arching into him as he artfully flicked his tongue over my clit and slid two fingers inside me.

The man, whose virginity I took when we Bonded, has now become quite masterful at turning me into a puddle of need. Slow rhythmic thrusts, timed perfectly with his tongue, had me crying out in pleasure as he teased me right to the edge, only to stop. My hand found his hair and I gripped it, urging him to continue and not to leave me hanging. He flicked his gaze up to me and I could see the grin on his face as he watched the need written all over mine.

"If you leave the job unfinished, you are not welcome in my showers for a week," I threatened.

It had been far too long since I'd managed to get one of them to give me an orgasm of any kind and doing it myself was no longer satisfying.

Hudson lifted his face to look at me seriously. "Do you really believe that I would leave you wanting?"

"All of you have been for weeks," I said, trying not to growl with my building frustration. "All of you treat me like I'm glass and if you do the wrong thing, I'll break."

His face turned into a scowl at my words, that not at all what he thought I would be saying. "You weren't ready, Lailah. A man can only watch the woman he loves panic so many times, before something has to change."

Sitting up, I grabbed his shoulders and slid myself onto his lap, his thick cock sandwiched between us. "Things have changed—I've changed. Just don't put me on my back and there shouldn't be a problem."

I could see the conflict in his face as his eyes searched mine. I lifted myself up high enough that I caught the tip of his cock with where I longed for it to be. Giving him a chance to tell me no, I paused, but then he wrapped himself around me and helped to lower me onto his rock hard dick. A whimper of pleasure at finally being filled escaped, causing Hudson to thrust up into me until he was fully seated inside.

"Oh, thank god," I sighed, resting my head on his shoulder as I moved, rolling my hips to take him as deep as I could.

Our breathing picked up and moans of pleasure echoed in the shower as we reconnected with one another on a level we both needed. I sped up and lifted off him higher, so I could grind myself against him harder, using the friction to work my clit. Then, much to my surprise, Hudson reached around back and started to massage my back door. Of course, with five guys in my life, there had been talk about all we could do with so many of us, but I didn't think Hudson would be one to give up his alone time with me.

The feeling of him inserting the tip of his finger to the first knuckle was the final piece to throw me over the edge, into an orgasm unlike I'd had in months. My whole body started to shake as Hudson also came, hitting the right spot to send me spiraling once more.

It took us a moment to come back to our bodies after that and even then, all we could manage was to sit on the bench, holding each other up until our legs worked once more.

"Now, that is the type of reaction I can handle seeing you have when I'm making love to you," Hudson announced, making me fall into a fit of laughter.

CHAPTER 2

LAILAH

"Trouble," Parker scolded when he entered the kitchen.

After Hudson and I finished our shower, he'd gone off to check on his lab before we left, and I retreated to the one place in this house that put me at peace—the kitchen. My parents owned a diner back in Wisconsin and my mother taught me how to cook at a very early age. I was a good cook, but my passion was baking, and being unable to sleep once I'd woken up from nightmares, I found myself down here baking myself a snack. Sarah was the cook, along with her husband Garrett, but she never stood in the way of me baking for the boys so she didn't have to keep up with their bottomless pit of a stomach-- her words not mine. I don't know what it was about the process, but it allowed me to be completely focused on the task at hand, forgetting all about what's happened.

I glanced up from the oven where I'd just pulled out a batch of cinnamon chip scones, to find Parker, arms crossed and scowling at me. "Good morning to you too."

Parker, the light hearted playful one out of the group, fit

the jock profile to a T. He was buff and well filled out, like a football player, with a shock of red hair styled in his signature faux-hawk. His warm brown eyes shimmered with mischief, telling me that he wasn't really upset with me, but playing the part.

"It's six-thirty, which means if you are taking something out of the oven you've been awake for some time now," Parker reasoned. "You should be cuddled up in bed even if you can't sleep, why not read one of your sexy harem books. For research of course, didn't Cami help you find a bunch of them to put on the kindle we got you?"

I set aside the oven pads and walked over to him to snuggle in against his broad chest. For the man who was all heart, figuratively and literally, this had been the hardest on him, as much as it was on me. Blessed with the element of spirit, or heart as he liked to call it, he could manipulate emotions but nothing he did could make my situation better. He beat himself up over it and took it personally, as if he'd failed me somehow. So, seeing me up and about early, knowing it was because of my nightmares, made him grumpy, which was far more Micah's thing.

"I thought it would be nice for us to have these on the flight," I muttered into his chest. "Besides, reading is great but baking helps to sooth me."

Pulling me away so he could see my face, he booped me on the nose. "You know I will never turn down anything you make, I already asked you to marry me because of your pie crusts. I just can't help but worry about you not getting enough sleep to deal with everything else going on."

"It's the summer, classes are done, and we get a break from training for me to go spend time with my family," I countered. "What if I promise that I will let you be in charge of making sure I have fun and relax while we are in the States?"

"You drive a hard bargain, Trouble, but I think I can work with those terms," Parker answered, flashing me a bright smile, before pulling me back into a tight hug. "By the way, the walls are not that sound proof."

Blushing, I shoved him away from me. "It was about damn time someone made me scream."

"I didn't realize that was on the table for me." Parker challenged.

Leaning against the island I crossed my arms, staring him down. "You never asked."

"Wait, am I late to the game here?" Parker asked, now looking concerned.

"No," I groaned. "That was the first bit of action I've seen in over a month and a half."

"Good thing we rented a house in town to stay at while we're visiting, then we don't have to worry about keeping you quiet," Parker said with a smirk.

"What are we keeping her quiet for?" Cami chimed in as she entered the kitchen.

I gaped at her, making a dramatic show of looking at my wrist that had no watch, then back at her. "Is the world coming to an end? Do I see Cami Whittemore in all her neon pink haired glory awake, dressed, and dare I say, perky?"

"Ha, ha, very funny Lala," Cami answered dryly. "You know we have to leave for the airport in like thirty minutes, and a plane waits for no one, even if they are privately owned. *Ooo*, did you bake?"

Chuckling, I nodded and moved back to the oven to take them off the hot tray and put them on the cool granite counter. "You'll have to wait. They're for breakfast on the plane."

Both Cami and Parker groaned at that, making me shake my head, grinning. Those two were so much alike it was crazy, it was one of the reasons they got along, but also seemed to get into large amounts of trouble.

"I'm going to check on Micah and make sure he's awake, I know how many are sitting there and when I come back there better be the same number," I glared at them both as I left the kitchen. "Sarah made muffins yesterday. They're in the Tupperware on the counter."

"Fuck yeah," Parker yelled behind me. He was right, this house wasn't very soundproof and I hadn't been quiet...

Upstairs, I stopped at the first door on the right but didn't bother to knock as I entered, knowing the chances of Micah still being asleep were high—and I was right. Curled up in his bed, with a pillow over his head, was the fire lord himself. In an odd way, he reminded me of the Heatmiser from that old Christmas movie, full of hot air. He had a temper and tended to act before he thought about things, but we were working on it, and he'd come a long way from the boy I sat on sleeping in the library. I tugged the pillow off his head, revealing his long thick brown hair that I gently brushed out of his face.

"Time to wake up grumpy pants," I whispered.

"Fuck off," he grumbled and pulled the blankets over his head.

"Remember I tried to be nice," I warned, standing up and walking to the end of the bed. I gripped the sheets and yanked, letting them fall to the floor, leaving him exposed in only his boxers.

This had him shooting up in bed, his dual swords in hand, ready to fight off whatever evil might be upon him.

"Green Day boxers, those are new," I commented, cocking my head to the side taking in the full picture, grinning.

"What the actual fuck, Lailah?" he muttered, cobalt eyes flashing in anger. "I could have attacked you!"

I raised a brow at that, knowing how much he prided himself at being in control of his powers. Being the bearer of the fire element came with its own set of problems, being one of the most volatile to control. "Micah, I trust you with my life. Do you really think I'm worried about waking you up in the morning? I tried to do it the easy way and you told me to f-off so this was the next option. Although, I could have asked Parker to help..."

Micah all but growled as he got out of bed and charged over to me, boxing me in against the wall. "That would not be a very wise move there, Cookie."

"No? I thought you and Parker were trying to work on mending bridges?" I questioned, knowing I was tiptoeing the line of stirring the pot.

Something about Micah brought out the combative side of my nature, the one that I kept strictly limited to my inner monologue or t-shirts. My collection of sassy shirts was only growing, now that my boys wanted in on the game that my brothers started.

"We are—like you asked us to, but having him in my room is not a bridge I want to fix. A man needs space where he knows that he can be himself, without someone judging him," Micah retorted.

I let out a heavy sigh. Things between them had gotten marginally better since they all worked hard to take care of me, but it didn't stop the snarky comments and cheap shots at each other. They had a long history, with many potholes, but the fact that they were both Elemental Warriors meant they would always be in each other's lives, no matter what. Add on the fact that they would be Bonded to me, and it was just something they were going to have to figure out.

"You packed? We're leaving in a half hour or so, Cami's already here," I asked, reaching up to wrap my hands around his arms still keeping me captive.

Micah grunted his answer as he took another step forward, melding out bodies together. Dipping his head, he captured my lips with his, making me moan as the connection, that was begging us to Bond, hummed between us. Back closer to Christmas, I'd asked for his Oath and he turned me down, saying he wasn't ready, then I wasn't the one who was ready when he brought it up. Now, I couldn't think of the reason why on Earth I didn't want this man to be declared mine for the rest of our lives together.

"Rumor through the walls is someone finally got lucky this morning," Micah whispered, lips brushing along mine. "Does this mean we can talk about making this official?"

"We can talk about it, but I'll tell you right now it's not gonna happen in the next thirty minutes," I chuckled, pressing a kiss to his lips and ducking under his arm. "Don't worry about breakfast, I made scones."

"That is not fucking breakfast, that's what you have for dessert after the real food," Micah yelled when I shut the door behind me as I left.

Smirking to myself, I ran right into a muscular chest covered in a tight black t-shirt that fit snuggly enough for anyone to know he had a six pack. I let out a surprised squeak as arms wrapped around me to keep me from falling back. Jay's handsome face greeted me with a smile tugging at his lips, showing just how much he enjoyed being able to surprise me. It had become a game to him, once he discovered how easily he could do it when we first met. His almond shaped, slate colored eyes gave me a critical look, always searching to make sure that I was safe from harm. Jay was showered, dressed, and alert, probably already having gone on a five mile run. Having grown up in a very strict militant family he couldn't help but act like the soldier he was raised to be, from the buzzed hair to the fatigues he always wore. His father owned the largest private military group in all of the eastern hemisphere based in Dubai. This left his family back in Japan, until he brought Jay to live with him and raised him on base for his teenage years.

"Beautiful, did you eat?" Jay asked.

Even before any of this happened to me, Jay was the overprotective one, always making sure I was looked after. He was always taking me on runs to keep me fit and stable when I came into my power, always having food on hand now that I burned more calories, and making sure I didn't get lost by driving me to and from school, no matter what time it was.

"No," I raised as he scowled at me. "I made a smoothie. It's in the fridge. I just wanted to wait until I had everything packed."

"I'll go get it," Jay announced and headed down the stairs.

Rolling my eyes, I headed into my bedroom where my suitcase was on the bed, open and waiting for any last minute things I needed to pack. Since I was coming back here, and I had plenty of summer clothes back home, I didn't need to bring a whole lot. I had Christmas presents for everyone ,along with other things I picked up along the way. My family was small town living to the max, and I didn't really see them doing much international travel, but if I ended up living out here permanently that might change. Telling my parents that I was going to have five husbands seemed even more daunting than explaining about the Elementi and demons. Like Brayden loved to tell me, I currently had two husbands, was engaged to two, and dating another but hoped to be engaged or married soon to all of them.

"Need any help?" Cami asked as she flopped onto my bed, stuffing the last bite of a muffin into her mouth.

"I'm good, just the last few things from the bathroom and I'm good to go," I said over my shoulder as I grabbed them.

"You know I've been all over the place, but I've never spent much time in America besides the DC office. I'm so excited to see what your life was like before you found out about the Elementi and became Synergy," Cami shared, bouncing on the bed hardly containing her joy.

Cami, my pixie of a best friend, was the definition of small but mighty. She was an Elementi soldier who was assigned to be my bodyguard when I hadn't come into my powers yet. She was my first friend and with her personality, need for adrenalin, and always pushing me out of my comfort zone, the only friend I needed. Between her, the boys, and of course Maggs, I was kept plenty busy. I didn't think I'd have time for anything else.

"Oh, do they have clubs? We have to go dancing, it's not summer break without dancing! What about a beach? Someone said we'd be close to water, is that true?" Cami asked, barraging me with questions.

Zipping up my suitcase, I hopped on the bed next to her. "My hometown is really small but it's not too far for us to go to one of the bigger cities where we can find a club. Yes, there is a beach we can hit up a few hours away, it could be a fun day trip or even a camp out!"

"Fuck yes, we are going to have so much fun!" Cami exclaimed, clapping her hands.

A knock sounded on my door, drawing our attention to Jay and Brayden standing there. "Time to go ladies," Brayden called.

Grabbing my suitcase, I headed for the door, but Jay appeared, thrust the smoothie into my hand and took my bag from me. Kissing the top of my head, he marched out and down the stairs without a word. Cami caught my eye and smiled. We had come a long way, these boys and I, but this was just the start of it.

CHAPTER 3
LAILAH

"Can we just talk about how crazy it is that we are showing up and starting the same day over again," Cami announced from where she was sprawled out on the plane. "Like, it will be dinner time back home but it will be late morning of the same day."

"Good thing we've been napping the whole flight," I chuckled from where I was curled up between Micah and Brayden.

Cami gave me a disapproving look. "Yeah, everyone but you, missy."

"What can I say, I got sucked into a good series and I just started book two," I answered with a shrug. The boys knew I didn't sleep unless I had to, knowing what awaited me when I did.

Jay caught my eye and motioned for me to join him where he was, tablet in hand. I extracted myself out of the tangle of limbs I was in and slid into the seat next to him.

"What's up?" I asked, peering over at the tablet.

"I thought it was time to show you the house we picked out," Jay explained, offering me the tablet.

My jaw dropped when I saw the house, then he flicked a finger across the screen to show the next image. "Oh my god, it's a lake house!"

Jay chuckled as he continued to scroll through the pictures. It was made to look like a log cabin but massive and modern, giving it a much more expensive look. It had a beautiful stone driveway, with a large garage for at least four cars. Six bedrooms and five baths, giving everyone plenty of space and won't feel too crammed. The inside was just as stunning as the outside, and oddly enough it reminded me of the house we stayed at in Austria, which I'd loved. This one was obviously bigger with a gourmet kitchen, large dining room, and sprawling living room with a massive fireplace.

"Is that a loft with a pool table and bar set up?" I asked, zooming in on the picture. "Holy shit, look at the windows on that side of the house facing the lake. Whoa, it has a movie room too?!"

"So does that mean you like it?" Hudson asked from his seat across from us.

"Who wouldn't love a house like that? I can't believe it's even in the same town I grew up in. All those lakes are private and the homes are crazy expensive, so I forget they're even there," I answered. "I'm still in awe that you guys could rent something like that for the summer." Micah and Brayden were now awake and even Parker was up from his section of the couch, watching me intently. "What?"

Jay reached out and took my chin in his hand, pulling me back to look at him. "Beautiful, we didn't rent it. We bought it."

"Shut the fuck up!" I gasped. "You did not just buy a house in Wisconsin to spend the summer in!"

"No, we bought the house because that is where your

family lives and you'll want to come back and forth to see them. You're a married woman now, Angel, and we need our own space, since there are six of us all together," Brayden clarified. "This isn't going to be the last time we're here and we all agreed that buying a home was the best option... you're not mad are you?"

Cami burst out in laughter, rolling off the couch. "Lover boy, it's way too late to be asking that question. You done already bought the house."

"Knock it off, pint-size ankle biter, we can just turn around and sell it if she doesn't like it," Micah grumbled, tossing a pillow at Cami.

"That wasn't my point, flame-boy," Cami shot back, using the pillow to prop herself up against the couch. "What I meant is, that if you were worried she would be mad, you should have asked first *then* bought the house together."

"She does make a valid point," Hudson cut in. "How do you feel about us buying a house, Sunshine?"

His question brought all the attention to me once again. "Ah, well...the house is stunning and I like it very much."

"But..." Parker ventured.

"Why did you feel the need to do this without talking to me about it? I wouldn't have said no—at least I don't think I would. I just would have preferred to be included in the discussion, this was a big decision and if we're a family, like you all keep saying we are, then we need to make these choices together," I explained meeting each of their gazes, so they knew I wasn't mad, just a little thrown off.

"That is a fair request," Hudson agreed. "In the future, we will do as you've requested, but just know that we bought this house completely with you in mind and if you don't want it, then it defeats the point."

I let out a dramatic sigh. "No, we can keep the house."

Brayden and Micah high-fived, Parker grinned at me, and both Hudson and Jay looked pleased with my choice. Cami jumped to her feet and snatched the tablet from my hands.

"Let's take a gander at this new house of yours, shall we. I have to pick out my bedroom before you guys take all the good ones," Cami declared as she flipped through the images. "Did you guys get it furnished or do you need to buy everything when you get there?"

That thought hadn't even crossed my mind until she said it.

"No, we got it furnished, it was a summer home that the previous owner hardly used, so everything is practically brand new," Micah answered. "That being said, I'm totally redoing my bedroom. The wilderness theme is not gonna stay."

I sat there, leaning my head against Jay's shoulder, lost in thought about the fact that the guys bought a house. Not just that, but it was my house too, for all of us to live in for as long as we wanted. It had taken me months to wrap my head around dating them all, now we were investing in our future. I didn't quite know what to do with that. It did surprise me that they could do all this without me knowing, and Parker was well aware of it, so that meant he'd been involved as well. I still don't understand what happened between all of them in France, but whatever it was seemed to be working itself out slowly but surely.

"Did you see the lake has a private beach for us to use?" Brayden asked, drawing me out of my thoughts.

Flashing him a smile, I nodded. "That will make the summer even more amazing, and I saw a dock for a boat too. That lake isn't very big, but it would be fun to get a kayak or two to paddle around in."

"I have a feeling we'll come up with lots of ways to make that house just what we need it to be," Brayden assured me. "It's only twenty minutes away from your parents place, so it's close but not *too* close."

"You guys really tried to think of everything, didn't you?"

Brayden shrugged. "We knew it was a risky move to make, so we tried to think of everything you would want to incorporate. Two cars got delivered yesterday, so we have transportation to use as well."

"Oh, then I'll give my car to Kyle for when he's ready to drive, just like I got it from Dylan," I shared, warming at that thought.

My family might own the only diner in the town, and be successful leaving us well enough off, but buying a car was a big expense for most people. Besides, it was always better to get a beater car that didn't matter as much if you crashed it. Although Kyle was a freshman in high school, he was only thirteen, having advanced a grade when he was younger. His teachers wanted to do it again with how smart he is, but my mother refused. Kyle might be book smart, but it wasn't fair to put him in a setting with much older kids when he just wasn't there yet. He ended up getting a scholarship to a prestigious private high school, so that was making a world of difference according to mom's weekly emails.

"I'm excited to meet this savant little brother of yours," Hudson interjected. "I have a feeling he will be a lot like my sister, Grace."

"Hope you brought your A-game for chess, it's his favorite thing to do with every smart person he meets. Says it tells him all about the person with no words needed," I laughed, knowing how terribly I fail at that game.

"Is he into computers?" Parker asked.

The thing I loved about Parker is that he was an under-cover nerd. You never would guess that he was at the top of our school for his computer programming and technology skills. I guess it comes from having a father who owns the largest tech company in the world, but Parker was truly gifted. One thing we do to spend time together is play video games of all kinds. I suck at them, but that wasn't the point.

"He does love computer games but since we have to buy all that stuff with our own money, he doesn't have many," I answered.

"Do we get to meet Dylan too?" Brayden inquired.

I knew how much family meant to him and being able to introduce himself to my big brother was something he really wanted. He'd almost called my dad multiple times to tell him we were together and practically married, but I reasoned with him that it was something to do in person, like we had with his family over Christmas.

"Mom did say that he had a summer internship with a law office in Madison, but he was going to take some time off to spend with all of us," I shared.

"*This is your captain speaking, we are preparing for our final descent into the airport*," the pilot announced over the speaker.

We all started to gather our things that we'd taken out or used during the long flight, and settled into the chairs, buckling in.

"So, the plan is that my parents are picking us all up at the airport and we'll head back to my house. Knowing my mother, she's probably made a huge feast for us to eat once we get there," I said as I peered out the window, looking over the small private airport that we were flying into.

"That will be good, you've only had your smoothie and half a scone the whole trip," Jay scolded.

"Yeah, I'm fucking hungry too," Parker admitted, his stomach growling its agreement.

Cami scoffed at Parker, tossing the Tupperware that had held the scones. "You ate all the damn food before some of us could even have one, you bottomless pit. This spread better be big, because my stomach might be eating itself."

"You act like there wasn't any food on this flight, all you had to do was ask for something and they would have given it to you," Micah snapped.

"Did my beloved Lala make what they have to offer? No, then shut your trap," Cami shot back, crossing her arms in a huff.

I squeezed Jay's hand, drawing him away from the argument happening around us. "It's always been hard for me to eat on travel days. I just get so excited." Jay clearly didn't accept that as a good enough answer, if his frown was anything to go by.

"So, what do your parents know about us?" Micah asked, leaning forward in his seat, watching me intently.

"They know you're all coming, that we are extremely close, and I'm dating Brayden," I answered, getting a look of disapproval from most of them. "Let me be clear— in no way am I ashamed of our relationship. I'd told my mom about Brayden before things progressed as quickly as they have with the rest of you. I felt like it would be easier to explain with all of us together, so we could answer their questions."

This seemed to settle them—for now.

"I'm not going to act any differently around you just because you haven't told them," Micah warned.

I knew he was going to have the hardest time dealing with me wanting to ease my parents into this. He'd lost so many people in his life already and the one blood relative he still had any contact with hated him. I had zero love for her myself after our brief meeting at the Christmas party Brayden's parents hosted. My hope was that Dylan might be able to help us find a way to get his aunt out of his life, and cut off from his money that she was 'guarding' until he was twenty-one. His fear was that she would drain the money out of the trust, or try to take the company before his birthday in September.

"Never expected you to, Micah," I reassured him. "This wasn't some plan to keep all this hidden, it's just hard when they haven't met you to understand how amazing you all are, regardless of our Bond."

With a *thump* and roar of the engines, we landed, cutting off our conversation as the plane taxied into our designated spot for de-boarding. This was the best part about a private plane, we could land in the smaller airports, making it a much shorter trip for my parents. Thirty minutes versus an hour was a big deal, and an even bigger bonus... no waiting for baggage to arrive. The flight attendant opened the door and latched on the stairs, signaling we could now get off the damn plane. I didn't bother to grab my suitcase, knowing I could come back on and grab it, as I dashed out of the plane and into the sunlight finding my parents and Kyle waving when they saw me. Running down the steps, I threw myself into my dad's arms and my mom quickly got in on the hug, squishing me in-between them. Finally, they let me go and Mom took me by the shoulders, looking me over. I'd made sure to wear a light sweater and leggings, so they didn't see the scars right away.

"Oh Ladybug, how I've missed you," Mom sobbed, as big fat tears rolled down her cheek. "I don't think I like you living so far away."

"Bonnie, we talked about this," Dad warned, putting an arm around Mom's shoulders. "You promised not to make our little girl feel bad for getting an education."

"I know, I know, but look how much she's grown up and we missed it," Mom pointed out, lifting her hands to cup my face. "Our Ladybug's all grown up."

The sound of someone clearing their throat drew our attention to where Kyle was waiting. "Can I say hello to her now?"

I laughed at that and pulled out of Mom's arms to hug my, not so little, brother. Kyle had gone through a growth spurt, and I now had to look up to meet his gaze. Granted, I was only five foot three, but still when I'd last seen him he was a bit shorter than me. It wasn't just his height that had changed either, he was buff and his hair was longer, letting the curl show. Hockey season had just finished so that could account for the new buff bod, but it still caught me off guard, having never gone this long without seeing him or my parents.

"What is Mom feeding you that you turned into a giant?" I teased, punching him gently on the shoulder.

Kyle just shrugged and blushed at my words. "Whatever."

Deciding to free him from more embarrassment, I turned to see the guys and Cami were off the plane giving us some space. "Come on over guys, I want to introduce you!"

CHAPTER 4

LAILAH

 ami and the boys joined us gathering around me, Brayden slipping his hand into mine and Micah taking the other.

"This is Brayden Dolton and Micah Lazonick, they are who I stayed with for Christmas," I shared. "Parker Jones, Hudson Lacy, and Jalen Minh—but he goes by Jay. Last, but certainly not least, is my best friend for life Cami Whittemore, she looked after me when I first got to school."

"It is so nice to meet you all, we've heard so much about all the adventures and traveling you've been doing. It's nice to put a face to a name," Mom smiled warmly at everyone. "I have no idea what time it is for you, but since it's ten o'clock here, I made a breakfast feast for you all, hope you're hungry!"

Clapping her hands excitedly, Mom led the way through the small airport building and out to where they had the van waiting.

"Now I didn't know how many bags you'd bring, so I brought my truck as well to save space in the van for you all," Dad informed us as he stopped in front of his old beat up red Ford. "Toss them in the back an' Kyle and I will meet you at the house."

Jay had, of course, grabbed my suitcase as well as his, so I didn't have to grab it from the plane. I kissed him on the cheek as he set them in the truck. "Thank you for always looking out for me."

He turned his face and kissed me full on the mouth. "Always."

Leaving me there to blush, he headed off to the van where Mom and Cami were chatting. Turning to talk to my dad, I found Kyle leaning against the truck with a raised brow. He didn't say anything, so I didn't answer the assumed question, just flashed him a smile and walked away. This talk needed to happen sooner rather than later, because these boys of mine were not holding back.

The drive was full of easy conversation, and it carried into the house when we arrived.

"Did she tell you that I had to make a map for her with just landmarks she knew so I could trust leaving her on her own?" Cami shared.

Mom laughed covering her mouth, eyes shining with mirth. Out of either of my parents, I look mostly like her, crystal blue eyes and curly hair, although hers was a deep brunette color. The blond came from Dad, and I was the only one to get it. Dylan got Dad's green eyes and Kyle was split down the middle with hazel.

"Oh, our Ladybug always seemed to end up in the oddest places when she got lost, making it twice as hard to find her. That's one reason she got a cellphone so early, that way she could call for help," Mom teased.

"Please tell me the whole summer isn't going to be telling every embarrassing story you can on me," I groaned.

Parker slung his arm around my shoulder and nuzzled

the side of my head. "Oh come on, Trouble, just think, when you spend time with our parents you can do the same thing in return. I know my mother would love to gush about baby Parker."

"Now that you say that, I guess it's not so bad," I sighed.

Mom gave me a lingering look as she waved everyone into the dining room of our simple ranch style house. "Come on, let's eat while it's hot. Ladybug, would you mind helping me bring things in from the kitchen?"

"Sure thing," I answered, following after her.

Not much in our house is current or top of the line but when it came to the kitchen, it was another story. The eating area had been removed to make a prep-station for the elaborate meals Mom and Dad loved to make. I really don't give my Dad as much credit for his skills with the grill and what he could whip up, I guess it's just because I'd always helped mom out with her work. She went right for the double oven and started pulling out casserole dishes full of enough food to feed an army. We had sweets, with chocolate chip pancakes, fluffy French toast, and muffins. Then there was the savory, cheesy eggs, sausage links, ham, and of course, bacon.

"Do you think I made enough? Those are some growing boys out there, if I do say so myself. I can barely keep enough food in the house for Kyle these days," Mom rambled as she pulled off the tinfoil.

"I think it will be fine, we did have snacks and things on the plane. Plus, I made your famous cinnamon scones before we left," I assured her.

Taking a deep breath, she set the dish down and looked at me. "Lailah, you know I don't like to get involved in your personal life, but I thought you were dating Bray-den. Is it normal to show that much affection among friends overseas? I didn't want to say anything in front of them, in case I'm just behind the times on things out in the world."

Taking her hands in mind I smiled. "Can I answer that question when Dad and Kyle join us?"

Mom blinked at me a few times, not expecting that request. "I suppose, if you feel it's necessary."

"It is, once I explain it, everything will make sense, I promise."

"Then you might as well wait a little longer. Dylan texted us that he would be here in about a half hour. That way we'll all be here, since I have a feeling this is not something typical."

This is one of the reasons I loved my mom so much, she just seemed to be able to read between the lines to the heart of the matter. I knew she wouldn't get mad at me for asking her to wait, instead it told her how important this was to me.

"Now, let's see if you still have your serving skills and see if you can take the rest of those while I take these," she challenged, leaving me four dishes to bring out.

Chuckling to myself, I rose to the challenge and mastered it, of course bringing the jug of orange juice along with me.

***

"Mrs. Mackenzie, that was an awesome breakfast, thank you," Parker said as he leaned back in his chair patting his stomach. "Now I can see where Trouble learned her skills."

"Well thank you Parker, and please call me Bonnie, there's no need to be so formal," Mom chided.

The sound of car doors alerted us that someone had

arrived, but I thought it was odd I didn't hear them coming up the drive.

"That'll be Dylan, he just got one of those new electric Toyota cars, since he's driving back and forth from Madison," Dad offered, getting up from his seat and walking to the door. "You're in luck son, we left you some food."

"Knowing Mom, there was way too much to begin with," Dylan answered as he walked in the door hugging Dad. "Now where is the world traveler who finally decided to grace us with her presence?"

Winking at Micah who didn't look all too pleased with my brother's sentiment, I got up. Before I could turn around, I was pulled into a bone crushing hug from behind. Normally, this wouldn't be a problem but after the catacombs, situations like this didn't go over so well. I knew that it was Dylan but not being able to see him and prepare for the hug, it triggered the beginnings of a panic attack.

"Let her the fuck go," Micah snarled as he shot to his feet.

I tried to tell Dylan what was going on, but I was frozen as my muscles locked up and my heart started to beat like crazy. My vision started to tunnel and flashes of the Dark Lord sneering down at me as he tried to work the spell clouded my mind. The arms around me were gone and I was swept up into someone else's arms, cradled against their body.

"Lailah, listen to my voice," Hudson's even timber echoed in my ear. "You are safe in your home back in Wisconsin with your mother, father, and brothers. We flew here on a plane not too long ago and finished a meal that your mother made. Can you tell me what you ate?"

With the help of a psychologist, we found that placement therapy worked the best. If I could focus on what I was doing now and who I was with, it pulled me from wherever I was trapped in my head.

"Come on Sunshine, tell me what you just had for breakfast," Hudson pressed, leaning his forehead against mine.

It took me a moment to pull up an image of my plate. "Fruit."

"What kind of fruit was it?" Hudson asked.

"Grapes, blueberries, and strawberries. Strawberries are one of my favorites," I added.

Hudson kissed my nose softly as I stopped shaking. "They're mine too, Sunshine. Tell me something else on your plate."

"Cheesy eggs and bacon, but Jay put a pancake as well when I passed them along," I said, taking a deep shuddering breath sitting up taller. "Then I saw Mom made strawberry syrup, so I'm glad he made me eat one."

Hudson smiled at me. "Why do you think we put him in charge of making sure you eat?"

Leaning in, I kissed Hudson and wrapped my arms around his neck, burying my face in his neck. "How badly did they take it?" I whispered.

"They're worried, but they're your family and that's what families do," Hudson answered. "They're not going to think less of you for surviving Lailah, none of us do. I'm glad you made it back to us alive, even if we have to adjust to dealing with some minor issues."

Sitting up I frown. "Minor? You call having a panic attack because my brother hugged me from behind, minor?"

"Yes, I do," Hudson stated. "Things could have been so much worse, Lailah. You didn't see what you looked like when we found you, adjusting to new ways of interacting with you is a small price to pay, and one I will happily do for the rest of my life. Now, stop hiding and have a conversation with your family, we'll get through this together."

Nodding, I shifted so I was now sitting beside him on the couch with the other four hovering nearby. My parents and siblings looked shocked from where they stood, still by the dining room table.

"Sorry about that everyone," I announced. "Do you mind having a seat...there're some things I need to fill you in on."

It was then I saw the strange woman standing just behind Dylan, looking extremely uncomfortable at being here.

"Dylan, did you bring a friend?" I asked, looking at my older brother.

He blushed and rubbed the back of his neck with his hand. "Ah yeah, sorry I should have probably said something, but I thought it was the best time, since we could both get time off. This is my girlfriend, Phoebe Turner."

"Hi," she greeted, giving a small wave. "I'm sorry to intrude."

Phoebe was stunning, she looked to have a Latin heritage with her olive skin, bright green eyes, and thick long mahogany hair. Her voice had an accent to it, but it just added to her allure, making me even more impressed that she was dating my brother. Don't get me wrong Dylan was a catch, but he was a solid seven from a small town and old fashioned ideals. Not what I would picture a woman such as her to pick for a serious relationship, and if he was bringing her home, it was definitely serious.

"No, please I'm the one who's sorry," I apologized getting up and walking over to her. "Here you are coming to meet Dylan's family, and his little sister has a mental breakdown the moment he touches her. What a way to introduce myself."

"I told Dylan to tell everyone I was coming, but he needed to make it a surprise," Phoebe tisked, narrowing her eyes at my brother.

"Why don't you check into the hotel, and I'll call you once we've talked things over?" Dylan offered.

Phoebe nodded her agreement and gave him a kiss on the cheek as she took the keys. Reaching out, I grabbed her hand to stop her from leaving. "Let's pretend this never happened, do over later tonight?"

She grinned at me. "I would like that."

Dylan walked her out, giving us all a chance to get comfortable for the uncomfortable conversation I had to have with my family. *Where did I even start? Hey Mom, Dad did you know there are demons running around in the world and it's my job to stop them? So, about the panic attack, the thing is, I got dragged to hell and offered up as a sacrifice to Lilith, Mother of All demons. Ugg!* Right now, telling her about the boys seemed to be the easiest part of this whole thing.

When Dylan returned and sat down my family turned their eyes to me expectantly. "So, Brayden and I aren't dating—we're married."

CHAPTER 5

LAILAH

"Excuse me!" Dad blurted out. "What did you just say?"

"Luke, let her explain. I'm sure there is a wonderful explanation for all this," Mom soothed, resting her hand on his leg. "Go on Lailah, we're all ears."

Taking a moment to look at the boys, and the love and encouragement that shone in their eyes, set me at ease. "I am in a serious and committed relationship with all five of these men. Brayden, Hudson and I are married, while the other three and I are engaged. Trust me when I say that I understand how hard it is to wrap your head around this, but believe me when I say this is the easier part to explain."

"I doubt that," Dad grumbled, crossing his arms glaring at the boys.

"Have any of you heard the term Elementi before?" I asked, hoping and praying that Hudson might be right and they knew something.

Mom froze and gave me a wide eyed look. "What did you just say?"

"Elementi, the warriors fighting against evil since the Knights Templar days," I offered.

"Wait right here and don't say anything important until I come back," Mom instructed as she headed off towards the bedrooms.

Dad also stood and started to pace in front of us. "You mean to tell me that my only daughter is married not once, but twice, and engaged to three other men and NO ONE asked me?"

I felt Brayden flinch beside me as his fear was coming to reality.

"Dad, it's true that I'm bonded for life with these two men and eventually to all of them, but we have not had an actual wedding," I explained, hoping that it might help take the edge off.

Unfortunately, it did not.

"What does that even mean, Lailah? How can you possibly think of being involved with more than one man? It's just not right!" Dad roared.

Micah and Jay stood, blocking me from Dad's view.

"Sir, I understand you are upset, but I'm going to have to ask you not to speak to her in such a way," Jay demanded. "Allow us to explain the whole situation before you cast your judgement on us or your daughter. It is the fair thing to do for your own child."

"What is with all the yelling?" Mom asked as she walked back out.

"Our daughter is sleeping with five different men," Dad stated waving a hand at us. "You telling me you're okay with this?"

Mom gave him a patronizing look, before she walked over to hand me an old tattered book. "This has been in our family for generations, and I was supposed to give it to you when you turned thirteen, but I didn't see the point. When I got it, I read the first chapter and never touched the thing again, it's faded and hard to read."

The worn leather cover had something that was once embossed on it but had since faded. When I opened it, the pages were weathered and stiff as I flipped through them. It was a handwritten book and the ink was faded but still legible, although it was written in old English with thees and thous all over the place. Turning back to the first page, I looked at the name written on the page and almost dropped the book with the shock that I got.

"Mom, why do we have Aiden Ryevick's personal journal and why do we pass it down through the family?" I demanded. "Do you know who he is?!"

"According to your grandmother, he was a very distant relative. He was the brother of one of our ancestors, but we migrated from Europe in the early nineteen hundreds. As far as I understand it, there aren't any more by that name living, Aiden never married and his sister took her husband's name. Your great aunt was big into family history and did a whole study on our family tree and gave everyone a copy of her findings. I'm sure I can scrounge it up from wherever I put it," Mom said, frowning deep in thought then shook herself out of it. "As for why we hand it down through the family, I don't really know, I'm sure I would if I actually read the thing."

"Sis, you already seem to know who this Ryevick person is," Kyle interjected. "Who is he to you?"

Closing the book, I clutched it to my chest. "For starters he is the founder of my school and a member of the Elementi. As they needed to grow with the times and changes happening in the world, he formed a base of operation for them at the school."

"Hold on, this means that you're related to him—distantly that is," Dylan pointed out. "Doesn't that seem odd to you?"

I shook my head. "No, that actually makes so much more sense when I explain what the Elementi really are."

"Don't tell me there's a cult and you've now gotten sucked into it and that's why you're married to all these men through some hokey mumbo jumbo," Dad grumbled.

"They are not a cult, but it does have something to do with the connection I have with them, yes," I offered. "Like I mentioned, the Elementi started back during the days of the Knights Templar. There was a large battle and after that, this group split off from the main faction before the whole thing was dissolved. These five men were blessed in order to fight a battle that has been waging on right under our noses since the day Adam and Eve were kicked out of the garden. As time went on, the darkness grew and because the angels couldn't fight this darkness, forbidden from interacting, they gifted these brave knights powers to assist them in the battle. The power they were given was in the form of elements, fire, water, earth, air, spirit or heart if you will. They traveled where they were needed, fighting off this evil, growing their forces to help them create the Elementi to what it is today. On that day, the knights were given their blessing and the angels promised that if they stayed true to their mission and pure of heart, a weapon would appear when they needed it most. With this weapon, they would be able to turn the tide of the war and bring it to an end."

My family looked at me stunned, none of them sure what to make of the story that I'd just told them.

"Horse shit!" Dad spat. "You said that this wasn't a cult, well this sure sounds a hell of a lot like something a cult would say. Let me guess *you* are the hidden weapon they've all been waiting for to save the day? How much money did they want from you? Or was it just enough to sell yourself to five men?"

His words hit right into my heart, making me flinch. I knew this would be hard for them to understand, it took me months to adjust to it and I had powers and seen demons. It was true what they say: people fear what they don't understand, and can't believe what they do not see. I guess I was going to have to give them something to see. Closing my eyes, I drifted inward to where my powers flowed from. There was the ball of golden light, reminding me of the sun, with two small orbs of green and blue power circling around it, showing my Bond with Brayden and Hudson. There were also wisps of silver and purple energy floating around, waiting for me to move past the Oath I'd made with Jay and Parker, sealing it with the Bond. Even though Micah and I hadn't completed either step, I still could easily reach out to him, pulling on his powers that burned bright just under his skin.

Drawing from each of them, I pulled forth our powers and thrust them out into the air around us. From the gasps of my family, I knew my plan worked, so I opened my eyes to see all of us glowing and the shadow of our knighted selves shimmering in the air around us like a hologram. I'd discovered this new level I could unlock on our powers when we battled our first demon conduit Tabitha, the governess for Brayden's siblings. We'd played around with it some in training but without us all being Bonded it put a strain on me, having to force that much power into them for long periods of time.

"Lailah, are you doing that?" Mom whispered.

I dropped the hold on the boy's powers and let mine

swirl around me like shimmering fairy dust. "Yeah Mom, I have the power of synergy. I can give or take from these guys and use it to strengthen them or myself, depending on what's needed in the fight."

Dad looked pale as his eyes flicked over all of us, trying to wrap his head around all this.

"That is wicked cool," Kyle grinned. "Dylan, our sister is a total badass."

"Yeah, I guess you could say she is," he answered, nodding his agreement. "I'm glad I sent Phoebe back to the hotel, not sure how this would have gone over."

Pulling my energy back into my center, I took a deep breath shaking out of my connection to the guy's power. "Being Synergy, I'm connected to the guys on a level that surpasses anything we can do in a typical relationship. Our powers are now combined, a piece of them lives in me and vice versa. It's an Oath given in the presence of an angel and then finished off with a Bonding of our powers, which is why we explain it as being married. Hudson and Brayden have done both of those things, while Jay and Parker have given their Oath, but I wanted to wait a bit on the forever part."

"What about him?" Dylan asked, nodding to Micah.

I turned and met Micah's gaze, trying to show him through my eyes how much he meant to me. "We both agreed to take things slow, when you'll end up together forever, there is no rush."

"Do you even like them or did this power you hold pick them out, forcing you into this?" Dad questioned, narrowing his eyes assessing the guys.

"Dad, I couldn't ask for better men in my life," I started. "I'm in love or falling in love with all of them, we each have our own relationship and are taking things that are right for each of us. Trust me when I say, that forcing this is the last thing that any of us want. Yeah, the connection once it's made can't be undone, but who is ever one hundred percent certain about the person they want to marry? Everyone has doubts and issues they need to work through, we're no different. It just involves a few more people, but the guys have known each other for years and so do their families. I've met them all and they're good people, who raised amazing men who I get to spend my life with."

Mom had tears welling up in her eyes again as she got up and pulled me into a hug. "Oh, my baby girl has grown up so much, and here you are married. It might not be how we pictured things, or would have liked, but what's done is done and clearly there isn't much you can change about it. We just love you so much Ladybug, we want the best for you and your future, so bear with us as we adjust to all this."

"Believe me, Mom, I get that, I do," I sighed hugging her back, thankful that at least she was on my side. I trusted that she would work on my Dad, since he was always the one who was more stubborn about changing his mind on things.

Holding me at arm's length she gave me a watery smile. "I think you should also tell us what happened to you."

My heart squeezed at the thought of how they would take this news after the reaction about the boys. Nodding, I gestured for her to sit back down and I did as well, taking Hudson and Brayden's hand in each of mine. Parker sat at my feet, leaning into my legs so I knew he was there supporting me.

"Since Christmas, the six of us have been in a few battles against the darkness that is trying to take over. We won some and lost others, which enabled the creation of a serum called Day-Brite. It messes with your brain, making you susceptible to outside influences and manipulation. They are using it to create an army out of normal everyday people so they can infiltrate our world in a covert fashion," I began.

"Why haven't we heard of any of this?" Dad cut in.

Brayden spoke up to answer my Dad's question. "If the world knew of this, it would cause mass hysteria and so far, we have been able to locate processing plants where the serum has been made. The Elementi have a large private military presence and are sending teams out to deal with them. Our labs are also working on finding an antidote, which we didn't think would be possible until Lailah had a dose forced on her. She didn't react to it the way anyone else has, meaning that she's had almost no symptoms."

"You got injected?!" Mom cried out covering her mouth in horror, eyes wide.

"Unfortunately yes, but as Brayden stated, this has given us hope for an antidote," Hudson buffered. "On New Year's day, we had an incident at the school that we needed to address, which got us separated and left Lailah vulnerable to be caught by the man we were hunting down."

Mom flinched at this, grabbing my Dad's hand. "Oh, this sounds so dangerous, you're all so young."

"It was really my fault Mom. If I had stayed with the group and not wandered off on my own, everything would have been different. By taking matters into my own hands and running off after the madman who wanted to blow up the school, I put everyone at risk," I explained. "The man we were after wanted to get me alone, once he did, he gave me the option of taking the serum or killing innocent people, and I couldn't let him do that. When the serum didn't work how he planned, I had the opportunity to end things and save myself, along with everyone else."

"That doesn't explain the reaction I got from hugging you," Dylan challenged.

Letting go of their hands, Hudson and Brayden helped me remove my sweater, which I was grateful for because I was getting far too warm. The tank top I was wearing showed the red raised scars on my skin, running down the length of my arms and on my chest. Hidden from view were the ones on my stomach and down each leg. I thanked God every day that he didn't put any marks on my face, leaving that free from any damage whatsoever.

Mom gasped and then let out a sob, burying her face into Dad's chest. Kyle looked, stricken eyes unblinking as he took it all in, poor Dylan looked sick to his stomach as he now understood my reaction.

"It wasn't that you hugged me Dylan, I have a hard time when I can't see the person who is touching me. If I can see you and know that it's coming, I'm just fine. My other big trigger is being held down on my back, it's how I was held when this happened to me," I said my voice soft and full of shame, even to my own ears.

Hudson wrapped his arm around my waist and pulled me tight to him, so I leaned my head on his shoulder while Brayden took my hand, running his thumb along the back of it.

"What happened to the man who did this to you?" Dad asked through clenched teeth, his body vibrating with anger.

"He's dead," Micah announced, his voice making it clear that was all to be said.

"Lailah, why didn't you tell us any of this? I would have

flown out to be with you had I known," Mom sobbed, taking the tissue that Kyle handed to her.

A tear rolled down my own cheek seeing how upset my family was for me. "I didn't know how to ask for help. If I didn't have the guys and Cami around, I don't know where I'd be right now. Right after it happened, I wasn't in a good place at all, thankfully they have a counselor and other amazing people on staff to help me process. Jay and I work on self-defense and training every day, which has helped a lot to make me feel strong. I've come a long way Mom, and I knew coming home for the summer was the best thing for me. Getting out of my normal and someplace that made me feel safe."

Mom sniffled but nodded her understanding. "Well, I'm so glad you're home, thankful that you're safe and well looked after."

"There isn't anything we wouldn't do for her," Jay declared, looking down at me from his seat on the armrest of the couch with a soft smile.

"Whelp, I think that's all the drama I can handle in one day," Cami piped up. "I declare that summer vacation starts now, and no more depressing talk is allowed!"

CHAPTER 6
MICAH

Watching Lailah put everything out there for her family to know, amazed me. The faith she had in them to still stick by her after everything she told them was so foreign to me. My parents and I had been close like that, but once I lost them there was no one in the world who could or would love me like they had. At least, that's what I believed before I met *her*. The only reason I hadn't gotten out of my seat and decked her father in the face for the things he accused her of, was simply because I knew she would be upset with me. Family was just as important to her as it was to Brayden—they both had the blessing of a family that gave a shit. I knew Oliver and Adriana cared about me, or they wouldn't have taken me in when I couldn't live with my aunt any longer, but I wasn't their kid.

I watched as everyone seemed to collect themselves after Cami's announcement and I couldn't help agreeing. This trip, getting away from the school where everything happened, was important. Lailah was fighting so hard every day to not let what happened slow her down any more than it already had. Thankfully, she was taking her altered schedule with far more courses with the Elementi instructors in the base under the house, so she didn't have to go on campus for many things. Being home around her parents and siblings might be just the thing she was missing and we couldn't do for her. Something I missed all the time, the hug and affection only a mother could give, and by the looks of Bonnie she had it in spades.

"Now you all tell us how tired you are? Ladybug said something about you boys renting a place while you're out here?" Bonnie asked, once she'd collected herself. "I know it's been a long day of travel and it's night time back at school, isn't it?"

"It's only seven o'clock back home, so I believe staying up for as long as we can, would be best. It will speed up adjusting to the time change," Hudson suggested.

Leave it to the brain to come up with the logical plan for us to follow. Although, I had to admit that since we'd come back from France and he Bonded with Lailah, he's become a better version of himself. He was far more involved with everything we did, instead of hanging back like Jay and working on his studies. He will always suck at video games, but he was becoming a match to be respected in training. Guess that's what happens when you finally have something you want to protect with your life after almost having it ripped away from you.

"Oh, I've heard people say that, but I wasn't sure if it was true," Bonnie commented. "I feel so bad about what happened with Phoebe earlier, what an awful situation to walk into when you're meeting the family for the first time."

"I'm sure she will understand she's a sweetheart and I think you'll all really love her," Dylan interjected, a love struck look on his face.

Parker coughed, trying to cover up a scoff and if I hadn't been an expert at the act myself, I wouldn't have noticed. He'd had a funny look on his face when she was first introduced to everyone, almost as if he might recognize her from somewhere. In front of Lailah we'd been putting on the best act we could, trying to get along because none of us wanted to add any more stress to her life. If I'm being honest, I don't know that I'll ever get to the point where I'll be able to trust him. Yeah, he pulled through for us in the catacombs, from what the others told me, but one time out of a hundred doesn't make a case.

"Why don't you tell her to come back over and we'll have a board game day," Bonnie suggested. "That way, we can all chat and get to know one another but it doesn't have to be too involved if you lot get tired. Please feel free to tell us you want to go home and sleep. It won't bother us a bit."

"Where did you say the rental was?" Luke asked.

Everyone paused and seemed unsure of how to answer this question, since we weren't sure if he was on board with us guys yet.

"Funny you should ask that, Dad," Lailah grinned. "One thing you'll learn about my boys is that they don't do anything halfway. It would seem that they bought a house for us to live in for the summer and whenever I would like to come home and spend time with you guys."

I watched her dad specifically to see how he would react to this information, but he seemed too stunned to do anything other than gape at us.

"Oh my good heavens!" Bonnie screeched, clapping a

hand over her mouth. "Well, I suppose with all five of you chipping in that you could make that work, but was that really wise while you're still in college?"

Lailah snorted, as we all realized that her mom didn't know that we all were extremely well off financially. Having all of us chip in made the purchase a drop in the bucket cost wise.

"Mom, trust me, it's fine. I'm the pauper in this relationship," Lailah added.

That statement made me frown, not liking how she viewed herself. "Cookie Monster," I growled. "I don't want to hear you say that ever again. You have to put up with all five of us, go to school, and be Synergy—that's more work than any of us have in this relationship. Taking care of your needs is part of being together and how we care for you, so I don't want to hear that bullshit ever again."

Kyle seemed to choke on his drink and almost spit it out as his brother slapped him on the back. "Holy crap, she lets you talk to her like that? Man, if either of us said that, she would read us the riot act."

"Kyle, you'll understand when you get a girlfriend, but everyone has their own way of showing affection. For the record, that was Micah being sweet," Lailah explained, winking at me. "When you put it like that, I can see your point. I do have to put up with all of you, it's only fair."

My girl thought she was slick, trying to brush this conversation under the rug, but clearly we were going to need to have one of her 'family meetings' about this subject. If we needed to make one account for us all to put money in for her to use, then that's what we'd fucking do. Her role in life was ten times harder than ours, and who knows what would happen after all this was over. All that didn't matter though, because she was mine and I was gonna make sure she had everything she ever needed or wanted.

"Where is the house?" her father finally asked, coming out of his stupor.

"It's in the Northwoods gated community, off of Eagle lake," Brayden answered.

"Northwoods! Those are some of the nicest houses in the area," Dylan exclaimed. "You guys aren't just well off if you can buy a house there."

I chuckled at Dylan's surprise. My boy Brayden had been the one to find it, but once he showed us the pictures and all it had to offer, we knew it was the right choice. A house like that was perfect for having her family over to spend time with us and relax. The other reason we all considered, is it gave her a private place to go swimming without anyone staring at her scars. The next house was a good distance away through the woods, making it completely secluded so she could be at ease. To us, her scars didn't make a difference, but I knew she fought with herself about them and only left them visible around us. If that bastard Ubel wasn't already dead, I would have taken my time skinning him alive so he could feel what she went through, then burn his ass slowly like a spit roasted pig until he died.

"Micah!" Lailah's voice cut through my thoughts. "Your hands are smoking."

Sure as shit, I was burning a hole in my jeans as proof that I wasn't keeping my anger in check. "Fuck!"

Hudson leaned over Lailah and waved a hand where the embers still glowed, dousing them. Now I was wearing singed wet jeans that smelt like burning hair, as it seared my skin underneath. My fire wouldn't hurt me, but it didn't mean my hair would survive like my skin would.

Lailah knelt in front of me, checking my legs. "Are you alright?"

"I'm fine, just was thinking of Ubel and lost control," I admitted, taking her hands in mine and kissing the back of them. "Looks like I'm gonna need to grab my suitcase and change. While I do that, why don't you and your mom pick out a few games we can all play."

Giving me a look that told me she wasn't convinced I was alright, she gave me a peck on the lips and stood. "Alright, but don't think you can get out of playing with us, I'll just hunt you down."

I grinned at that, loving to see the fire in her eyes when she challenged me. It was our thing, I pissed her off, she fought back by yelling or hitting me in retaliation using her new skills— it was glorious. "Wouldn't dream of it, Cookie."

"Truck's out in the driveway," Luke yelled as I walked to the front door.

I waved my acknowledgement and stepped out into the cool spring air, with the sky covered in big puffy clouds. Having never been to America before, I didn't really know what to expect but the term house with the white picket fence was incredibly accurate. My phone buzzed in my back pocket and when I pulled it out I saw it was Ned, my financial guy I'd hired privately to keep an eye on things, until I could take it over once I turned twenty-one.

"Hello?"

"Micah, thank god I got a hold of you. It's your aunt, she finally made her move and is trying to put through paper-work to challenge your parents' will, stating that you have not met the requirements that they put in place for you to take over the company," Ned blurted out. "We know that isn't true, so something else must have changed without us knowing it."

The anger that I'd been trying to gain control of burst forth again at this, and I slammed a fist into the tree I was standing under. A black charred indent appeared once I pulled my hand out of the trunk, the smell of burning wood sharp in my nose. "Tell me you called the lawyers."

"Of course, but I remembered you telling me you would be out of the country for the summer. Did she know about that?"

Wracking my brain, I tried to figure out how the hell she could have known until it dawned on me. "What account did you use to put money down for the house?"

"Ah..." Ned started, then paused as I heard the rustling of papers. "That would be your personal spending account, you don't use it often, so it had the most funds to easily access."

"Is my aunt a joint holder on it?"

"God damn it, she is," Ned swore. "I removed her from it, I know I did. Let me do some digging and find out how the hell that happened."

"This isn't good, Ned, she's using the fact that I'm gone to pull this shit because she knows I can't get back to fight it fast enough."

"What do you want me to do?"

"We'll need to call a meeting with all the board members of the company, and then I want a meeting with the ruling parties in our country. Seems I'm going to need to be far more aggressive in this matter sooner than I thought."

"Very good, Sir. I will see that it gets done. Is this still the best number to reach you while you're in the States?" Ned asked.

"Yes, call if you need anything I will answer day or night. This matter needs to be handled swiftly and quietly from our outside sources. Do you hear me?" I growled.

"Understood, I will call the moment I know anything." With that Ned hung up, and I was seriously contemplating whether Lailah would really hunt me down or not if I went for a run to clear my head instead of coming back inside.

CHAPTER 7

LAILAH

The second I saw Micah walk back in, I knew something was wrong. I moved to intercept him, but Brayden grabbed my hand and shook his head no. As much as I wanted to fix what was wrong, I also knew to trust Brayden, who was Micah's best friend and knew him better than anyone else. Chewing on my lip, I watched Micah head down the hall to the bathroom, wishing that we were bonded so that I could feel what was wrong. Each of my bonded partners and I had gotten better at controlling what we let through to the other, but I knew if I wanted to know they would show me. Just like now, Brayden was fully aware how anxious I was about Micah and he sent soothing energy, assuring me that it would be alright. As much progress as Micah and I made in our odd push and pull dance, I feared him sliding back again if things got too much.

"Give him time, Angel, if you try to talk to him now, he will only shut you out," Brayden whispered into my ear, kissing me on the temple. "Let him cool down a bit and give him the chance to bring it up before you corner him."

I gave him side-eye at his words. "I would never corner him."

Brayden just gave me a cheeky smile and pulled me over to the table where Mom had a few games laid out.

"Oh yes, Twenty Second Showdown!" Kyle exclaimed. "I forgot I got this for my birthday. We have to play this game, there's no better way to get to know people than a game like this. Dylan is Phoebe on her way back over?"

"Yeah, she should be pulling up any second," Dylan answered. "I've never heard of this game, what is it?"

"Basically, you have twenty seconds to do whatever's written on the card. It could be something silly like: listing food that start with C, pretend to meditate for three seconds, or get one of your teammates to do something random," Kyle explained.

"Now this is the kind of game I'm talking about!" Cami shouted, bouncing on her toes.

Knowing how competitive my boys and Cami were, this could be a very interesting game. "Sounds great to me."

"You sure about that, Trouble?" Parker challenged, mischief already shining in his eyes.

Setting my hands on my hips and jutting out my chin, I met his gaze head on. "Bring it on, buddy."

"Oh, now he's done it," Dylan laughed. "She's got that look on her face."

Parker's smile widened as he glanced at my brothers. "Yeah, it's my favorite look on her, means she's gonna give it all she's got."

Grabbing the box, Kyle set things up in the living room. "We're gonna need a lot of space for this to happen. Sis, you want to grab a pen and paper for us?"

Nodding, I headed into the kitchen to the famous junk

drawer, where you could pretty much find just about anything if you look hard enough. I felt someone moving up behind me, causing me to spin around quickly on the defensive, only to see it was Micah. He didn't say anything, just gave me a moment before he pulled me into his arms and buried his face in my neck, holding me tightly.

Wrapping my arms around him, I stroked up and down his back, whispering into his ear, "you don't have to tell me what's wrong but know I'm here to listen whenever you need me. Whatever it is, we'll figure it out together, I promise."

He seemed to relax the longer I talked him down, until his lips pressed a kiss to my pulse, and he moved up my neck. Then he kissed along my jaw until our lips met in a heated kiss, like he was worried he wouldn't be able to survive without kissing me. My hands curled into his hair as I gave back just as much as I was getting from him. He shifted me so his leg was between mine and pressed it to my apex, making me squirm, as my leggings didn't provide much of a barrier between my clit and his jeans. I humped him like a dog in heat, desperate to feel this closeness between us, even though I knew it was being used as a distraction from whatever was upsetting him. A hand slipped under my tank top and bra to grope my breast, flicking my nipple with his finger, making me groan as I ground on him harder. The need I had for Micah was insane, something about him made me crave his touch and I couldn't get enough of it.

Someone clearing their throat broke us apart rapidly as I tried to readjust my clothes. Then I saw it was Jay and relaxed, giving him a lazy smile as I was drunk off Micah's touch. My silent protector had a penchant for exhibitionism and voyeuristic tendencies, which I was quickly finding out I didn't mind one bit.

"As much as I hate to stop what's happening, your absence has been noticed," Jay warned with a sly grin.

Plucking the pen and notepad from the counter where I'd set them down, I sauntered up to Jay, fisted his shirt and pulled him down for me to kiss. It was a down and dirty kiss with teeth and tongue, but I knew he loved it from the sounds he was making. What surprised me was Micah coming up from behind, rubbing his dick against my ass as he held my hips.

"Do you see what you do to us Lailah?" Micah whispered against the shell of my ear. "Even your family being just behind this wall can't stop us from wanting you."

Yup, I was about to come just from his words alone, if he kept talking like that to me with Jay rubbing the outside of my leggings.

Just when I thought I was going to hit the finish line, Jay stopped and pulled away. "Not yet beautiful, we have a game to play with your family first."

I all but whimpered as he took my hand from his shirt and led me back into the living room, where I discovered Phoebe had arrived to join us. The looks on the other guys' faces told me, without a doubt, my lips were swollen and cheeks flushed, telling them exactly what had been going on in the kitchen.

Great , just great. Now I'm horny as hell and have to act normal around my family and brother's new girlfriend. I hope those two have the worst blue balls ever for this kind of torture.

"Grab someone from your team and slow dance for ten seconds," Phoebe read the card aloud, popped to her feet and grabbed Parker. She wrapped her arms around him and started to sway like you would as a kid trying to slow dance.

"One, two, three, four," Mom counted aloud for them.

What struck me as odd was the look on Parker's face, it was almost as if being touched by her was causing him pain. When Dylan first introduced her, I'd noticed the weird way he responded to hearing her name and seeing her, his face going pale like he'd seen a ghost. With everything happening and then explaining things to my parents, there wasn't a moment to check in on him. When we divided the teams, they tried to keep it so it wasn't me and the guys against them. Since there were twelve of us it worked out perfectly.

"Okay, time! Flip the timer, flip the timer," Kyle yelled, waving his arms.

Phoebe was slow to let Parker go, not getting to the timer in time to flip it and stop the sand from running out, giving us a point.

"Ha, ha, ha, suckers. That's ten points for us, making us the winners!" Cami crowed, leaping out of her seat and doing a jig. "Oh yeah, who's the best team? We're the best team."

"You totally cheated on that round where you had to have a thumb war, there's no way you could win that fast," Kyle argued. "You only had maybe five seconds of sand to work with."

Cami gave him a sly grin. "What can I say, I'm *really* good with my fingers."

"Oh eww Cami, don't say things like that to my little brother," I said as I faked a gag at her words.

"I don't get it?" Kyle frowned looking at the two of us.

"It's because I'm a les—" Cami did not get to finish that sentence, as Micah chucked a pillow right into her face.

"Enough, tiny-terror, you'll scar the kid for life," Micah muttered.

Cami spluttered and made to retaliate when she got a look from my Mom and sat back down, blushing in embarrassment. It made me wonder what her relationship was with her parents. I knew her sisters, but I'd never really heard her talk about anyone else in the family.

"Now it's about time I get things started for supper, are you and your boys staying, Lailah?" Mom asked once the room settled down.

Glancing at my watch, which I'd forgotten to change to Wisconsin time, I saw it was a little after midnight back at school. Now that we'd played three rounds of the game and my adrenaline was wearing off, the tiredness was creeping in. Even though I didn't get much sleep and tried to stay awake as long as possible, waking up at four in the morning made for long days. Add on the fact of traveling, the stress of talking to my family, and a panic attack—I was beat.

"I think it's best if we get to the house so we can check things out before it's too late," I suggested.

"That's a good idea," Dad agreed. "Right now, you'll have light to see by for another few hours but out by the lake when it gets dark, it's pitch black."

"Dylan, would you mind driving the van with your father to take them all over?" Mom asked, resting a hand on his shoulder.

He smiled at her and patted her hand. "Sure thing, Mom."

"That's my boy, it will give Phoebe and I a chance to talk without you around, so I can tell her all the embarrassing stories I can think of," Mom teased, giving Phoebe a wink who smiled at her.

"I think I like the sound of that," Phoebe said.

Dylan groaned, rolling his eyes. "I knew this was going to happen, try not to tell her anything that would make her dump me."

"Why on earth would that happen, you're my precious first born who can do no wrong," Mom gasped in mock horror.

"Yeah, yeah, yeah," Dylan mumbled, slipping his shoes on.

The lot of us piled into the van as Dad started up the truck, rolling down his window and waving for me to do the same. "You guys lead and I'll follow."

Giving him a thumbs up, we were off. Like they said, it was an easy twenty minute drive leaving the town behind us and entering into more of the wooded lands near the lakes. I left the window down, feeling the wind on my face and breathing in the country air that I grew up with, telling me that I was really home. When we pulled up to the guard shack, a man stepped out wearing a grey and black uniform with a badge from a security company on his chest.

"Name and resident you are coming to see?" the man asked.

Brayden unbuckled and opened the left sliding door getting out to greet the man. "We're actually new residents here, this is the paperwork we were told to give you so we can receive our car stickers."

"Oh yes, your cars were delivered yesterday, along with the other items I was told about," the guard informed us. "One moment and I'll grab the things you need that your property manager left with me."

Dylan turned to look at me and mouthed—what the fuck—making me snicker.

"Here you are, there are also documents there if you want to add on visitors to the approved list that will get special stickers allowing them access," the guard shared handing Brayden a large envelope and other papers.

"Thank you so much," Brayden said, shaking the man's hand before climbing back into the car. "Oh, and the gentleman in the truck is with us as well."

The guard nodded and waved us along once the gate was open.

"How cool was that?!" Dylan blurted. "You guys had cars delivered?"

The guys all laughed at my brother's amazement. "How else did you think we would get around here?" Parker asked. "We kept it simple and just got two cars, one for everyday use and another for fun."

"Sis, how the hell did you find these guys?"

Turning in my seat to look at them, I smiled. "I didn't, they found me and refused to take no for an answer."

"Now that I think of it, literally half of us found you lost somewhere," Brayden mused.

"Or got sat on while taking a nap," Micah pointed out. "Then I couldn't get rid of her, she kept showing up every-where I was, so I decided it was easier to just accept it than fight it."

Rolling my eyes I stuck my tongue out at him. "Ever the romantic."

"Whatever, you love it," he shot back.

"You're right, I do," I shared, meeting his gaze so he knew I was talking about something more than his sassy wit.

Understanding flickered in his eyes as he opened his

mouth to say something, then didn't. That was alright, I'm not sure this was the right atmosphere to have the conversation we'd both been dancing around for months.

"Ten-thirty circle drive, this is us," Hudson called out.

Dylan pulled onto the brick drive, that seemed to go on for a good mile, until we broke through the trees and there was the house.

"Holy fucking shit," I gasped. "The pictures did not do it justice at all."

CHAPTER 8
LAILAH

The entrance to the house felt whimsical, like I was entering a cottage more than a mansion, with its cobbled pathway and stone arched front. Just like in the pictures, it was fully furnished with a more rustic feel, heavy on the wood and stone, but all high end furniture in leather. You stepped down from the front door into the living room where the massive sectional couch and fireplace was, but it was also where the two story windows looked out to the lake. Cami clung to my arm as she tried to contain her excitement over the house, until she finally gave into it and dragged me towards the back door.

"We have to check out the lake Lala, you know that's where we're going to be living for the next few weeks!"

Outside was a large stone patio with chairs and a table with, you guessed it, another fireplace to keep warm by in the cooler weather. The back had been cleared of trees, so it had an open grassy area with a lawn swing and other seating at the top of the gently sloping hill down to the water. I knew I would be coming back to see how the sunrise would look while having a piping hot cup of chai.

The previous owners had made a literal beach, with sand and all, leading into the water. Cami raced right in, yelping when she realized how cold the water was up on her legs.

"Holy balls, why is it so cold?" she demanded, as she quickly scampered back out of the water.

I laughed at her antics. "Cami it's still spring here, the nights are still cold so the water doesn't have a chance to get warm yet. Give it time and we'll be able to swim to our hearts content, I promise. Until then, I think we should get some kayaks or something to use on the lake."

"Oh, good idea," Cami said, clapping her hands. "They even have a pier and everything."

We walked out on said pier and found a raft for us to swim out to and a slide that was installed as well.

"This place is paradise isn't it," I whispered, wrapping an arm around Cami as she did the same to me.

"Yeah, you're one lucky bitch, I'll tell you that. Now just don't screw it up," she teased, poking me in the rib.

I was tempted to toss her into the lake, but decided to at least wait until we had our clothes unpacked first. "Come on, I saw a fire pit back on the lawn. Ever had s'mores before?"

"No but I've heard of them, marshmallows and chocolate, what's not to like?"

"The things I'm going to introduce you guys to while you're here, it's gonna be awesome. I've missed having my mac and cheese, ranch, root beer, things that seem so common to have around until they weren't."

"Lala, you're all kinds of special, you know that right?" Cami joked as we headed back to the house. "They better not have taken all the good rooms or I'll punch them right in the dick."

Thankfully, they'd been distracted taking my dad and

brother on a tour of the place, so Cami was safe to pick out her room. I trailed after her, taking in the beauty of the place and how the builders managed to make sure every bedroom got as many windows looking out at the lake as they could.

"Found your room, Lala," Cami called.

Walking down the hall I came to the room at the end where she'd called me from. I gaped at the room with a massive bed that had a frame built all the way around it, like it was sunk in the platform. It could easily fit three or four people at a time without being crammed. It also had more windows than any of the other rooms, with vaulted ceilings, making it seem so open and bright even in the evening light. There was a set of leather armchairs placed to look out the window with a coffee table, perfect for me when I woke up from a nightmare but didn't want to leave the room. It also had a balcony with seating. There was an attached bathroom that was also set up to be roomy with two sinks which will be nice.

"How on earth did they find a place that was so set up for our situation?" I mused walking back into the bedroom, where I found Brayden perched on the bed smiling.

"So, do you like it?"

Running, I tackled him to the bed peppering kisses all over his face. "Like it, I fucking *love* it."

"Uh-oh she's swearing, is this a good sign or bad?" Parker asked as he entered the room. "Well, by the look on her face I'm leaning towards good."

Rolling off Brayden so I was sitting on the bed, I gushed, "you guys have outdone yourselves finding this place. It couldn't be more perfect for this summer and for us to come back to. Could you imagine Christmas here together?"

"Man, I love when you talk about our future together,

it's just so damn cute, Trouble," Parker said, grabbing my face between his two hands and forcing it into a fishy face. "Look at you, the cutest thing I've seen all day."

I tried to smile but with my face all smushed up, it didn't really work. Giving me a quick peck, he released me and pulled me into a hug. "Come on, your dad and brother want to head back but wanted to say goodnight first."

Letting him pull me to my feet, I followed him out and back down to the front door where they were waiting.

"Well ladybug, we don't want to intrude longer than we have while you're settling in. Give us a call if you wanna come by, but I'll be back to work at the diner, hard for both of us to be off for too long," Dad shared, hugging me tight and kissing me on the forehead.

Dylan pulled me from Dad and gave me a bone crushing hug, lifting me up off my feet. "So, what's it gonna take to let us hang out here for the week hmm? Phoebe and I don't have to go back until Sunday so we can work Monday."

"If I'm not mistaken, the point of this place was to be able to have my friends and family come hang out here," I pointed out, looking at the guys for confirmation, which they all nodded to. "Just give us a heads up you're coming, so we can tell the guard to expect you."

"That is the bougiest thing I have ever heard out of your mouth sis," Dylan laughed, giving me one more quick hug before they both left for the night.

Now that my family was gone, the events of the day fully caught up to me and I headed over to the couch flopping onto it. "Is it nap time yet?"

Hudson leaned over the back of the couch looking down at me. "I believe now would be a better time to sleep than earlier today. You want something to eat before you head up for the night?"

"Let me guess, the house is already stocked with food, isn't it." He just grinned, giving me my answer. "Did you get the mac and cheese in the blue box?"

"If you mean, did we get a case of it yes, yes we did," Hudson confirmed.

I rolled off the couch and ran to the kitchen, opening all the cabinets and doors scoping out where everything was in the space. The pantry was so large it could be considered a walk in closet, and there sitting on the shelf was my beloved *Kraft* mac and cheese. I grabbed four boxes, knowing if I made anything all the guys would want some too, I'd learned quickly to make enough or they would be eating off of my plate until Jay caught them doing it. That man's obsession with my food consumption was on another level. Setting the boxes on the counter I went in search of a large enough pot, only to discover the drawers rolled out so I could see all the way in the back.

"Hey Trouble, can I talk to you about something..."

I peered over my shoulder at Parker as I grabbed the milk and butter out of the fridge. "Of course, what's up?"

As if they all had super sonic hearing, the rest of the guys entered the kitchen and took a seat at the counter or leaned elsewhere, in view of what was going on. Suspiciously, Cami was not sticking around for this conversation, telling me that I'd missed something earlier in the day they noticed.

Parker bristled at the others, his face turning into a deep scowl. "I'm sorry, did I say your names when I asked to talk?"

"Dude, everyone saw how weird you were acting around her brother's new girlfriend—so how do you know her?" Micah challenged.

"What are they talking about? You know Phoebe?" I

ventured, stepping up so I was standing right in front of him. Parker rubbed the back of his neck and wouldn't look at me. "You're scaring me, Parker."

At my words, he winced which only ratcheted my anxiety up even more. "She was my first love. We dated in high school for two years before she dumped me when she had to move away."

My mind whirled with this information trying to make sense of it in my brain. "Why didn't either of you say anything earlier? You acted as if you didn't know each other at all...why would you do that?"

But no answer came. He just hunched his shoulders at the hurt in my voice, refusing to look me in the eye when I reached out to him.

"Do you still love her?" I whispered. This was the only explanation that made sense for how he was acting.

Micah growled and grabbed him by the back of the shirt, tossing him into the cabinets before he held him with an arm across his throat. "Answer. The. Question."

"No," Parker wheezed. "Well, in a way I guess I do. God this is so messed up, I didn't expect to ever see her again."

Jay stepped up behind Micah and placed a hand on his shoulder, gripping it tightly. Micah brushed him off, but let go of Parker and stormed out of the room. The sound of the back door slamming echoed through the house.

"I believe it might be in your best interest to explain what happened between the two of you. Leaving this to our imaginations can do more damage than being honest," Hudson advised.

Parker sagged to the floor and dropped his head between his knees. "Like I said, she was my first love, Phoebe was everything to me at that point in my life. We were in a strict boarding school, that my parents sent me to in order to help teach me better discipline after I came into my power. The jokester and party boy wasn't what the Elementi had planned on getting, so they suggested this place. During the summers, I was placed with you guys as we attempted to bond and train like every generation had before us."

"Me being the odd man out in this dysfunctional group has been normal since day one—until you came along, Lailah. But before you, it was Phoebe that kept me going. When her family pulled her from school and moved her back to Spain, she broke it off with me, saying she didn't want to do long distance being so young. It broke me to lose her, which turned me into that desperate sap who drunk called and left messages on her phone, begging her to take me back. I didn't think I would ever get over her and now having seen her, I'm not sure I really am. After she left, I decided not to get too involved with anyone, just keeping things loose and casual. Then no one would get hurt and we all had a good time, which I was able to do until I crashed into you that first day."

With those words, he raised his head and looked at me. "I might be confused and need time to process seeing her again, but I stand by my Oath to you, Lailah. Phoebe is everything I thought I wanted in the past, but you are how I see my future. Yes, I might still love the idea of her, not having truly dealt with things, yet it is nothing on the love I have growing for you, Trouble. The unconditional love you give me is more than anyone has ever shown me in my whole life."

"Why didn't she say anything?" I pressed, my mind cataloging every interaction they had today. It was true, Parker acted appropriately in every situation, but now that I knew the history, I wasn't so sure of that. The way he kept saying he wasn't sure he was truly over her, and wanting to process things, that was girl lingo for there's a chance I might still love them, but I don't want to lose you in case they turn me down.

"I can't speak for her, but I wanted this conversation to be between me and you first. Your parents are already dealing with a lot. Given everything we explained today, there was no way I was gonna give them another strike against us. My hope is that Phoebe is having the same conversation with your brother at some point today," Parker answered, holding out a hand to me. "Please tell me you understand, I can take crap from these guys and have it roll off, just not from you."

Reaching out I took the offered hand and helped pull him to his feet, allowing him to wrap me up in a hug. "I believe you, but I'll be honest and say that I don't like this situation at all. You have to promise me that if having her around is going to be a problem you tell me right away, or you and I will have issues. Don't lie to me or hide things while they're here. Also, if she so much as touches you, and it makes you feel uncomfortable, tell me."

"I promise, if there was a way I thought I could tell you sooner, I would have," Parker murmured, his lips pressed to the top of my head. "Please don't let this come between us, I don't know that I could survive that."

Pulling back, I took his face in my hands and looked him dead in the eye. "You are the one in control of that Parker, don't let it come between us and it won't."

"God, I don't deserve you," Parker whispered as he placed a hesitant kiss on my lips. I kissed him back deeply, wanting him to have no doubts I was still on his side and appreciated him coming clean to me.

Breaking the kiss I turned, letting him pull me against

his chest and resting his chin on the top of my head. "Anyone else have something to say about this matter?" Even an idiot could tell the others weren't as willing to let this slide as I was, but they weren't going to upset the apple cart. "Great, then we're going to have some mac and cheese and go to bed. I think that's enough drama for one day—don't you?"

CHAPTER 9

LAILAH

That night, I slept the best I had in months. It would seem a mix of full body exhaustion and jet lag was all I'd needed to get a full eight hours of sound sleep. When I woke up on my own it was still pre-dawn, but having gone to bed at eight last night, I felt completely rested. I crawled out from Micah's arms and discovered that Jay was already up and out of bed. I guess I shouldn't be surprised. He was always the first awake before I started having nightmares. I slipped on a hoodie over my pajamas, the morning air cool as I headed down to the kitchen. To be honest, I was super excited to be up early enough to make a perfect cup of tea and sit outside to watch the sun rise over the lake.

It took me a few minutes to find where whoever got our groceries put the tea. I was gonna need to rearrange things at some point, knowing I'd be spending the most time in the kitchen. There was no electric kettle, but I'd preemptively put the standard kettle on the stove last night to use. As I waited for the water to heat, I meandered over to the windows looking out over the lake, taking a deep calming breath. I'd been worried that coming here would be harder than staying at school with everything that was going on. One thing we *had* to do today was make sure we put the wards up around the house and property, knowing that I was a beacon to demons. The last thing we needed was for the reality of our work to come crashing into this part of my life. My parents might now know a little of what was going on, but seeing it first hand was another matter entirely.

The whistle of the kettle made me jump, snapping me out of my thoughts to race over to the stove so I didn't wake the others. Opening the cabinet, I pulled out a large mug that almost needed both hands to hold and noticed on the outside it had: *tea only up in this bitch.* I would put my money down on Parker being the one to make sure this was in the house for me. Tea finally prepared, I carried it outside and headed for the anorak chairs on top of the hill, just as the warm glow of the sun started to appear on the horizon. Curled up and using my mug to warm my hands, I relaxed my head against the wood of the chair and closed my eyes, letting the sounds of nature ease my worries. Birds started to chirp in the trees, the water lapping at the shore, and the leaves were rustling in the soft breeze of the morning. This is how I wanted to wake up every day, knowing that not everything in the world was hiding darkness just behind the corner waiting to take over.

At the sound of footsteps, my eyes flew open, and I found Jay standing in front of me with a blanket in his hands. "It's too cold to be out here with just a hoodie, you're not even wearing pants."

"Good thing I have you to look after me then," I grinned, getting up from my seat to push him to take it.

Giving into my demands, he settled in the wide chair and held his hand out to me, already guessing at what I wanted. Curling up in his lap, he tucked the blanket around my legs before wrapping his arms loosely around me. We both let out a sigh of contentment, it had been too long since I'd had Jay all to myself where he wasn't pushing me to train or eat something. I knew he was doing it because he cared, and from all that I've witnessed and gathered about his life—I don't think he knew how to show his love to anyone differently.

"You seem happy," Jay stated.

I took a sip of my tea giving him an acknowledging hum.

"There were also no nightmares," Jay continued, stroking a hand down my arm. "Is it because you're away from school or being with your family?"

"Sleep wise, I think it was the travel and time change, as for feeling happy...It's all of this," I answered, gesturing to our surroundings. "I'm not knee deep in everything Elementi, wondering when the next problem will show up, when will we get sent to deal with another demon, what is the Dark Lord preparing for this time. It's been too quiet and I can't tell if losing Ubel and his connection to Dantalion really hurt him, or if it's something else. Being here in the quiet of the morning, as the sun is going to rise, with the sounds of nature, you just can't help but be reminded that this is what we're fighting for."

Jay didn't say anything to that, he just rested his chin on my head and held me tightly. We sat like that for some time, watching the beautiful array of colors wash the sky, proving that once again the sun will always rise. The sound of someone traipsing through the woods put us both on high alert, causing Jay to slide me off his lap and step in front of me. Most of the time, demons attacked at night using the shadows to hide themselves, but they could just as well act in the sunlight. In Jay's hand, his bow appeared as he pulled on his power, quiver materializing on his back where he took an arrow and nocked it. The sound was getting louder and closer, making my heart beat faster as my own sai appeared in my hands. I was never going to let my fear make me a victim.

"Oh!" a middle aged man gasped when he saw us, eyes wide with surprise.

Both of us let go of our powers, allowing our weapons to dissipate as quickly as we could. The man shook his head and rubbed his eyes like he was seeing things as shook off his fright. He wore an olive green work coverall that had a logo for some landscaping company on it.

"So sorry to startle you, I forgot they said this place finally had people in it," he shared, rubbing his hands on his coveralls nervously. "I'm with the grounds crew, we're hired by the community and take care of all the yards, mowing, trimming bushes, things like that. We come on Thursdays or Mondays during the summer, depending on what part of the community you're in."

"I see," Jay said, looking the man over carefully. "That doesn't explain why you're coming through the woods when there is a gate to the back yard behind the garage."

"Ah, yeah...well it seems that you had all the locks changed and the guard at the gate didn't have a key for us, so I was coming around to open it on this end," he explained.

Jay seemed unconvinced by his explanation. "Do you always come so early?" I asked, stepping out from behind Jay.

"Since you're the first house on our route, yes, we try to get started early, so when the summer gets hot we're working in the cooler part of the day."

Jay took my hand and gathered up the blanket. "We'll

leave you to your work, but we will not give you a key. The gate will be unlocked by six am on Mondays for you to do your work. If that plan changes you will need to let us know."

The man gave him an odd look but nodded his head. "Will do, Sir."

I gave the man a friendly smile as Jay led the way back into the house.

"What the hell was that, Jalen?!" I demanded once the back door was shut. "Do you know how rude that was?"

Jay cocked a brow at me, crossing his arms over his muscular chest. His short sleeve shirt showed off his black and gray tattoos on his left arm, that I knew curled on to his pec. "In all the paperwork we got there was no mention of a grounds crew that looked after the homes in the community. Are you saying it was wrong of me to question someone who is trespassing on our lawn at six in the morning?"

"What's going on?" Hudson asked as he stepped out from the kitchen. "Someone is in our yard?"

"A landscaper," I answered off handedly, not taking my attention of Jay. "Why on earth would someone who is looking to cause trouble show up now? Wouldn't that be smarter to do at night when you can easily tell if someone is in the house or not? This is Wisconsin, nothing major happens in rural Wisconsin, unless you're into cow tipping or something like that."

"Sunshine, there's no need to get so upset about this," Hudson soothed. "I will simply call the HOA and ask them about what this man has said, then the matter will be settled."

"That's not the problem," I huffed.

"Do you mind explaining to us what *is* the problem?"

I knew my irritation over this was out of proportion, but I couldn't quite put my finger on why it had rubbed me the wrong way. Then it struck me, "I don't want to live my life believing that every person is out to get me. It was a perfect morning, everything was peaceful and calm, then in one second we were on high alert, weapons drawn ready for a fight and it was just a man trying to do his job."

My shoulders sagged as my eyes started to burn with held back tears. Since I laid there, holding Ubel's hands mourning the loss of what I'd done, I hadn't cried. In all my panic attacks, therapy sessions, and training, the one thing I couldn't do was cry. Like now my eyes would burn, the pressure would build, but nothing ever happened past that. Hudson stepped forward and took the mug from my hand, setting it down, and wrapped me in his arms with Jay pressing up against my back.

"Beautiful," Jay said into my ear. "It's my job and part of the oath I swore to you, that I will protect you know matter what. To me, anyone I don't know is a danger to you, but I can also see it from your perspective. I'm not going to change my mind on this, you're just going to need to trust me that everything I do is to keep you safe." I nodded my head against Hudson's chest as Jay kissed the back of my neck and stepped away. "I'll make breakfast today."

Hudson shifted me so he could scoop me up into a bridal hold and carried me back up to my bedroom, where Micah was still passed out. He climbed into bed and set me down, wrapping himself around me as Micah muttered something in his sleep, moving closer to me.

"Never change, Sunshine, we need you to continue to see the good in people. The rest of us have been in this life for too long. We've lost the ability to see the humanity in those around us—even our own families at times," Hudson whispered. "This is what makes you who you are, the pure goodness and light that no demon or Dark Lord can diminish. We, as your knights, are to protect you from the darkness, but also to advise you when the way is not certain. None of us know how prevalent the demons are in this area, we don't have the house warded, and we are in a different country. You'll have to forgive us when we don't have the same sense of calm that you do being back on your home turf."

As always, when Hudson took the time to break things down for me, it made more sense. It made me think back to when I first arrived at Ryevick and how lost I felt, not knowing where anything was or the customs around me. Lifting one of his hands I kissed the back of it, "That makes sense when you put it that way. I forget sometimes that you're just as human as I am about these things."

Hudson chuckled, his body shaking as he tried to keep quiet. "You forget we're human?"

"You know what I mean," I huffed. "Sometimes, I feel like you are all superheroes or something, with how you handle all the crazy stuff we've been through the past eight months of knowing each other."

"I think I like being thought of as a superhero," Hudson teased, kissing the top of my head.

"Would you two shut the fuck up," Micah grumbled. "Some of us are trying to sleep here."

Reaching out, I poked Micah's cheek playfully which made him crack open an eye, teeth snapping at my finger. "So, you don't care that there was a mysterious man that showed up in our backyard at six in the morning while I was sitting out there?"

Just as I guessed, Micah's eyes snapped open and he sat up, giving me his full attention. "What the fuck, Lailah! Are you okay, because if that asshole touched you I'm going to burn his ass until he's ashes and no one will be able to find him."

"It would seem we have a grounds crew to take care of the yard," Hudson shared, a hint of laughter in his voice.

Micah's face changed from concerned to pissed as he looked down at me. "Seems like you forgot to mention that little detail in your story there, Cookie Monster."

"Oh, but you were sleeping. I didn't want to bother you," I taunted.

Micah grabbed my ankle and snatched me away from Hudson slipping his hand under my sweatshirt to tickle me. "You think that's funny, do you? Well, let me show you what you get for pulling dirty tricks like that, Cookie Monster."

Wiggling under his tickle assault, I tried to get free but he was sitting on my legs, making it impossible. I turned my head to Hudson, who was now leaving the room and me to my fate. "Hudson, you get back here and help me!"

He just looked over his shoulder, laughter in his eyes and smiled, shutting the door behind him.

CHAPTER 10

LAILAH

"Traitor!" I yelled after Hudson.

Micah leaned forward, looming over me and that's when the fun and games ended. I could see in his face when he saw the change, and quickly jumped off of me, pulling me into a sitting position holding my shoulders.

"Are you good?" Micah asked, eyes full of worry. "Please tell me I didn't trigger an attack."

I closed my eyes, placing a hand on his chest so I could feel his heartbeat thundering in his chest, not as helpful as Hudson was in this situation, but it was a connection to the here and now. Taking a few deep breaths in through the nose out through the mouth, I was able to center myself before the panic set in completely.

"I'm good," I sighed, leaning forward to rest my head on his shoulder. "Don't beat yourself up over this, I was fine and then I wasn't."

"Lailah," Micah started, seemed to think better about what he was going to say. Instead, he pulled me up so I was in his lap, legs wrapped around his waist and held me. "Every time I think I have things figured out I fuck it up."

Pushing back on his chest, I sat back looking him in the face. "What does that mean?"

"How the hell can I be a guardian for you when I keep doing things wrong?"

Frowning, I tilted my head as I looked at him. "You're going to need to explain that more?"

"Look at the others, they can hold their temper around others, Hudson pulls you out of panic attacks, Jay makes sure you eat and don't get lost, Brayden is your soul mate and gets you in a way only he can, hell even Parker gets you to try new things. What the fuck do you even need me for?" Micah ranted.

"You done?" I asked, sarcasm heavy in my voice. He opened his mouth to continue but I covered it with my hand. "Would you like to tell me what the hell this is really about? Does it have anything to do with what made you so upset yesterday?"

"Of course you wouldn't forget about that," he muttered. "I found out my aunt is trying to steal the company from me while I'm here and out of the country."

Not having expected that answer, I blinked at him for a moment, trying to remember what company his parents had. "I thought it was a country, not a company?"

"It's both, I guess. My parents own the land and almost all the businesses in that country, thus holding a large sway over everything. They have a leader who is, I guess you could say, a king that makes the laws and such, with a group of advisors, to help in maintaining the country. When my parents died, everything got put in a trust, as well as a parent business, to collect everything my parents own in that country into one place. Once I take hold of every-thing, I can change how it's done, but it was the best they could come up with on short notice. My aunt wants to make a move to take that business over from me permanently, by showing that I'm unfit to handle the responsibility," Micah explained.

"What a bitch," I muttered. "I should have done more than knock her on her ass at that Christmas Party."

"Once I get her out of the picture, everything will be fine," Micah assured me. "I have no idea why my parents picked her to be my guardian in the first place."

"Are you sure they did? I mean, with all the shit she's pulling it wouldn't surprise me if everything was manipulated from the start," I asked.

Micah looked at me like I had just told him that the best news he's ever heard, as a smile bloomed on his face. "How could I not have thought of that?!"

He pulled me to him kissing me soundly, sliding one hand into my hair to deepen the kiss as I wrapped my arms around his neck. Falling back on the bed, he slid his free hand up under my sweatshirt, letting it run along my skin, sending shivers up my spine.

"Lailah," Micah said in a breathy voice as he broke the kiss, "I'm ready to be yours wholly and completely. It's time that I stopped running from the best thing that's ever happened to me because I'm an idiot."

Gazing down at his deep blue eyes that were so vulnerable in this moment, I slid my hands up to cup his face. "Micah Knight of the fire element, do you swear to love me, protect me, and always be by my side no matter what happens in our lives? That we will fight for each other every day, even if we argue and butt heads about things?"

"Yes," Micah agreed, his features resolute in his statement. "Everything I have to give I will, until the day my life is taken from me."

Our powers burst forth at our personalized version of

the Oath, since he'd experienced it once before. His red energy glowed around us like an ember, while my golden power sparkled like the sun. Not able to hold back any longer, Micah yanked my hoodie over my head, taking my t-shirt with it. Running his hands along my sides, he pulled me up so his mouth could latch onto my breast, groaning like he was eating some magical desert. A moan was pulled out of me as I tried to get his shirt off him, needing to feel his skin against mine. We'd waited for this moment for far too long and it was going to be raw, rough, and needy.

My hand was furiously working at his sleep pants while he dragged my shorts off, tossing them aside. I was going to ask him once more if he had second thoughts, but I stopped breathing when he entered me. The feeling was so addicting that I didn't want him to stop. Micah found his way to my neck, biting down hard enough to leave a mark, but it only fueled our fire. His hips worked hard into me as I ground on him to drive him deeper. My hands found his hair, needing to hold on as he bucked underneath me. He was pounding into me with all his strength, and I could feel it in every part of my body.

Neither one of us could catch our breath, sounds coming out in short pants and moans. His hand moved between our bodies to find my clit and I shattered apart. My walls pulsated around him, and I was sure he was close to his own release. His hand snaked down, grabbing my ass and lifted us both into a sitting position, changing the angle. Thrusting a few more times, I felt him swell inside of me before he growled in my ear and buried his head in my neck.

I felt his body shudder under me, filling me with his power along with other things, making me cry out as another orgasm exploded within me. Running my hands up and down his back as our powers settled within each other, I reveled in the knowledge that Micah was now fully mine, I didn't want to let go.

"I love you," I whispered, feeling it deep in my soul.

"I love you, too," he whispered back before kissing me softly. "Now and always, my beautiful sexy Cookie Monster."

Rolling off of him, I curled up against his side, resting my head on his chest as he lazily stroked a hand over my skin. This was a different side of Micah I'd never seen, but when I pulled on our bright new shiny connection, I found he was at peace. Not just the sated and happy high that came with having sex, no it was deeper than that, almost like I was able to help balance out his power level making it easier to control.

"Are you spying on me?" He asked, frowning at me. "Got to admit, that's an odd feeling, having someone in my brain. What are you so curious about?"

"Since I've met you, I've wanted to know what is going on in that brain of yours and now I can feel your emotions. You can't blame a girl for peeking when she finally gets the chance," I answered with a smirk.

Micah chuckled, shaking his head. "Guess I have to admit I did the same thing. Do you have any idea how much worse things are going to get for you once Jay can do this?"

The thought hadn't even crossed my mind but now that he said it, I groaned. "Brayden and Hudson do so well respecting my privacy, but I know he won't give a flying fuck about that if it will keep me safe and healthy. We actually argued about that this morning after the whole gardener thing."

Micah shifted so he was now propped up against the

headboard with pillows. "As your newest husband, allow me to give you some advice. If Jay doesn't feel right about someone, then I would trust his instincts on it. I don't know if it's part of his elemental power or what, but he is a bloodhound when it comes to sniffing out suspicious people. Ubel impersonating Mr. Creed has been the only person to sneak past him, and even then, he felt like something wasn't quite right."

"I know," I muttered, sitting up. "I'm gonna go take a shower... you wanna join me?"

Micah flashed me a smile, grabbing me around my waist and tossing me over his shoulder as he headed for the bathroom. "Like I would turn down that offer."

When we finally made it downstairs, after testing out a few different options in the new bathroom for later use of course, we found the rest of our group at the table finished with breakfast.

"Your food is in the oven, Beautiful," Jay said the moment he saw me. "Micah's, too."

"Oh, did someone work up an appetite this morning?" Cami asked, wagging her eyebrows. "From the reactions of Hudson and Brayden, I gather we have a new fully bonded member of the family?"

I expected Micah to have some snarky comment in reply to that, but instead he just cupped my cheek and kissed the ever loving shit out of me. Cami hooted and hollered, while the other guys laughed at his display of dominance.

"Yeah, you could say that," he murmured against my lips.

Stunned, I stood there like an idiot as he grabbed out

plates and set them down at the large table, putting me next to Brayden and himself on the other side. Shaking off the lust he'd just provoked, I took a moment to give Brayden a quick kiss as I sat down.

"Breakfast looks great Jay, thank you," I shared, giving him a smile, hoping things were okay between us.

Jay gave me a half smile in return and nodded as he turned back to something he was watching on the tablet.

"So, I called the HOA and we do in fact have a grounds crew that comes on Mondays to take care of the yard," Hudson informed me. "They did ask if we had a key that we would be leaving with the guard up front, but I told them what Jay said about unlocking the gate for them." I gave him a thumbs up, since my mouth was full of eggs. "This does, however show how important it is that we get the wards up around the house today so all of us can feel more relaxed and prepared. You feeling up for the task?"

Along with weapon and combat training, we'd also been working on using our powers together. So far, we had been doing everything on instinct, not knowing what I was able to do, but since we'd discovered a few things it gave a direction to follow.

"Absolutely, I'm totally ready to make it happen," I answered. "I'm more rested than I've been in months, add in the power boost from bonding with Micah, and I can't think of a better time to do it."

"Excellent, once you're finished eating, we can all gather in the back yard and get to it. I want to look over the books and other things Nona gave us," Hudson said as he got up from the table.

Nona was Cami's half-sister, and our resident know it all when it came to the 'magic' of the Elementi knights. She'd been working with me since the beginning to channel my powers and test what they could do. It wasn't until I'd fought with Tabitha that I was able to unlock the next level of my powers, but it seemed to grow each time I Bonded with the guys. Now the only two left were Jay and Parker, but I wasn't in a rush; this wasn't Pokémon. I didn't have to catch them all right away.

"Okay, so when you guys are done working your voodoo magic on the house, what are we gonna do next?" Cami asked, resting her chin on her hands.

I perked up thinking of an idea. "We could go to my parents' diner for dinner."

"Oh yes! I like this plan, then we can figure out what to do tomorrow," Cami clapped her hands excitedly. "Should we invite your brothers and Phoebe too?"

Not sure how to answer that, I looked over at Parker for some indication of what he thought. Cami hadn't been there for the whole conversation last night, but really it was a matter for us to deal with anyways.

"Should be fun," Parker agreed, giving me a reassuring smile. "Your brother is only here for the week, so we should make the effort to spend time with him."

Reaching across the table I squeezed his hand in thanks, before getting up and taking my dishes to the sink. Since I was one of the last ones to breakfast, I figured it was only right that I help in cleaning up. Then it was time to ward the house—if everything went like we planned.

CHAPTER 11

LAILAH

The six of us gathered in the middle of the back yard, looking down at three sheets of paper that had symbols drawn on it. "So, all we need to do is mentally draw these around the property?" I asked.

"Do you think you can remember them all? We need to do this in one go," Brayden questioned.

"Thankfully, most of these I've learned, there are just a few new ones but they're simple enough. Who knew the language of the angels would be so complex?" I sighed. "Alright, let's do this."

I stood in between Hudson and Brayden, since I've been Bonded to them longer and could easily access their powers, then I would draw on the other three. Things should work easier now that I had a connection to them all, even if it wasn't the full thing. Taking a deep breath, I closed my eyes centering myself, and sank into the part of me that held my energy. I couldn't help but smile at the small red orb that had joined the others circling my ball of power. Drawing on my golden energy, I let it fill my whole body until I felt my skin tingle, like I had an electric current running through me. Then I brought Bryden's power into the mix followed by Hudson, Micah, Jay, and Parker. I wondered if this is how a rocket felt right before it was shot off into space, holding that much energy until it was needed.

Letting go of the guys, I brought the first symbol into the front of my mind and drew it out with my Sai. In my mind, it was swirling with all the colors of our individual powers that I'd collected, when I felt like it was at its peak point in power, I stabbed my Sai into the ground. The symbol sank into the earth, and I was able to thrust it towards the front of the property, where we'd marked on the map I looked at before we got started. One down, five more to go to set the foundation. I repeated the process until they were complete, which meant I was now onto the hard part. That just set up the perimeter of the barrier. Now, I had to build the dome to cover the property. These were the symbols that I wasn't as confident in, but I understood their meaning and Nona always said intent is eighty percent of the work. I could feel sweat trickling down my back as this task used all the skill that I'd gained in the past six months, which compared to the others, wasn't long at all.

No, I can't think like that. I need to keep the intent pure and focused in my mind. There is no room for doubt or insecurities, I have to keep us safe.

Pushing through the negativity, I started on the chain of symbols that I needed to draw, infusing each of our powers into them one at a time, layering them with the strongest protections we could. Once I'd done the five elements, it was time for mine to seal the deal and bind them to the ward, creating the dome. For some reason, I was having trouble with a few of the symbols rejecting my energy with

Jay and Parker, which in a way made sense, since we weren't Bonded.

"I need you two to put your hands on either shoulder," I instructed through gritted teeth, knowing they would understand who I was talking about.

Sure enough, as soon as I had physical contact with them the symbols stopped rejecting me. Now that I had the chain set up, I had to thrust it into the network of the grounding symbols I'd already done. This is where I would know if I was successful or not, I was hoping so, but we were all prepared for it to fail since it was the first time we'd done this. The wards back at Ryevick just needed to be recharged, not redone completely, so this was new territory. Taking a few deep breaths and focusing my mind on the intent of this ward, I slammed my Sai into the ground once more, shoving every ounce of energy I had into making this work. The ground rumbled and shook under us, as it absorbed the power behind the barrier. Just when I didn't think I had enough strength to hold it together long enough, it snapped into existence, cutting off my connection to it so abruptly that I slumped to the ground.

"Holy shit," Parker cried.

My eyes snapped open expecting something bad to be happening, but instead, above us was a shimmering rainbow bubble of the barrier. We'd done it, the wards were activated and functioning just like they should. I grinned as the shimmering dissipated until it was something that you just caught out of the corner of your eye when you weren't looking at it. As an Elemental Warrior I could see such things, but to the normal human eye they would have no clue it was even there.

Parker reached down and pulled me to my feet, grabbing me around the waist and swinging me about. "You did it, Trouble! You really fucking did it on the first try."

I laughed at his excitement, wrapping my arms around his neck the best I could with how tired I felt. Giving me a toothy grin, he kissed me deeply before putting me down.

"Sunshine, not only did you do this on the first try, but these are even stronger than the ones back at Ryevick," Hudson pointed out as he ran a hand along the barrier. "Just think what you'll be able to do with a little more time and training."

"Of course our girl is a badass," Micah added with a wink. "Never underestimate the quiet ones, they'll get you every time."

Cami came bursting out into the back yard looking around slightly panicked. "They don't have earthquakes here, right?"

"No silly, why do you ask?" I inquired as I headed over to her.

"What do you mean? Did you not feel the ground doing the jitterbug on a Friday night?" Cami demanded hands on her hips.

I stopped in front of her and frowned. "You felt that?"

"Whoa, are you saying you did that?"

"Maybe, when I finished off the last part of the ward the ground shook, but I didn't think that was something other people could feel. I thought it was more of a power energy thing shifting," I explained.

"Yeah, sorry to break it to you, Lala, but you set off car alarms all over the neighborhood. How much juice did you put into that spell?"

"If I had to guess, this is one of the strongest barriers I've ever seen or heard of," Hudson interjected. "It has to be from combining your power as Synergy right from the foundation."

Cami looked at me wide eyed a moment before she beamed at me. "Get it girl, kicking ass, taking names, and shaking the world up—literally."

"Can I take a nap first? Shaking up the world has kind of taken it out of me."

"Sounds like we need to break in the theater room of the house to me," Cami announced. "What do you think—Magic Mike or Princess Bride?"

Parker marched right up to us hearing her suggestions. "What the hell kind of lesbian are you to want to watch Magic Mike? Doesn't that go against all the rules or something?"

"Just because I don't want to fuck a man doesn't mean I can't appreciate their dance moves," Cami challenged, rolling her eyes. "Besides, seeing you get all worked up about it is just part of the fun."

Before either of them could start an even bigger argument, I grabbed her arm and dragged her into the house. "Why do you always have to pick on them?"

"Lala, we were raised together like siblings. I'm only doing my duty as their adopted little sister."

"Sure you are," I drawled heading to the kitchen. "If we're doing movies then we need snacks."

Cami and I raided the kitchen, making copious amounts of popcorn and grabbing some drinks, before we made it up to the loft where the movie room was set up. After some trial and error, we figured out how everything worked and discovered a giant wall of movies, hidden behind a curtain, to pick from.

"Holy shit! You're never going to run out of things to

watch," Cami laughed. "Alright, I say you pick two and I'll pick two then we close our eyes and pick one."

"Works for me."

It took far longer than I expected to pick out two movies with the options that were available. I wasn't in the mood for romance, and scary movies were definitely off the table, so that left action and comedy. Then I spotted one that was a mix of both with awesome actors, *Day and Knight*. Then I saw a movie that I hadn't watched in years, that was one of my favorites growing up—*Hook*.

"Alright I got my two, what did you end up with?" I asked, turning back to Cami.

"Well, it doesn't matter because we are sure as hell watching Hook. Who doesn't love Robin Williams?!" she asked, snatching the movie out of my hand. "Go tell your crew and see if they want to join us."

Wandering over to the railing that looked out over the living room, I yelled, "We're watching Hook if anyone wants to join us."

"Oh, fuck yeah!" Parker cheered.

"Wait, that's the one with Robin Williams, right?" Brayden asked, walking into the living room and looking up at me.

Grinning, I nodded. "Sure is—cult classic if you ask me."

"Yeah, I'm totally down for that, I love that movie. Need us to bring anything up?" he inquired.

"We have popcorn to spare so whatever else you need or want is up to you."

Brayden gave me a thumbs up and hustled off to the kitchen.

"I brought you beef jerky to snack on," Jay stated from where he'd snuck up on me.

Whirling around, I clutched my chest. "Seriously, do you think I'll ever be able to keep track of you?"

"I know a way we can find out," Jay said with a wicked glint in his eye, as he drew me closer to him with a hand on my waist.

"You're not mad that I Bonded with Micah before you, are you?" I murmured, as I held his gaze.

He shook his head, leaning forward so our foreheads touched. "No Beautiful, our time will come when it's supposed to. I'm not worried. He needs you more than the rest of us do in some ways, that's why he fought it so long."

Tilting my head back, I kissed him, letting my lips linger against his. "I love you Jaylen Ming, never doubt that for a second."

A look of amazement flickered in Jay's expression before he gave me one of the first full blown real smiles I've seen from him. "I love you too, Lailah Mackenzie."

"Let's go watch a movie hmm," I suggested, grabbing his hand off my waist and interlacing our fingers. "Oh, and hand over the jerky that sounds amazing."

We all ended up watching the movie together chanting, Rufio, along with the lost boys and yelling curses at Hook before Peter learned to fly so he could save his kids. When that one was done, the guys all picked out a movie and we voted, ending up with Brayden's choice of Bourne Identity, which evolved into us wanting to watch the whole series, taking up most of the day. Just as we were talking about whether to count Bourne Legacy as part of the series, my phone rang. Looking down I saw it was Dylan, I'd texted him about dinner earlier in the day and didn't hear back from him, so I assumed he wasn't interested.

"Hey sis, sorry I didn't get back to you sooner, Phoebe and I have been running around helping mom out by taking

Kyle to all his things," Dylan explained. "If you still want to do dinner at Percy's we're starving."

I glanced at the time on my phone real quick, having lost track of time. "Yeah, we can totally meet up, why don't we say six-thirty, that way we have time to get there."

"Awesome, we'll see you there," Dylan said before hanging up.

The guys and Cami watched me questioningly. "Anybody up for dinner at my parents' place?"

"Ah food is involved, of course your boys are interested," Cami laughed when everyone gave their agreement.

"I can't believe it's already six and we didn't even notice," I mused, grabbing my empty popcorn bowl and tossing in other snack wrappers. "We have a car that can fit all of us, right?"

"Trouble, we got two for a reason just to make sure we could all travel together, but I think we can all fit in the SUV just fine," Parker answered, following me down to the kitchen.

Setting my things on the counter, I turned to face him with a smirk on my face. "Dare I ask what kind of vehicles you guys picked?"

"A little faith in us would be nice," Parker scoffed. "We did pick out this house without your help, but we weren't sure if it should be two cars or three. Guess if it turns out we need a third you get to pick it out, sound fair?"

"I highly doubt we will need three cars for a vacation home," I answered, scrunching up my face in dismay.

Jay walked into the kitchen with a set of keys in his hand twirling them around his finger. "Ready?"

"Just need to get my shoes, Cami's going to be the wild card here," I commented.

"Lala, I know you did not just say that I'm high maintenance!" Cami gasped, clutching her chest. "Clearly you need to spend more time with Maggs, I love that woman to death, but damn."

Laughing, I pulled Cami into a hug. "I didn't mean anything by it, and you know I enjoy Maggs. I hope it works out for the two of you to come back and visit us while we're here."

"Yeah, she would love that," Cami sighed, then shoved me away. "Go get your shoes, you're holding everyone up."

I flew up the stairs, slipped on my shoes and headed back down, just as everyone was walking out to the garage. When the door lifted there were two brand new cars: a pearl colored Mercedes SUV and a sleek black Audi sedan. My jaw dropped, yet again blown away by the fact that they could spend this much money like it was nothing, hell just one of them could do it alone and not feel bothered by it.

"We're taking the Mercedes," Jay informed me, as he took two fingers to lift my jaw, closing my mouth. "Don't want you catching any bugs now, would we."

CHAPTER 12

PARKER

Seeing how excited Lailah was about the car, we all decided to let her have shotgun so she could scope things out. I decided to sit in the back so I could make sure I had my shit together by the time we got to dinner. Everything I told Lailah was true, I didn't love Phoebe the way I loved Lailah. It showed me how wrong I was to think that was real love, but seeing her out of the blue like this and spending time with her dating someone else wouldn't be easy.

I could still remember the day that she told me her parents were coming to get her in two days. We spent every moment we could together, and the night before she was getting picked up we gave up our virginity to each other. She was the one who wanted to wait, being raised a good Catholic girl and because I loved her I waited, thinking we would be together forever. Oh, how things changed. I begged her to let us try long distance, we managed it for the summer, why not give it a try. It was then I found out that she didn't tell her parents about us, and I was her dirty little secret. They were super strict and wouldn't let her date. She had to fight tooth and nail to get into a co-ed school when they wanted to send her to an all girls one. Me not being available during the summer was the perfect plan for her to have her cake and eat it too.

That hurt more than I thought it would when she told me. Even if we were to keep this thing going, it would have to be a secret and she wasn't willing to put in the work. So, after this beautiful moment that I thought we were fully committing ourselves to each other, she got dressed and left my life forever. I refused to see her off with the rest of her friends, knowing I wouldn't be able to keep the pain and hurt off my face. It was then I learned the hardest lesson of being the bearer of the spirit element—don't fall in love. When you can control other people's emotions, it's so easy to get lost in them yourself, seeing only what you wanted to, pulling forward the best parts when you're with people. It made me wonder if she even felt about me the way I had or if I'd unknowingly created that with my powers.

Fast forward four years, to the moment I ran into the woman I was supposed to love with everything I am. I know the others are still pissed at me for keeping the fact that I gave her my Oath a secret, but there are some things that are just between two people. Yeah, I get that Lailah has five people in her life that she loves equally but for us men, she is our everything. Allowing myself to give my heart to another person is scary, but wonderful at the same time, and I just wanted us to have a moment to always remember that, was the two of us. We both needed time to deepen our relationship and I believe, without a doubt, it was the right move to make.

When we pulled up to the restaurant, I couldn't help but smile as I took in the building. It looked like it came out of a movie from the sixties, with the neon lights and the large glowing sign announcing we were at Percy's Diner. There was also a claim to the best pie in the county, which I had no doubt was true, having had Lailah's pies at Thanksgiving. A bell rang, announcing our arrival and a young woman in jeans with a Percy's t-shirt came right up.

"Lailah! Your mother told me you were back for the summer," she exclaimed, pulling Lailah into a hug. "I'm glad they didn't talk you into working all summer, leaving a job for the rest of us poor college students."

"Oh, it's good to see you Sam, how is UW—Madison treating you?" Lailah asked as Sam led us over to the table where the others were waiting for us.

Sam shrugged. "It's alright, I like my major for the most part, but who can go wrong with business, right? How is life overseas? That has to be amazing, is that how you know these handsome fellas?"

We'd all been settling in around the large corner booth that the others picked out but we paused to see what Lailah would say. None of us would blame her for not owning up to dating all of us. We knew she wasn't ashamed of us, having made that extremely clear multiple times. We hadn't really talked about what to tell people outside of our family or Elementi, who didn't understand how we ended up in this situation.

"Yeah we all met at school, funny enough they've all been friends since childhood and I'm lucky enough to be included in the gang," Lailah answered, giving us all an affectionate grin.

Sam leaned in pretending to whisper. "Let me know

which one you're dating, or want to date, so I don't go after the wrong guy."

"Oh, I'm sorry I must have given you the wrong impression," Lailah announced with a frown. "I'm already dating them all quite seriously, so none are available to you."

Dylan seemed to get uncomfortable at this moment and Kyle was just trying to hold himself back from laughing. Phoebe, on the other hand, gawked at me eyes wide with shock.

"Damn, Lailah if you didn't want me to make a move on them you just had to say so, no need to be rude about it," Sam muttered blushing with her embarrassment.

"She wasn't trying to be rude," Bryden interjected, ah the man with the white knight complex coming to save the day. "We are, in fact, all dating Lailah."

Sam blinked at us for a moment, then a grin broke out and she punched Lailah's arm. "Get it, girl!" then her face crumbled into a look of concern. "Do your parents know?"

"Of course," Lailah laughed. "We aren't trying to hide our relationship, some of us have even gotten married in a non-traditional sense."

Letting out an impressed whistle, Sam nodded her head, setting the menus down on the table. "What a world we're living in today. You, my friend, are going to be the talk of this little town by the time summer's over. I'll give you guys a sec and come back to get your orders."

That right there was the reason this whole thing worked. Lailah was proud of us and did everything in her power to show everyone just how much we meant to her. I have no doubt that in telling Sam, the whole county would know about us by tomorrow morning. Did Lailah give a flying fuck? Absolutely not.

"You know what you just did, right?" Dylan asked, confirming my guess.

Lailah just smiled as she scooted in next to me. "It saves me time from having to explain it to everyone individually. Like dad always says—work smarter not harder."

"Yeah, I don't think that's what he was talking about..."

"Well, it's already happened so we can't put the cat back in the bag," Lailah stated, ending that topic. "Mom and Dad add anything new? Oh, it's strawberry-rhubarb pie season!"

"You're in luck, Dad started doing Burger Monday," Kyle shared sliding over a sheet of paper. "He comes up with three unique burger flavors that change each week, and says it's been a real hit."

"Are the burgers good here?" Phoebe asked.

All three of the Mackenzie siblings looked at her in horror for even asking. "One thing I can promise you, is that any burger our dad makes is the best you've had in your life." Dylan declared.

"Sounds like we're all having burgers tonight," Hudson said, snapping his menu shut. "I say we let the master chef surprise us."

"Oh hell yeah," I cheered. "That is an awesome idea."

Sam came back over and took our drink order and loved our plan for the burgers. "You guys are going to make his night, having new people to test his burgers on. The town is still trying to keep up with his combinations, not too many adventurous people around these parts. Hell, most don't ever leave the state."

"Tell Dad to make sure I don't get anything spicy, he knows I can't handle that," Kyle interjected.

"Yeah, yeah, we know you can't handle anything past

pepper in the world of spices," Sam teased as she headed off to the kitchen.

"Hey Trouble, where are the bathrooms?" I asked.

Scooting out, she stood and pointed to the other side of the diner. "Around that glass brick wall, they're singles, but there are two of them."

"Thanks," I murmured, kissing her on the temple.

"I'll join you, I need to wash my hands," Phoebe said as Kyle and Dylan got up to let her out. "Better to do it now so you don't have to move when the food gets here."

We walked in silence to the bathrooms and once we were around the wall and hidden from view, she grabbed my arm and pulled me to a halt.

"Aren't you going to say anything to me?" Phoebe asked, her voice sounding hurt.

Balling my hands into fists I looked at her over my shoulder. "I could ask you the same thing, Pheebs."

"How would that have looked if I told them we knew each other and dated for two years when your girlfriend just had a panic attack?" Phoebe accused. "When you didn't say anything about it, I decided to let it go, but it seems we're going to have to figure out something since we'll be spending time together for the next week or so."

Turning to face her, I frowned. "What do you mean, figure something out?"

"Well at some point it's going to be obvious we know each other," she pouted, letting go of my hand to rest it on my chest. "Parker we were madly in love, that teaches you a lot about a person."

"Lailah already knows about us, I don't keep secrets from her," I explained, removing her hand. "If you give a damn about her brother, then I suggest doing the same thing. Unless leading men on and dropping them high and dry is your thing."

"Is that what you think happened between us?" She demanded, hands on her hips trying to show off her curves. "I told my father about us, even asked him not to take me out of that school so we could be together. He was having none of it and in a last ditch effort I gave you the last piece of my heart when I gave you my virginity. Then *you* never came to see me off, ending things for good."

My jaw dropped at this information. "Why didn't you tell me? The last thing I remember is you clearly explaining to me that you wouldn't even consider doing long distance when you left."

"If you had come to see me off, I would have told you I changed my mind. I wasn't ready to give up on us. I thought I could talk my dad out of being a dick and let me stay," Phoebe huffed, running her hands through her long wavy hair. "How can this be happening? You're here in the States, dating his younger sister, for crying out loud."

"Guess fate likes to have a laugh every once in a while," I shrugged, and turned to head into the bathroom.

"What, that's it? You're not even going to ask me how I am or what I've been up to?"

Grabbing the handle to the bathroom, I looked back at her once more. "Sure I'd be happy to, at the table holding my fiancé's hand while you sit next to your boyfriend. Phoebe, what we had was amazing, but it's clear that no matter how much we loved each other, we didn't fight to stay together."

Ignoring her indignant huff as I entered the bathroom, I turned on the sink to splash cold water on my face. It was over, we talked. I told her how things were going to be, and now we can both move on. No need to keep holding on to old wounds when it seems we both fucked up all those years ago. Lailah was perfect and all I would ever need for the rest of my life and I was not going to fuck it up.

Right?

Did seeing Phoebe and finding out she didn't plan to leave me change anything? No, she was with Dylan and I was with Lailah, I had to get over these lingering feelings before it did cause a problem.

CHAPTER 13

LAILAH

As promised, Dad's burgers were out of this world, the guys hardly even talked once the food arrived because they were stuffing their faces.

"Okay, I kind of want to order another one but I don't think I could actually eat it," Parker admitted as he leaned back and rubbed his stomach.

"I can't believe you ate all that," Kyle blurted. "That was two patties, a fried egg, and BBQ pork."

Dad had gone all out, using everything he could find in the kitchen to impress the boys. Each of us had gotten something different but all amazing in their own way. Mine had my favorites on it and was simple compared to everyone else.

"If this isn't one table of happy customers, I don't know what is," Dad smiled as he walked up to us, drying his hands on a towel as he kissed me on the top of the head. "Hey Ladybug, you settling into the house all right?"

"Yeah, the house is amazing," I answered.

"Sir, that has to be the best burger of my life," Parker announced. "Allow me to shake the hand of a grilling god."

We all laughed when Parker reached across me to actually shake dad's hand.

"Son, you can call me Luke," Dad said, gripping Parker's hand. "The way things sound, the lot of you are already part of the family. I'm sorry my reaction yesterday wasn't all that welcoming, but I only have one little girl and as her father it's my job to look out for her. It will be nice to have you all around for the summer so we can get to know one another better."

"Thank you, Luke, that means a lot," Brayden shared, giving Dad a nod.

Dad stayed to talk for a few minutes but then he had to head back to the kitchen to help out with orders. Seems his burger night might be taking off faster than he thought.

"Hey, what do you say we take a day trip into Chicago?" Dylan asked. "Wisconsin is the mecca of cheese but there isn't all that much to offer in the way of entertainment."

"I have a better idea," Kyle announced. "Do any of you like roller coasters?"

Micah rested his elbow on the table leaning in. "I'm listening."

Kyle grinned at him like the cat who got the canary. "If we're going to drive all that way, I say we hit up Six Flags instead."

"Oh, I knew I liked this kid," Cami exclaimed. "Lala, if you weren't my homegirl for life you might have competition from your little bro."

"Don't let the boyish looks fool you, that little bro is the most down-to-earth person you'll ever meet. He might even give Hudson a run for his money on brains when it comes to math," I pointed out. "Theme parks are his major weakness though, brings the kid out in him like nothing else."

"So that's a yes?" Kyle asked, ignoring everything I just said.

"Let's put it to a vote," Hudson reasoned. "All who are interested in going to Six Flags raise your hand."

Everyone raised their hands but Phoebe, but once she saw that, she smiled and begrudgingly raised a hand.

"It's settled then. We'll have to head out fairly early, since it's a two hour drive and we want to make sure we have plenty of time to spend there," Dylan instructed.

Kyle had his phone out and was looking something up. "Looks like they open at ten thirty, so we need to leave by eight at the latest. Although it will help that it's a Tuesday and all the high schools won't be out yet."

"Wait then how come you're off?" Cami questioned giving him a skeptical look.

"My school runs on a different schedule so we got out last week, but I also go back to school sooner than everyone else," Kyle answered.

Sam came over and started to take plates from us. "Now, I know you aren't going to leave without having pie. Mrs. Mackenzie makes the best pie in the whole county, says so right on our sign."

"I don't know, we've had Lailah's pies and they are damn good," Parker challenged. "Seems like we're going to need one of each flavor to test out that claim."

Sam laughed and shook her head. "How you have any room to eat another thing I will never know."

The table was soon loaded up with pie and everyone was sampling each flavor, but I took a whole slice of strawberry-rhubarb to myself. It was my favorite next to sugar cookies, but for this it was only good while in season, so I was going to eat my body weight while I could. As we sat talking and laughing, I felt a sharp stab of anxiety coming from Micah and noticed he was looking down at his phone. He typed out a text message and then looked up.

"Hey, I need out," he stated, causing half of us to move out of the booth for him.

Without another word, he headed to the front door, phone already up to his ear. I knew he didn't know that he was broadcasting his emotions to me right now, but it was clear to me that things were not good.

"I'll be right back," I murmured to Brayden, giving his arm a squeeze so he wouldn't follow.

Stepping outside, I didn't see him right away but I felt the pull to the side of the building that was farther away from the main road the diner sat on. Rounding the corner, I saw him pacing as he talked on the phone his anger growing by the second. Taking a deep breath, trying to block out his emotions so they didn't overwhelm me, I sent him soothing energy in exchange. This caused him to snap his head up seeing me standing there, he paused in his conversation as if unsure of what to do now that I'd caught him. He sighed and held out his free hand for me to take as he put the phone on speaker.

"Ned, just so you know Lailah is here with me," Micah informed.

There was a pause on the other end of the phone before he spoke again. "Hello Lailah, I'm Ned, Micah's financial advisor and lawyer he hired to look into things with his aunt. Do you want me to continue, Sir?"

"Go ahead, I'll tell her about it anyways, she's pretty much my wife."

Hearing Micah say that gave me butterflies in my stomach that were not at all appropriate for this current situation.

"Congratulations, Sir," Ned said without hesitation.

"I've contacted the council and King Rupert about the situation to see if there is anything your parents worked out with them. They were all given the same documents that you were at their death, but I did discover that the will was updated weeks before you were to be gone. The trouble is, that I'm just not equipped to deal with this kind of dispute on such a massive level. Your aunt's team is throwing up roadblocks and I don't have the skill to get around them," Ned explained. "I think it's time we pulled in more help on this, she isn't going to back down easily."

Micah hung his head resting it on my shoulder as he gripped my hand. "Thank you, Ned. Do you have any suggestions?"

"If you want someone to fight dirty, then personally, America is the place to do that. I know our laws are different, but if you're not planning on playing fair then it doesn't really matter."

Then an idea struck me. "We can ask Dylan. The firm he works for is a branch of one that's main headquarters in New York, who's to say we can't fly out there if we need to."

"What's the firm's name?" Ned asked.

"Holmes, Cooper, and Lewis," I answered.

Ned let out a harsh laugh. "Oh yeah, they will be the right kind of people. They do tons of work in the business world, trust me you do not want to go against them if they have their eyes set on what you have."

"Alright, can I tell them to reach out to you if they have questions?" Micah inquired.

"Absolutely, it would be best for us to work alongside each other. They'll need someone with the correct law license to file some paperwork," Ned shared.

"Thank you, Ned, you took a risk on me being a kid and all," Micah said, pulling me into a half hug.

"Sir," Ned started and paused as if he was surprised by the kind sentiment. "I just wish I could be more helpful to you. I'll keep an eye on things, the council is trying to stall where they can, to give you time, but there isn't much I'm afraid."

"I'll get the ball rolling as fast as I can," Micah promised then hung up.

Neither one of us said a word as he wrapped me up in a hug and buried his face in my neck, holding on to me for dear life. I could feel his pain and anger rolling through his body, so I tried to counter them as I rubbed his back. It was at this moment I understood what Jay said earlier in the day, about Micah needing me more than the others in some ways. He had Brayden, but with problems like this, he would never turn to his best friend for help. Brayden's mom was now fully recovered but their family had some healing to do from everything that happened over the two years she was under the influence of Tabitha messing with her brain.

"We won't let her win, Micah," I promised. "Even if I have to take her down myself, I won't let her steal the only thing your parents left you."

Micah lifted his head at that and looked down at me with a smirk. "That has to be one of the sexiest things you've ever said, but I won't put that on you after everything you've gone through."

"Oh, know that's not how it works Mr. I heard you call me your wife and that means we do this together, no matter what," I told him with a glare.

His answer to my threat was to kiss me, and not just a peck on the lips. It was all tongue and teeth as he tried to devour my mouth as if he could force me to agree with him that way. Lucky for him, I didn't back down that easy and I gave just as good as I got, which is how I ended up plastered to the brick wall of the diner with my leg tucked up over his hip as he ground into me. If it was Jay, I have no doubt that I would get fucked or at least finger fucked, but Micah wasn't as into the almost getting caught part of things. He just liked to be in charge and decided what was going to happen.

"Ah guys..." Brayden's voice called.

We broke from our kiss to turn to where he stood with a faint blush on his cheeks as he rubbed the back of his neck.

"Sorry to interrupt, but everyone's finished and ready to head home."

I couldn't help the snort that came out and quickly devolved into laughter. Here I was, dry humping one husband while the other had to come and tell us it was time to go, something about that just hit my funny bone and I couldn't stop laughing.

"What did you do to her?" Micah asked, giving me a quizzical brow.

"Me? I wasn't the one trying to fuck her with clothes on," Brayden said defensively. "I should be asking you that question, I could feel her lust even with my shield up."

Finally, I was able to pull myself together and wipe my eyes from the tears that slipped out. "Oh god, I needed a good laugh, can never have too many of those. Come on, lover boys, let's head home before the others get suspicious of us back here."

Micah grabbed me around the waist and tossed me over his shoulder, smacking my ass. "What if I want them to think the three of us are up to no good?"

"Well, that's up to Brayden," I answered.

This wasn't the first time that Micah alluded to having a threesome. It made sense that he'd be comfortable with

Brayden since they were best friends and all, but I wasn't going to decide that for Brayden.

"What do you say man? You in or out on what's going down when we get home?" Micah challenged. "If I remember correctly, I get you all to myself if I want, seeing as it's our honeymoon, but I'm willing to share if you are, Brayden."

Peeking past Micah's arm, I saw Brayden staring at me and licked his lips. "I say the faster we get home the better."

"That's what I thought," Micah said, handing me off to him. "I'll let you have her for now, since I got her all worked up."

I huffed at that once Brayden set me on my own feet. "I'm sorry, when did I turn into a piece of meat to be handed out?"

Micah stepped up into my space and grabbed my chin. "Oh, you're no piece of meat, you're my delectable Cookie who I plan on eating up tonight. But make no mistake, I'm going to be calling the shots in our little tryst and you're absolutely going to love it."

I leaned in for the kiss I thought I was going to get, but instead he pulled away with a hungry glint in his eyes as he walked back to the front of the building.

"What the fuck was that?" I demanded turning to Brayden, who was also grinning like a fool.

"That Angel, was the real Micah, the man who loves control but rarely ever finds someone who will trust him enough to surrender," he paused and tilted his head to look at me. "Do you trust him enough to submit to him?"

A shiver of delight trailed down my spine. "Absolutely."

To say that the drive back to the house was the longest of my life wouldn't be too far from the truth. The raging hard on that was trapped pressing against my jeans was killing me, but it was going to be worth the wait. Yeah, we'd already gone at it twice today but what can I say—I'd denied myself for too long, so now we needed to play catch up. I knew that once I gave my heart to Lailah it would be devastating in the best way possible. She now held me by the balls, and I was totally okay with that, hell I would wrap them up in a bow if she asked me to.

I'm sure that others might think it's weird to want to share her even more than we already have to, but this was a desire that I've had for a long time. I trusted Brayden with her completely, as well as trusting he would be able to handle what I was going to ask. Tonight was going to be a production and I was the director dictating what everyone did and when. The thrill of having that power to give or deny pleasure made me want to come in my pants before we even got started. The rest of the guys could feel the tension in the car as awkward conversation floated about, but I didn't give a fuck. Tonight was ours and the rest of them could just deal, it's not like we didn't have the rest of our lives to explore all of our dreams and fantasies. Once back at the house, she hugged and kissed all the other guys good night, before taking my hand.

"You guys better keep it down. I don't want to be listening to you forking all night," Cami yelled.

I laughed. "Do what I've had to do, wear headphones and turn your music up. Better yet, call your girlfriend and get some of your own action."

"What do you know, flame boy's got a point. Okay new plan, let's see who can be louder," Cami offered trailing behind us.

Lailah stopped and looked at her best friend. "Good-night Cami, if you talk to Maggs tell her I say hi."

Biting back a smile, I shook my head, loving how unashamed she was about what was going to happen tonight.

"Lala, you are no fun," Cami pouted.

"Oh, I beg to differ on that," I interjected, wagging my brows. "She's tons of fun."

"Okay, ew. That was too far, asshole. Too far," she muttered with a shiver.

Brayden joined us, ignoring the looks the other guys gave us in mild surprise at the combination of people involved, but they didn't say a word, smart men. I would bet my inheritance that Jay is one kinky fucker and would love to have an audience every so often, once they sealed the deal. It's the silent ones who are always freaks in the sheets, I was just an asshole who liked to boss people around. I led our merry band to Lailah's bedroom and stopped in the middle of the room, waiting for Brayden to close the door. We'd already agreed amongst us men not to ever lock the door, in case something happened, but with that came the rule no one would enter unless it was urgent. Each of us valued our time with Lailah so it was easy to trust the rule would be followed.

Turning Lailah to face me, I ran my hands down her arms and grasped her hands. "Look at me, Lailah," I demanded using her name so she knew I was being serious. "What I would like to try tonight is being in control of everything that goes on, but if at any time you are uncomfortable or you feel it will trigger a panic attack, you say red. The moment that word comes out of your mouth we will immediately stop and check in with you. Are you interested in allowing me to do this with you tonight?"

She gave me a sultry smile and nodded her head.

"I need you to tell me with your words, Lailah," I stated.

"Yes, I am willing to give you control over what goes on tonight."

"What is the word that you say if you want us to stop?"

"Red."

"Do you have any questions or triggers to tell us, besides being laid on your back or grabbed from behind?"

She paused to think about that for a moment. "Not that I am aware of, but I will alert you if that changes."

Ah, my little Cookie Monster was already learning the rules to this game.

"Brayden, are you comfortable and willing to participate in this?" I asked my best friend. "You do not have to join in if you're not ready or interested in following my direction."

He just grinned at me like I was being an idiot. "I am more than willing to be involved in things tonight."

"Same question to you, anything you aren't willing to do?"

"I don't mind sharing or being that close to you naked, but I am not interested in being more involved with you physically," he shared, looking a little uncomfortable saying it.

It's not like I could blame him, most vanilla people thought if two guys were involved in any sexual act it meant they were gay or bisexual. "Totally fine and I'm not interested in you either, other than my best friend."

Brayden seemed to relax completely once we said our peace. I took a few steps away from both of them and crossed my arms, taking in Lailah's simple beauty. She wore a simple ironic shirt that said *This is my Tea Shirt* with a tea cup on it and a pair of skinny jeans. Her blonde hair was up in a messy bun while curls escaped drifting around her face and neck. Yet the most striking thing about her was those crystal blue eyes that looked at me with such love and trust it blew my mind. This woman had waited for me even after I was an ass to her when we first met, rejected her Oath the first time, and yet somehow here I was Bonded to her for life.

"Brayden, remove her shirt," I instructed.

Instead of going behind her like most people would, he stood in front of her so she could see him as he gripped the bottom of her shirt and lifted it off of her. I stepped to the side so I could still clearly see her body being revealed. Her smooth alabaster skin was bathed in the warm light of the setting sun, making her golden hair shine. Brayden dropped the shirt and raised a hand to touch the swell of her breast, but I didn't tell him he could.

"Stop," I ordered. "You are not allowed to touch her unless I've given you the instruction to."

Brayden's hand was paused, hovering above her skin, but then he pulled it away and dropped it by his side.

"Kiss her, like you can't breathe without her mouth attached to yours."

Brayden didn't hesitate as he leaned over and kissed her as I'd directed. He kissed her as desperately as I had just outside the diner. He kissed her until her arms started to raise, wrapping around his neck, kissing him back just as fiercely.

"No Lailah, that rule wasn't just for Brayden. " I warned her, tapping her arm so she dropped them by her sides again. "You aren't allowed to touch him either until I say so."

This interaction didn't slow down my best friend from kissing her, and I wasn't doing anything to stop it. I was watching, enjoying, getting hard as a fucking rock.

"Now, take off the rest of her clothes."

Brayden broke the kiss to do as I said, peeling her bra off and exposing her breasts then quickly moving on to her jeans and underwear. There she stood absolute perfection, her breath coming faster as her eyes started to shine with lust watching both of us, waiting for the next order I would give.

"Now, take your cock out and let her see how badly you want her."

Brayden didn't hesitate as he unbuttoned his jeans and slid down the zipper. I gave her a few seconds to take in the sight of it, before I did the same so she could see my need too. Shifting so I was standing directly in front of her beside Brayden, I craved the sight of her reaction. I gripped the base of my cock and slowly started to stroke it up and down. Lailah's chest was rising and falling more rapidly as she watched me stroke myself. I was having trouble holding on to my control, but I refused to touch her just yet.

"Brayden, I think it's time you ditched the clothes too."

"Is that permission to take them off?" He asked.

"Yes, it is," I answered, trying not to laugh at how serious he was taking this.

Seconds later, he was also naked and I felt it was only fair to join them. I mean, it's not like I wasn't getting in on this action tonight either, so away the clothes went.

"Lailah, have you given a blow job before?" I asked. We men agreed never to talk about our inmate times with Lailah, unless it was something we all needed to know for her safety.

She gave me a cheeky grin. "A few times, but I can't say I'm a master or anything."

"Well then, get on your knees and show us what you've got," I instructed with a raised brow.

"You or Brayden?"

"Brayden, he's waited a long time to have you."

Dropping to her knees, she reached out to grab Brayden's cock and pumped it a few times before she brought her mouth down on him. I watched in fascination, the way her mouth moved over his dick, but nothing prepared me for what came next. She tilted her head back and opened her mouth wide, taking him in until her lips were touching the base of his cock. She pulled back, letting his dick slide out until her lips were no longer touching it, before taking him back in again.

"Fuck," Brayden gasped.

"Oh you lied, Cookie," I said with a chuckle. "That right there, was impressive as fuck."

She pulled her mouth off of him to look at me. "I wasn't able to have sex with them, but I wasn't going to leave them with nothing. Blowjobs are easy for me to stay on top and have control over the situation."

"Enough of that then, a few more rounds and the fun

would be over all too soon. Everyone on the bed," I directed with a wave. "Lailah, if you're on all four can Brayden be behind you?"

"I don't know, but I'm up for giving it a shot," she answered, jumping on the bed.

I positioned myself in front of her as Brayden sat beside her. "Let's try something easy. Brayden you eat her out from behind while I get a sample of what you just had."

Brayden rolled onto his back and pulled Lailah to sit on his face, while I knelt in front of her. Reaching out, she grasped my hard cock and rubbed her thumb over the tip, smearing the pre-cum that was leaking out of it. I knew the moment Brayden's mouth connected with her pussy as her eyes rolled back in her head and she moaned.

I pushed my hips forward, pressing my dick against her lips and she opened for me, letting my cock slip into her mouth. I kept up a constant rhythm as she licked and sucked, swirling her tongue around my cock. Lailah's moans were muffled by my dick, but I could tell Brayden was doing his job to make her feel good.

I reached out and ran my fingers through her hair, gripping the strands tight as I moved her mouth up and down my cock.

"You like that, don't you?" I whispered, "You like the way I take control."

I saw her nodding, but her mouth was full of my dick. I wanted to stay like this, giving her commands, watching her mouth move up and down my cock.

But that wasn't the only thing I wanted.

I pulled out of her mouth and she gasped. Instead of taking a breath, I moved down and pulled her off of Brayden, laying her on her back. It was risky but I hoped not looming over her would do the trick. I was now face to face with her glistening wet pussy, happy as can be. Running my tongue through her folds, I worked it up to her clit and licked the tip. She cried out and Brayden muffled her moans with a kiss. She was so fucking beautiful. The way her body moved as I licked her pussy. How she balled up the sheets in her hands as she was on the verge of coming.

I pulled back from the kiss and looked into her lust filled eyes. I knew what she wanted.

"You want me to let you come, don't you?" I asked as I slid a finger inside of her.

She nodded vigorously. "God yes please let me come!"

I pushed another finger inside. "That's a good girl," I smiled.

I wanted to make her come first like this, on her back like therapy, only good things happened like this now. She exploded seconds later, thrashing and moaning with Brayden now working over her breasts with his hands and mouth. I didn't relent, seeing the pure ecstasy on her face was all I wanted in life, knowing that I did that to her pleased me to no end. When I finally pulled my fingers out of her, giving her a chance to recover, I backed off and sat up, grinning at her.

"Think you can handle some more?" I asked.

She let out a huff trying to catch her breath as she sat up. "I'm no quitter, besides neither of you have gotten to finish."

"Angel, only you would be so concerned about that," Brayden shared with a soft smile on his face. His gaze flicked up to mine as if asking a question.

"I think you've earned it man. Enjoy our wife how you want to," I said, giving up control of the situation... for now.

Brayden reached out a hand to Lailah who crawled over to him. He positioned her so her head was down on the bed, ass up in the air, legs spread wide giving him space to fit. I watched her face carefully to make sure she was okay, along with checking in on her emotions. Everything pointed to her being totally relaxed and comfortable with what was going on, so I leaned back against the headboard and stroked myself. Brayden took his cock and ran it up and down along her pussy lips and clit, then slipped it into her. He pumped in and out, grabbing her hips tightly as they began to fuck. He slapped her ass playfully, causing her to moan and buck against him. Watching my wife getting fucked was surprisingly one of the hottest things I'd ever seen, maybe Jay was onto something. I was so turned on I didn't think I'd last long even by my own hand.

Brayden moved faster and harder with her encouragement and I could tell he was getting close to coming. Lailah was already there as she squeezed him with her pussy making him close his eyes and grunt. "I'm coming, Angel," and he did.

I decided to join them, rubbing my cock over Lailah's back as I exploded all over her, I'd never cum that hard in my life. Brayden flopped down beside Lailah as I did the same, trying to remember how to move again. Even though I didn't fuck Lailah, I was more than happy with how things turned out. Eventually, we all managed to pull ourselves together enough to make it into the bathroom to shower. Lailah, being the woman that she is, felt I needed a little more attention—who was I to argue?

Then we curled up in bed with Lailah in the middle, tired and satisfied.

CHAPTER 15
LAILAH

Walking up to the entrance to Six Flags with the sound of screaming people, the clicking of the roller coasters, and the music blaring over the speaker was exhilarating. I tugged on Jay's hand once we made it through the security check towards The Demon. "We have to hit this one up first, it's my favorite," I announced.

Jay had decided that I had to be attached to him at all times, unless on a ride or in the bathroom, because he's convinced I'll get lost in the crowds. Even though it wasn't peak season and people were still in school, all the college kids were taking advantage, making it busier than we expected.

"We can't leave the others behind," Jay answered, pulling me against his chest, trapping me in his arms as he looked down at me. "I wasn't kidding about the rules, Beautiful, know that I will be keeping track if you break them."

"You really should be careful saying shit like that around her brothers, they might not understand how you mean it," Cami pointed out an impish grin on her face.

Jay's steel colored eyes looked down at her and frowned. "They should appreciate that I'm keeping her safe."

"Oh, that I don't think they'll have a problem with, it's the spankings that come later I'm talking about," Cami explained. "Lailah's family is as traditional and vanilla as they come, let's not stress them out too much."

This actually got a bark of laughter to come from Jay, which shocked both me and Cami.

"What's funny enough that you got him to laugh?" Parker asked when he joined us.

"Nothing you need to know," Jay stated.

Soon enough, the rest of our crew gathered with Hudson and Kyle pouring over a map of the park. "I have a foolproof method of making sure we hit every ride at times that are known for being the lowest wait time. The trick is making sure we start with the right ride off the bat, or it will throw the whole process off," Kyle informed Hudson, and proceeded to tell him all about whatever brilliant math thing he used to find the right variables.

"Yo, Kyle," I called out. "What's the first ride? We need to get this show on the road. It's already fifteen minutes past opening."

Sure enough, that was all I needed to say to get the reaction I wanted, causing Kyle to blurt out the name of the ride. "Raging Bull!"

Jay led the charge after studying the map the whole drive down, saying something about needing to know all the exits and lay of the area. We might be at an amusement park to have fun and relax, but I wasn't sure that relaxing was a concept that Jay or Hudson completely understood. Raging Bull was one ride that took me a few years to actually go on, since it had one of the steepest drops right at the beginning but once I sucked it up and did it, I was hooked.

"Fun fact about Lailah," Dylan piped up as we got in line for the ride. "She is one you literally have to force onto the ride no matter what she says, because in the end she loves it. Just wait, she'll be fine, then as she watches the ride go and the people panic she'll get cold feet and try to bail—don't let her."

I gaped at him. "I do *not*."

Kyle snorted. "Oh yeah you do, sis."

"Trust me, that won't be a problem if she's attached to Jay all day," Micah said, giving me a wink when I glared at him. "He won't let her back out of anything she's agreed to do or rules to follow. Isn't that right, Cookie Monster?"

"Oh, you are *so* not getting lucky tonight," Cami snickered.

Micah just shrugged like that fact didn't bother him one bit, he already knew he wasn't going to be sharing the bed with me tonight. That didn't mean I wouldn't come up with some way to retaliate later on, when he'd all but forgotten about his comment. It didn't take us long to get onto the ride, thanks to Kyle's skills and I hopped right on and pulled the bar down around my lap without any hesitation.

"Dude, you really fucked up this time," Parker commented as he got in the car behind me and Jay. "Did you see the look on her face just now?"

"Fuck off, Care Bear, worry about your own issues hanging out with us today," Micah snapped back at him.

I snapped my head around and gave them a dirty look. "You keep that shit to yourselves, no matter what happened in the past she is here as my brother's girlfriend, and she will be respected as such. Do you hear me?"

They both nodded their understanding, so I turned

back to the front satisfied, feeling Micah's tinge of guilt. It was sure coming in handy having this connection to my moody man-child. Then we were off and all conversation stopped as we climbed up the massive incline, the rattling of the coaster all I could focus on. Jay reached out and took my hand, unclenching it from the handhold in the harness and interlaced our fingers. There was a slight pause at the top where we seemed to hang in midair before we plunged down, yanking a scream from my throat that didn't last the whole way to the bottom, where we entered into a tunnel and shot back up into the bright late morning sun.

Getting my breath back I grinned, tossing my arm up as we went down the second drop, still holding Jay's hand whooping my excitement. All too soon, the ride was over and we had to get off, my body still vibrating with the adrenaline. Glancing back at the others I caught sight of Phoebe, who was white as a ghost clutching onto my brother as he walked across the platform to the exit.

"Phoebe, are you alright?" I asked, rushing over.

She licked her lips and gulped down a few breaths of air before she could give me an answer. "I'm alive...barely."

"Why didn't you tell us that you were afraid of roller coasters?" I demanded, helping to steady her as we walked back to the front of the ride.

"I didn't want to be the one to ruin your fun together, your brother can't take much time off and I knew how much he missed you," she explained. "I just need some water and I'll be fine."

I looked up at Dylan and saw the guilty look on his face as he helped her to sit on a bench. "I'll go get a water bottle —be right back."

"Don't worry we'll stay with her," I promised, sitting

beside her rubbing her back. "Is there anything else we can do to help?"

"If anyone has motion sickness pills or a patch, those always helped her," Parker suggested.

I pulled out my phone and texted Dylan to see if any of the gift shops might have that in the park. It made sense to me that they would, but you never know.

"Wait," Kyle spoke up. "Parker, do you know Phoebe?"

Parker looked over at me then Phoebe before he nodded his head. "Yeah, we were good friends back in high school, we lost touch since then."

"Talk about a small world, they say there is a separation of seven people for you to know someone. Seems that this worked out to be a case of two people," Kyle said, far more interested in the math of the situation than the fact neither of them admitted it before this.

An awkward silence fell as we waited for Dylan to come back, unsure of where to take things from here. So, I did my sisterly duty and came up with random small talk. "How did the two of you meet?"

"Oh, well we both work for the law firm but under different partners," Phoebe answered. "He wants to go into business law to be more helpful to your parents while they still run the diner. I like the more messy dramatic family and estate law, people show their true colors at that point."

"Wait, did you say estate law? Like that has to do with wills and trusts right?" I asked excitedly.

Phoebe nodded, a little surprised at my reaction. "Ah, yes exactly those types of things."

"Did you do school in the States or overseas?" I pressed.

As if Micah caught on to what I was leading up to, he set a hand on my shoulder and gave a gentle but firm squeeze in warning. I could also feel his worry through our connection begging me not to talk about this in front of the others.

"Overseas at Cambridge, why do you ask?"

"Well, I've been going to school overseas now at Ryevick University," I shared now ,trying to come up with a reason I asked that wouldn't make me look stupid. "I was just curious to talk about the differences between types of schools."

Phoebe gave me an odd look when I told her I was at Ryevick, but she schooled her face quickly enough that I assumed it was because I said something dumb.

"I've been to so many different schools all over the world, but none of them have been here in America. That might be why I picked being here to be honest," Phoebe sighed. "My father could not understand why I didn't want to take an internship closer to home, but it was time for me to spread my wings and be on my own. Shortly after I was brought onto the team, I met Dylan and we hit it off right away, so I have to say it was fate."

My heart warmed hearing this, having experienced this myself with the guys. How people like us could travel halfway around the world and find love was amazing.

"Hey sis, good call on the motion sickness pills," Dylan called out when he returned. "They didn't have any in the shops, but I asked security if they had an EMS on staff and he had some in his pack. They must be something special because I've never seen it come in a liquid form like this before. You're just supposed to add it to water and drink it that way."

This seemed to catch Hudson's attention, seeing as his family runs a pharmaceutical company, it didn't shock me he might have some incite. "Do you mind if I look at the packaging?"

"Oh...ah sorry he mixed it up for me, said since it was hospital grade, he needed to prepare it," Dylan explained, handing over the water bottle to Phoebe. "Why would you want to look at it anyways?"

I could feel how uncertain Hudson felt and tugged on our connection getting him to look at me. Giving him a questioning brow I looked from the bottle to him hoping he would guess what I was thinking.

"My family is in the pharmaceutical business and I was just curious what they would use, it helps to have that information in case she had a reaction to something in the medication," Hudson offered.

Dylan bit the edge of his lip as Phoebe raised the water to her lips. "I'm sure it can't be anything too crazy, he's an EMT after all, wouldn't he have warned me if there was a side effect to watch out for?"

"I don't know what training they go through here in America, but I know most are not taught as in-depth about medication as doctors or pharmacists are," Hudson sighed, rubbing his brow as Phoebe gulped down the water and made a face at the taste. "We'll just keep a close eye on her for the next half hour, if there's no reaction I'm sure things will be fine."

"Does that mean we need to leave?" Kyle asked, sounding a little disheartened.

Dylan tossed his arm around our little brother's shoulders and grinned. "Nah little bro, you go with the others and have fun. Phoebe and I will relax and do some epic people watching while we wait for the meds to kick in. Once everything is fine, we'll catch up with you, sound like a plan?"

Kyle nodded, smiling from ear to ear as he pulled out the map and looked at his watch. I knew he was doing all the calculations in his head for the best ride to go on next. "Yes, it's the Joker next! It's new this year and I can't wait to try it out. Come on, we need to get a move on if we want to hit the perfect window."

Standing, I paused as Dylan took my seat on the bench. "Keep us updated okay, if I don't hear from you in thirty minutes, we're hunting your ass down. Trust me when I say that Jay can find anybody when he wants to."

"Don't worry sis, we'll be fine, you're the one who gets lost all the time," he joked waving me off. "Don't puke. I hear that ride is like the Zipper from the state fair, but worse."

That made me pause, I didn't get sick on rides but the one time I did, it was because I tried to win the eat a whole pie and get another whole pie for free. Going on a ride full of blackberry pie was not the world's smartest idea and Dylan never let me live it down.

"It was the pie," I said defensively.

"Then isn't it a good thing you had another one to eat when we got home," Dylan shot back with a wicked smile.

"Keep sharing dirt like that and who knows what Phoebe might learn, still got that special stuffy you *loved* so much," I threatened.

Dylan turned bright red and started to stutter. "D... don...don't you dare!"

"You've been warned," I cautioned, giving him the hand gesture that I would be watching him as we walked away.

Jay took up my hand once again with a soft chuckle that was almost lost in the noise around us. "Watching you three makes me wish I had a sibling—then I remember I have these assholes," Jay muttered as he gestured to the four guys walking ahead of us.

"I would say they're a pretty good glimpse into what it's like," I agreed.

Hudson slowed his walk to join us, taking my free hand in his. "Tell me why I'm so worried about Phoebe taking that medication?"

"Do we have any idea if the Day-Brite serum has crossed into the US?" I asked, looking at Jay.

"There have been no confirmed cases by the Elementi here, but it is one of the hardest things to detect. It doesn't show up on any screening we've tried so far, but there is a spike in missing persons cases across America. Enough that the FBI had been looking into it, even though there is nothing connecting them together," Jay shared.

"They've had the drug long enough that they could have found a new subtle way to administer it, versus injecting it like they had been doing," Hudson admitted. "That fact alone makes me worried, it only takes one medical professional like that to start administering it. People come here from all over and then go home, making it virtually impossible to trace where the dose could have happened."

"Has your father's people come up with any other helpful attributes from their studies?" I asked hopefully.

Hudson looked down at me, his eyes sad, and shook his head. Those poor people that had been secret test subjects forever had their lives altered for the sake of others. They were the reason I was pushing so hard to find a cure through my blood, I just hoped we could find it in time.

CHAPTER 16

LAILAH

Just as we got off the ride my phone started to buzz. It was a good thing I put it in my bra so I would make sure to notice it, since my body was still recovering from all the chaos of the ride. Seeing it was Dylan, I answered right away waving at the guys to get their attention. "Dylan, thing—"

"She's gone." Dylan blurted, cutting me off. "I don't know what happened. She went to the bathroom but that was like ten minutes ago. I went in to check on her, since Hudson was worried about a reaction but she wasn't in there. I tried to call her, even wandering around the area to make sure she wasn't waiting for me in a different spot."

"Hold on, back up a little," I said in a soothing voice. "How long ago did she go to the bathroom?"

"It's been like twenty minutes since she went in. Lailah, you have to help me. You said Jay can find people, right?"

"Where are you right now?" I demanded as I grabbed Jay's hand and started to run down the exit path back to the main area of the park.

"Ah...oh, I'm right near that kid's area. She wanted to

walk around a bit once she felt better. Do you think something happened to her? God, why did I let her take that medicine?" Dylan babbled.

"Don't move, we're coming to you," I snapped hanging up the phone. "Guys we have a problem, Phoebe's gone missing. Dylan is waiting for us over at the entrance to the kid's section of the park."

Once Jay heard this he charged off, almost dragging me with him, since I wasn't prepared for the sudden change in speed. Thankfully, it seemed that they had been walking closer to us, so it didn't take us long to spot Dylan pacing near a bathroom building. It didn't take him long to see us and the second he did his body seemed to sag in relief.

"This the bathroom she went in?" Jay asked without preamble. Dylan nodded as Jay handed me off to Micah and entered the woman's side of the bathroom.

"Asshole this is the women's," a lady yelled.

"What the hell are you doing here?"

"Get the fuck out before we call security and get your ass banned from this park."

I squeezed Micah's hand to get his attention. "I should really go help with that." He nodded and followed me, standing just outside the door as I entered. "Ladies I'm sorry about the intrusion but our friend is missing, and this is the last place she entered. You didn't see anyone sick or passed out in here, did you?'

This caught all the irate ladies' attention and gave Jay a chance to look the place over while they talked to me.

"I just walked in here, how long has she been missing? Did you contact park security?" one asked, clutching her daughter to her tightly.

"We have someone reaching out to them right now, she

wasn't feeling good so we wanted to make sure she wasn't still in here," I explained.

Another woman pulled out her phone. "I can post it on my Six Flags season passholders group and see if we can get more people looking for her. The government keeps trying to cover up all these strange disappearances going on right now. If they won't look out for us, then we better do it ourselves."

"I appreciate the offer but I'm not sure right now that's the best plan, she's only been missing for twentyish minutes. She could have gone to the help station for medical help," I suggested.

Jay walked back up to where I was and shook his head before he walked out.

"Thank you ladies for your help, and sorry again about my boyfriend barging in like that. Have a good day."

Ducking out of the bathroom, I was met with the others as they gathered around Jay. "Did you find anything?" Dylan asked.

Jay held out a little wallet that hooked onto your pants that Phoebe had been wearing. "We know she was here, but if something happened, she's now without identification. I suggest contacting security and seeing if they know anything first, if they have nothing for us, I will do what I do best."

Dylan looked absolutely crestfallen at this information, so I wrapped my arm around him so I could lead him to a park bench. "How could this be happening? Things like this don't really happen in real life, this is some Lifetime movie shit or something."

"I promise you, that we will do whatever we have to, to make sure she is safe," I vowed, looking my brother dead in the eye. "On my honor, as an Elementi Warrior, blessed by the angels we will find her."

I could feel the binding promise click into place as I invoked my power into my words. I'd read about giving an Oath to a king or other leader to back up your words, but I didn't understand the gravity of what that meant until now. Even if it took all summer or beyond, our focus would be on finding Phoebe. Dylan pulled me into a tight hug as if he understood the gravity of what I just did on some soul level.

"Thank you, Lailah, I believe you," Dylan whispered as he sat back. "I know Phoebe and I have only been together for less than a year, but I think she's the one, I want to marry her someday."

Jay stepped up and waited for us to give him our attention. "I talked to security, they're looking into things and asked for us to meet them at their office onsite."

It didn't surprise me one bit that Jay had already scoped out where that office was, since he led us right to it near the entrance to the park. It was awful for me to think of this right now, but there was something so sexy about a man who could take charge and make things happen. Micah wrapped his arm around my shoulders and pulled me into a half hug, kissing the top of my head as we waited for Jay to speak with one of the security people.

"If you could come in with us, there is a camera right by that bathroom for situations just like this. If you can point out what the female in question looks like we can send the photo out to our team," the security guys said, ushering us in. "Do you have an approximate time to have us start looking at the footage?"

Dylan rubbed his forehead as he though. "It's been forty-five minutes or less since she entered that bathroom."

The man nodded, typed something into the keyboard and rolled back the footage. We stepped back letting Dylan and Jay get the better view of the small tv screen of the bathroom.

"There!" Dylan shouted. "She's wearing a green flowy short sleeve shirt with black jeans."

"Let's keep it going and see if she leaves the bathroom," the security man said, slowing down the speed making it easier to spot someone with all the people wandering by.

I held my breath praying that we would see her walk out or something else to give us a clue as to what was going on.

"Wait, when did that attendant enter the bathroom with that cleaning cart?" Jay asked as one left the bathroom.

"We have people check every hour on the hour, and that bathroom is busier than usual with it being near the kid's area. Sometimes it gets more attention if someone hits the alert button that maintenance is needed," the security guy explained.

Stopping the tape, they rolled it back past when Phoebe entered another ten minutes or so and we saw the person enter. You couldn't tell if it was a man or woman with the coverall uniform and the cap they had on but seeing as the woman didn't cause a fuss it made me think female. *Could this be how they stole Phoebe? That medicine had to have been the Day-Brite serum, that's the only reason for this.* Just like me, once you took the serum you shone like a beacon to rogue demons looking for a person to take over. If it weren't for Jay's rule, that could have been me getting stuffed into a garbage cart, but this made things all that much harder.

"Show me where those carts are stored and where the staff keep their things," Jay barked, making us all jump.

The security guard looked at Jay with a frown. "Look kid, I was willing to help you find your friend but at this point, it's time to call in the police and have them handle things. This is now a missing person's case."

"Who is in charge of your security?" Jay demanded. "I will need to speak with him."

"Sure, and it's a woman, but Kendall isn't going to tell you anything differently than I just did. We deal with this stuff all the time," the guy muttered as he wandered off deeper into the office.

Jay turned to face us, his stoic expression hard. "Micah, I need you to call the closest Elementi hub to us and tell them what's going on. I need to contact my father and make sure we own this security company so we can keep the police out of things. Hudson, I need you to call your dad and find out if this serum could actually be consumed this way or if it's just a typical kidnapping. Parker, do you think you can get ahold of her father and find out if he knows of any threats against his family that we should be worried about? Brayden, don't let Lailah out of your sight."

This sent everyone into motion, leaving me and my siblings in limbo watching everyone else be purposeful. I sank into one of the chairs in front of the screens and pushed the button to play the film. It was still stuck at the slow speed so it gave me extra time to watch Phoebe walk in, tucking her phone in her back pocket.

"Jay!" I called swiveling around. "Did you find her phone?"

Jay had his phone up to his ear talking to someone and motioned for me to wait a moment. "Dylan, hand me your phone." With a questioning look he pulled out his phone and handed it to me. "Do you use Snapchat?"

"I mean, I have it on my phone but I don't really use it

much. I got it so when Phoebe went on a trip I could see her updates, she uses it a lot."

Now I was grinning, knowing that with the recent update if you didn't turn off your location it would be sending out your location to your friends. I scrolled through his list and found her profile, so I knew what her avatar looked like and flipped to the map and sure enough there was her dot moving away from us on the interstate. Shooting to my feet I let out a shrill whistle that my dad taught me at one of Kyle's hockey games. Everyone snapped their heads to look and me as I held up the phone.

"They have her phone and are driving away, who's coming with me to chase it down?" I inquired.

Micah promptly hung up his call and shoved his phone in his pocket. "Let's roll."

Dylan tried to come with us, but I stopped him. "No, you need to stay here with Kyle and the others. You are the only one who can answer certain questions about her, they need you more."

He tried to argue but then let out a breath and sagged his shoulders. "Fine, but call Kyle the moment you know anything."

"Take Parker with you," Jay instructed.

I was glad that he didn't try to stop me because it was too dangerous. We were a team and each of us needed to pull our weight. This was my chance to do that. Micah, Brayden, Parker and I jogged out of the security office, got our hands stamped so we could get back in if we needed to, and booked it across the parking lot to the car. Micah hit the button unlocking it and we all piled in, I took shotgun so I could give directions.

"We need to get on 194 south. It looks like they're

getting off on Belvidere Road, heading towards the lake," I shared, as I pulled up the nifty GPS this new SUV had.

Micah tore out of the parking lot, weaving around every car that was in our way like we were in the Indy five-hundred. Blowing through a red light we turned on what felt like two wheels onto the road that would get us to the highway.

"Man, you might want to slow it down just a touch so we don't get pulled over," Parker suggested.

"I don't see you driving, do I?" Micah growled. "You let me worry about shit like that and just hold on tight. We're not going to lose her because we were too stupid to see if she had her phone on her."

"Enough!" I yelled. "We need to stay focused, this is no time to argue."

At that, everyone shut up.

"Take this to the next exit then get off and head east," I instructed. "They're still on the same road and the traffic lights are slowing them down. It should help us gain some ground."

I tried not to look at how fast we were going, keeping my eyes locked on the moving dot that was Phoebe. I trusted Micah with my life, so I needed to trust him to get us there alive and well enough to save her. I spotted the exit and before I could say anything he was cutting across five lanes of traffic to get there, making more than one person honk and flip us the finger. We made it just in time for a green light but I doubted that would have slowed Micah down one second. Once more, with the weaving through cars, we were on Belvidere Road taking whatever risks he felt like he could.

"It looks like they're heading for Sheridan Road and heading north."

I grabbed my phone and pulled up my map so I could look around to see if I could guess where they were heading. "There is a fishing harbor with charter boats, a water treatment plant, generating station, and Illinois Beach State Park. None of these jump out at me as a place demons would want to hold someone captive."

"My money's on the power plant," Parker spoke up. "Think about it, a huge factory to work out of and limited people working there. No one would go there unless they needed to. If I was going to run a secret demon body snatching ring, I would do it there."

"I agree, out of the choices that sounds as logical as any," Brayden added.

Micah let out a sharp laugh. "So we are just gonna go with that because Parker watches scary movies? I say the pier, if they have a boat there, it gives them the freedom to take her wherever they need to or cross state lines where no one will be looking for her."

"Both are fair suggestions, the docks are first up so we'll know pretty soon if that's the case," I said, mediating the tension in the car.

Why on earth did Jay send Parker with us? He knows that Micah and him don't work well together. Too late now, I had to deal with things as they are and make the most of it. Although Parker might not be the tactical one out of us, he was a skilled fighter and had a large amount of power backing him up.

"They passed the marina," I shared as we pulled onto the next road heading north. "Looks like the power plant might be the winner, unless they want to ditch her in the forest, making us all wrong."

No one seemed to appreciate my shot at levity and Micah just gave me a look out of the corner of his eye. This road wasn't quite so busy and had less traffic lights as we got into the industrial area, helping us pick up some speed.

"Bray, call Jay, let him know where we are and if he doesn't hear from us in twenty minutes we need help," Micah instructed.

Brayden pulled out his phone and dialed. "Good call. Hey Jay, we're on..."

"Tell him we're at the Waukegan Generating Station," I interjected, turning in my seat. "That's where the dot stopped."

CHAPTER 17

LAILAH

J ay decided right away that he wanted to meet us there and wanted us to wait for him, but I had other plans. "You cannot tell me we are actually going to sit here while they could be attaching a demon to her, are you?"

The guys all looked at each other, then undid their seatbelts. Having mine already off, I tossed open my door and jumped out of the car, taking a look around the oddly empty parking lot.

"It's a Monday afternoon, there's no holiday, so why aren't there more cars parked out here? There wasn't even someone at the guard shack," I mused.

Parker came to stand next to me. "I told you, no one would check out here if they didn't have to. We ended up taking a service road in, so it's off the beaten path."

"Let's go you two," Micah ordered as he marched off towards the office building.

"Look, if we're going to do this, we should be smart about it," Brayden cautioned. "Let's take a look around the outside to make sure there isn't another employee parking area. What if this is a whole mix up and the phone got stolen by someone who works here? It could have fallen out of her pocket for all we know."

I understood where Brayden was coming from, but it was a little too late to be getting cold feet about this. "Fine, we'll scope out the outside then we're going in."

The building was in two sections, the front was a low office building that had the company name on it. My guess is it was used for meetings and the paper-pushers of the production. The real work though, was in a massive brick building four stories high with five giant stacks out front. There wasn't any smoke coming out of them and I wasn't sure if that was good or bad. Once we made it behind the actual station, there was a massive field of electrical towers holding lines going in every direction. You could feel the hum of the energy coming off them and an occasional snap as power leapt across the lines. This told me that even if the stacks weren't smoking, there was still power flowing from the station itself.

"I don't see anything useful out here, let's head inside," Micah decided as he walked up to the closest door.

When he tried to open it, it didn't budge. There were two more doors for us to try but all were locked tight. Micah pressed a hand against the set of double doors and I watched as steam started to rise and the door turned cherry red under his touch. Pulling his hand back, he kicked the same spot and the doors burst inward, giving us our way in.

"Okay that was badass," I said, following Micah into the building.

Now I understood why they based horror movies out of places like this, because they are legit creepy as all hell. The lights were off but for the soft warm glow of security lighting along the concrete corridor, with pipes and wires running all along the ceiling. I could tell we were walking up an incline and the hallway was wide enough that three of us could walk side by side. I could imagine machinery of some kind being driven around moving things or bringing in supplies, it was a long walk to wherever we were going. We reached a point where we could go left or we could keep going straight. Our choice was made for us when the door to the left was locked and the one ahead was not.

Micah went through first, pulling the door open enough to see what was on the other side then looked back at us, motioning us to be quiet. He slipped through, then a moment later waved us to follow him with another warning to be quiet. The room we entered was the main production area if I had to guess. Metal walkways in a grid-lock pattern filled the room giving us the opportunity to look down and see the massive coils and mechanical parts that generated the electricity. Turbines churned, pulling water from the lake to help keep them cool as they labored. If I wasn't so worried about getting caught and or killed, this would have been a super cool experience to appreciate. At the moment, I was just praying nothing jumped out at us since there was nowhere to hide. Then I heard what had Micah so cautious— voices.

"What do you mean you only brought one?" a man growled. "You had a whole fucking theme park to pick from!"

"Look, I'm not the only one working that area, alright," this coming from a woman. "I did my part getting the newly dosed person out of the park without getting caught. She was with someone and they called security, I couldn't risk them searching the back where we keep them until the end of the day."

They were talking about Phoebe! This also means that she was given the serum.

"Then you better get back there before they notice you took too long of a lunch break. We were short on our quota for last week. We can't come up short again, do you hear me?" the man growled.

"You know what? Fuck you, old man. The only reason you're even in charge of this place is because you got picked by a Higher Demon," the woman snapped.

An odd hissing snarl echoed in the room below us as we crept closer. "That's right little human, don't make me rip your pathetic low level demon out of you and send your rotting corpse to your loved ones. I can just as easily replace you with the woman you brought me. She will be used for a higher purpose, I can tell. Her soul is tainted and will draw the darkness to her."

"Go rot in hell, I'm over this shit. I was promised power and a place in the new dark world that would destroy this shit stain of an existence that we live in now. Yet all I've been doing is collecting bodies for other people—like a slave!"

"That's because you are a slave," the man's voice had now completely changed to sound like a snake with the hissing S's. "Or at least you *were*."

"*No.*"

The sound of a scuffle, followed by a sickening slam of something against the concrete floor made me ill. I could only guess what just happened and was so extremely grateful that I didn't have to witness it.

"At least she brought me you," the slithering voice crooned. "Come, come let's find you a master. This will make them happy, yesss, yesss, indeed."

I gave a pleading look to the guys, this was our chance. We could totally take the one demon. We'd dealt with far worse than a measly Higher Demon before, Ubel was a

Greater Demon one of the Dark Lord's court. Brayden gave me a sharp shake of the head no and pointed back the way we came. I knew they would want to talk this to death, and I knew it was the right choice, seeing how things went the last time I went off on my own. Once we made it back to the hallway, we gathered in the corner that would allow us to be hidden if someone opened the locked door on the left.

"Please tell me we're not going to let them use her as a puppet for a demon," I demanded. "You saw what that can do to a person."

"Angel, we are not going to abandon her if we can do something to help. All I ask is that we go about this with some kind of plan," Brayden explained.

Micah scratched his chin as he thought. "We need to find out how many demons are in here or if that is the only one. From what they were saying, this is a drop off point for people they've given the serum to. Wherever they took Phoebe, there could be others. Wouldn't you rather have the chance to save more if we can?"

"Of course I would," I scowled at Micah. "How exactly do you propose we scope out the area?"

"Two by two," Parker stated. "If we go as a group of four we won't cover as much ground and be easier to spot. I'll go with Lailah and you go with Brayden."

"I think the fuck not!" Micah snarled.

Parker sighed. "Think about it man. You and I are the strongest fighters out of the four of us. Do you agree?"

"So?"

"Why would it be smart to put two strong people together? You and I don't work well together, but you and Brayden are a dynamic duo, always have been. Lailah only has up close or defensive weapons to fight with, I have long range which means I can keep her protected," Parker argued. "Put aside your personal feelings and think like Jay."

Micah just glared at him for a few seconds before he nodded. "Fine, but know that if anything happens to her, I will kill you with my bare hands."

"I would expect nothing less, and if I let it happen, I would absolutely deserve it," Parker agreed. "Now, do our cells work here?"

We all grabbed ours and looked at the screen but there was no signal. "Has to be all the concrete, it might get better out of this hallway," Brayden reasoned.

"We will search for twenty minutes and if we don't find anything, make your way back here. It's the best we can do unless we have cell service, so try to text before heading back here," Parker suggested, surprising us all with his logic. "If I can find a computer I'm gonna see if they have blueprints of the place I can access to make it easier."

"Seems you aren't a complete idiot after all," Micah muttered, as he headed for the doors back out to the generator room. "We'll go right, you wait a few minutes then you guys go left."

Seeing that Parker wanted to argue, I placed my hand on his arm drawing his attention. "Don't let him get inside your head, this team doesn't work without all of us."

"Thanks, Trouble," Parker said, giving me a tight smile, brushing his knuckles along my cheek. "Come on, let's go find Phoebe."

Back in the generator room, we stayed low as we made our way along the gangplank. It was slotted so I could see the various parts and pieces working as we moved, but I didn't see any signs of workers in the room with us. The noise of the motors working covered our steps, but even still, we moved as silently as we could not taking a chance.

We reached the end of our walkway and there was a door with a glass window cut into it, so we could see into the next space. It looked like a control room filled with all kinds of buttons, knobs, dials, and computers—exactly what Parker had been hoping to find.

"The door is unlocked," Parker whispered as he opened it.

The room was far larger than we could see from the narrow window in the door, which is why we missed the man who was working at one of the computers. I'd entered first and when I spotted him, I closed the door behind me, keeping Parker out and hidden.

"What the hell are you doing in here?" an older man with graying hair that stuck out in all directions under his hard hat demanded. "Look, how many times do I have to keep telling you idiots that the control room isn't a place to fuck around in? You hit the wrong button and you'll turn off the power for the next fifty miles in all directions. We can't afford to get noticed like that."

He thinks I'm one of the demon helpers I realized, forcing myself to hold back a grin, thankful for the first time ever for what I went through. I probably gave off the same energy as the other dosed people.

"I'm sorry, I'm new to all this and I can't find anyone," I explained playing dumb. "I had a problem with one of the people that got dosed and I need to inform someone but not sure who or where they are?"

The old guy sighed and picked up a walkie-talkie. "Control room to harvest area one, do you copy? I have a lost puppet that needs to talk to Mozog."

"This is harvest area one, Mozog is busy, send them our way and we'll deal with it."

"Will do," the controller said, turning to us. "Alright

you're gonna have to take a left out of here and take the stairs to the lower part of the generator room. There is a set of double doors under this office that leads to a hallway, follow it all the way to the end until you get to the red door. It says, emergency exit only. The alarm will sound but that's just to keep people out, on the other side is harvest room one. That's where all the empty puppets go to get their masters." He paused and looked at me closely for the first time, squinting his eyes at me. "Why don't I feel the presence of your master?"

Quickly, I ran through everything I'd learned from the Elementi on different types of demons and their classifications. "Yeah, well you'd have to have a master that gave off any power, I got picked by a simple low level messenger."

"Ah, explains how simple you are and how you fucked up on your first job," he harrumphed. "Now get out, I've got important work to do."

Backing out of the door, Parker all but grabbed me and dragged me down the walkway before he slammed me up against the concrete wall. "What the actual fuck, Lailah. How could you do something so reckless after everything that's happened to you?! I should have been the one to go in first, I could have taken him out without you having to put yourself in danger!"

"I didn't think the whole thing through alright, but it turned out better than either of us could have planned. He thought I was one of them, the puppets, and he told me where they are keeping the people they take," I reasoned. "You have every right to be upset, but I suggest we go back in there and deal with him. I will back you up and stay out of the way, letting you handle things. He had a walkie-talkie that he used to communicate with the harvest room and I think we're going to need it."

Parker's expression was still full of anger and fear, but he let me go. "Don't think this is the end of this, just wait until Jay and Micah find out about that shit. You'll be handcuffed to one of them at all times for a month." He rubbed his hands over his face and growled. "Let's go get the walkie-talkie."

CHAPTER 18

LAILAH

As promised, I stayed outside while Parker entered the control room to deal with the man inside. I could hear the sound of a scuffle, but the thick metal door kept me from hearing much else, so I sent up a prayer that Parker was as skilled as he thought he was. The room fell silent and then the door swung open to reveal a grim Parker. "All clear, come on in, I want to take a look at the computer systems."

Entering, I found the man knocked out and propped up in the corner, his hard hat laying next to him. I could tell by the slow movement of his chest that he was still alive, which made me let out the breath I'd been holding. Knowing first hand what it was like to have that weight on you, I would never wish that on anyone, let alone someone I loved.

"See if you can find something to tie him up with while I do this," Parker instructed as he typed away at the computer terminal.

I knew he was mad at me about the stunt I pulled, and even agreed it was a stupid move, but it didn't make it sting any less to have him brusque with me. Back in a locker, I found a tool box with zip-ties in it and grabbed a handful to use. Once I bound his hands and feet together, I slipped the radio off his belt then began scrolling through the channels to see if there was anyone else talking.

"This is guard team five, to Mozog do you copy."

"Mozog is unavailable, this is High Demon Brutus."

My eyes shot up to Parker's when the second man spoke, recognizing it from the generator room.

"High Demon Brutus, we found a door on the backside that has been damaged. Please be alert we might have intruders. It seems they torched the lock."

A hissing snarl echoed through the walkie-talkie. *"Pull in every guard we have. I want this place searched from top to bottom, Lord Mozog is dealing with a conduit and we can't let them be disturbed."*

Gasping at what he said, I dropped the radio and covered my mouth to keep from making any more sound. That's what they'd meant when they said Phoebe's soul was tainted, making her a perfect match to be a conduit for one of the Dark Lord's Greater demons. I'd spent every extra waking hour learning all the names and traits for the seventy-two Greater demons that made up the Dark Lord's court. After almost being one for the Mother of All, I didn't want to ever end up in a situation where I wasn't informed about what was going on. If we'd known more about Dantalion, Ubel wouldn't have gotten the drop on us like he did.

"Lailah," Parker called, pulling me out of my head. "Look at me Trouble, right in the eyes." I did as he asked, reaching out a hand to him. "We won't let her go through what you did, I promise."

"You can't promise that Parker, no one can," I stated

bluntly. "I was lucky, being Synergy and bound to you guys. It saved my life, but Phoebe won't have that, none of these poor people do."

Parker cupped my face with his hands. "Lailah, on my Oath I swore to keep you safe, as well as the people on this planet we call Earth. How can I not promise to do right by her? I might not love her the way I love you, but she still holds a special place in my heart. It's a downfall of being the Spirit element, once someone becomes important to me, they always will be. I've watched what you've gone through for months, so I'm telling you right now, we will do whatever it takes to try and prevent her getting taken by some slimy bitch of a demon."

Unable to speak, I nodded my head. I could appreciate what he was saying but the reality of it was, she'd been dosed by the serum and if we didn't find a cure, in many ways it was already late for everyone in this building. Not that, that fact would stop us from saving them all, it just made the outcome more challenging. "What's your plan then?"

"I figured out how to cut the power to just the building but not to the city around it, leaving the backup power working to supply during the shutdown. It will only be out for a half hour before the whole system will do a reboot and fix what I changed. This should unlock every door, making it easier to move around and get people talking on the radio so we can hear where they are better."

"It's as good a plan as any," I sighed, pulling out my cell phone. "I'm gonna send the others a message so they know our plan and where the location of the harvest room is."

"That's good because we're not going there."

"What? Why not?"

Parker spared me a look as he continued to type. "There

is another area of the building that I think they have Phoebe in. The power draw in there is too strong for something important not to be happening there."

That sounded logical to me, but I didn't love the idea of us going after a Greater demon with just the two of us. If the Dark Lord hadn't pulled Ubel back to talk to him, I never would have had the upper hand. Mix in the fact a Higher level demon was running around, I'd want all the help we could get. I typed out everything we learned and sent it, having one bar of service, and prayed that it would be enough to get it out into the data stream to alert them if they get a signal.

"Ready, power is going out in three...two...one."

The constant hum that had been vibrating through the building stopped, making it almost too quiet for my liking.

"What the hell just happened," Brutus yelled through the radio. *"Control room, do you copy? Control room."*

"There is a team close by, we'll check it out."

Parker reached out a hand to me. "Time to go."

Grasping it, I let him pull me to my feet and we bolted out the door, running as fast as we could, no longer caring about keeping silent. I trusted Parker to know where to go so I just kept pace, thankful that running was my favorite hobby. Shoving through a set of double doors, we rounded a corner but Parker screeched to a halt as three men in all black uniforms with flashlights and guns appeared in front of us.

"They went through that door, two of them both dressed all in black with this weird symbol on the shoulder. We tried to get them to stop, but they were too fast and well trained, almost military if you ask me," Parker explained, pretending to huff and puff like he was out of shape.

One guard lowered his gun slightly. "What did the symbol look like?"

"It was some star looking thing, but had symbols on the points that connected to one in the middle. Never seen anything like it before in my life," Parker answered, describing the Elementi symbol to them.

"Fuck," a guard swore. "How the hell did they find us out here? The closest branch is in Chicago."

"Doesn't matter, we need to alert the other teams about this. You two turn around and head back to the harvest room, if they are going to attack, that's the room they're aiming for," the lead guard of their group said, raising his walkie-talkie to his mouth.

Quickly, I turned ours down where I clipped it to the back of my jeans, hidden under the sweater I'd worn to hide my scars.

"Guard teams, be advised that the Elementi have been spotted and are gunning for harvest room three on the upper level," he said, then turned to the other two. "Good thing only harvest room one is full since we sent off our shipment two days ago. What are you two still standing there for, GO!"

We turned on our heels and started off back the way we came, until we rounded the corner and Parker pulled me to a stop while we waited for them to leave. Once the hall was quiet again, we booked it down the hall and up three flights of stairs to a steel door.

"This looks like a roof access," I pointed out. "How would the roof be drawing power?"

"It's not, but the room can be accessed through skylights that are on the roof. If we're going to drop into a party with a Greater demon, and who knows how many Higher or Mid-Level demons, I'd rather have every advantage we can," Parker pointed out. "My hope is that since they are on the hunt, no one will be up here, or only one person. I'll head out first going to the right, you go left, and we'll take anyone down along the way."

"You make that sound so simple," I grumbled.

"None of that now, Trouble," Parker warned. "You've come a long way in your combat training, I know you'll be fine."

Taking a deep breath and shaking out my body, I gave him a nod that I was ready. He pushed open the door, which gave a loud screech from the hinges, making us both pause to wait and listen. After a few moments and nothing happening, we executed our plan. Keeping low, I headed for the closest cover keeping my eyes peeled for any movement or sound that would alert me to someone being up here. The roof was massive and seemed to be in a U shape, with the middle lower where the generator area was. What I wouldn't give for some binoculars right now, to check out the other side of the U. I circled back when not crossing over to the other side, feeling that the chances of someone being up here were slim.

"All clear?" Parker asked as we met in the middle.

"Yeah," I confirmed. "I kept a look out for the other side too but didn't see any kind of movement."

"Then I'd say this is as good a time as any to check out what's going on in the secret room," Parker announced.

I'd seen the Plexiglas bubbles that made up the skylights but avoided going near them so I didn't cast a shadow. The plastic was warped and not very clear due to weathering, but it was better than nothing and kept us from being noticed right away. The first three sky lights we didn't see anything useful, it looked like a large conference room with a table and chairs. When we came to the fourth, I knew right away what I was looking at and it sent chills down my spine. I had to back away from the sight of it, pulling my knees up to my chest so I could rest my head on them, trying to take calming breaths.

"Lailah, what is it?" Parker asked, his voice full of worry.

The only answer I could give him at the moment was to just shake my head. I'd talked to my therapist about everything that had gone on, but the guys didn't know the whole story. It was too hard to talk about still. With the reassurance from my therapist, they let it be and knew I would talk about it with them when I was ready. The problem was, I was nowhere near ready to face what I saw down in that room again, which made me even more upset. It was a stone altar, just like the Dark Lord had placed me on to perform the ritual connecting me to Lilith. That's where he carved up my skin, bled on me, and chanted those dark heinous words, trying to get me to be the perfect puppet for his lover. It was by the grace of God, and the Angels that blessed me with the power of Synergy, that I was saved from that awful fate, along with my bonds to the guys. Phoebe had none of those things to protect her. She wasn't laid out on it yet but I had no doubt that is what they meant to do to her, since she was already tainted by some experience, along with having been dosed with the serum.

Lifting my head, I met Parker's worried gaze and reached out a hand to him. When he grasped mine in both of his, I felt strong enough to explain my reaction. "That's the room we're looking for and where they plan to make her into a conduit for one of the Greater demons of the Dark Lord's court. That stone slab with the carvings in an altar and it connects them to Hell and the demon they are going to pair her with. If we can destroy the altar, it will cripple their ability to make more conduits for stronger demons. It won't stop them from being possessed by others but it's better than nothing."

"Do you think you can destroy it if I hold off whoever is in the room?"

My panicked brain screamed out in protest but I pushed it as far down as I could, knowing I needed to stand up to this fear. "I will give it everything I've got, if you give me the time to try."

"We could wait for the others, now that we're outside I'm sure Jay and the others got your message," Parker offered.

"No," I blurted, shaking my head furiously. "We might be too late at that point. We need to do this now, before they get any further with Phoebe, or we won't be able to save her."

Parker licked his lips and searched my face, as if he wasn't sure I could handle doing this. "Let's check the other skylight and see if it's the same room, so I can pull their attention from you entering right over the altar. If not, then I'll drop in using the conference room, making a racket and see if I can draw them out so you can do your thing. I know you want to destroy that thing, but if it looks like you can't and we have a chance to still save Phoebe, then do that. Phoebe is the reason we're here, we can come back with more help to deal with everything else going on here, alright."

I knew what he was saying was reasonable, but I knew if we left without obliterating that altar, they would either kill off the other people they had, or let lesser demons possess them. They wouldn't wait around to have the

Elementi attack them a second time. This was the only shot we had to ruin this operation and the one reason the Elementi Warriors were created—we're their only hope. "Let's do this."

CHAPTER 19

PARKER

Seeing the look of determination on Lailah's face, fighting against the fear she was feeling, astounded me. The woman I met at the beginning of the school year had turned into a warrior. Like the rest of us, she had scars and wounds that were seen and unseen, but she used them to fuel her as we headed into a situation that we most likely would be outnumbered. I was torn, wanting to hold back until we could meet up with the others, but I knew we didn't have much time before the power turned back on, making it harder to get out. Lailah was trusting me to make the best call, but I agreed with her that Phoebe didn't have much time left.

The tug on my heart, thinking about her having to go through what Lailah did, worried me a bit. I'd been working hard at figuring out my feelings about this whole matter, and it's just gotten all muddled in my brain.

Shaking myself out of this funk, I peered into the skylight. I found it was in the same room as the altar, with ten feet between them. It seemed to be a workroom, with tiled floors, and computers set up in units for people to work at. They'd all been shoved up against the wall haphazardly having no use for them apparently, but explained how they could access more power in this room. Feeling along the outside of the frame, I found the seam for where the Plexiglas fit into the window. It was brittle from being exposed to the sun and harsh weather, so I decided the best thing to do was create the biggest distraction I could by kicking it in, sending it crashing to the ground below.

"What the fuck?!" A woman screeched. "We're under attack, call the guards!"

Seems like now is as good a time as any. I dropped in from the roof, landing in a superhero crouch. I took a moment to look around the room, gauging how many people were there, before I made my next move. Like any good demonic ritual, all five of them were in black cloaks looking the part, with Phoebe passed out on the floor.

"You guys know the robes don't actually make a difference in your demon voodoo, right?" I pointed out as I stood, letting my six foot staff, with a two foot blade on the end, materialize.

"Elementi Warrior," a man hissed from under his hood.

I gave them a bright smile, like I wasn't at all bothered by the fact that I was extremely outnumbered. "I'm flattered you've heard of us."

The man tossed back his hood exposing a face that looked like it could be Voldemort's brother, but much more snake-like. He was Brutus, the voice we heard in the generator room when we first got here then again on the radio. He'd admitted that he housed one of the Higher-level demons, which I'd encountered a few times, but had never seen them possess a person before. "You are foolish to come alone but I will end you before you can bother our master."

Brutus lunged forward, his hands growing claws like Higher level demons had, that oozed with what I knew to be poison. Lailah had been scratched by one before and she still carried those scars, along with the others. Swinging my staff out, I blocked his attack, moving back to get a better look at the room trying to find the leader Mozog. Brutus seemed to notice he didn't have my full attention, so he sped up his attack, letting his demon take more control over his body. It was only the years of training I had that kept me from getting sliced by his claws in the gut as I kicked out, hitting him in the leg and dropping him to his knees. Higher demon he might be, but this time he was trapped in a human body and couldn't dematerialize to avoid my counterattack.

Tired of being on the defensive, I struck while he was down, trying to cut off his head. As much as I wanted to save the human he was inhabiting, I knew it was too late for Martin when Lailah killed Ubel. The host, no longer having a demon to keep them alive, would wither and die after having something so evil eating them from the inside out. Brutus might be trapped in the human body but he was still able to move faster and force the body to be bent and break in ways it shouldn't have been able to. Doing a move that could only happen in the Matrix, he avoided my attack and sprang to his feet, flipping backwards.

"You'll have to do better than that, warrior," Brutus said with a hissing laugh. "Don't tell me this is the best the Elementi have to offer."

Catching movement out of the corner of my eye, one of the other robed figures was trying to sneak up behind me with a dagger in his hand. Whirling, I used the butt of my staff to hit him right in the cheek, knocking the wind out of him and sending him sprawling backwards. Brutus used this to his advantage, making his next move, keeping me on my toes slashing and cutting away at me, until all I could do was keep him off me. Two more of the group came at me and I knew I needed to take some of these people out or I was going to lose this battle before Lailah even had the chance to get to the altar. The hasty plan we made was to listen in until I had their attention, and she would make her way through the skylight over the altar. Well, I had their attention alright, but Lailah still hadn't made it down into the room yet. *Could she be dealing with another panic attack? I knew it, we should have waited for the others, but the need to get to Phoebe fast was still riding me.* Pain burst through my brain as I felt something get jammed into my thigh, looking down it was the dagger that one bastard had been holding.

"Okay, that's fucking it!" I yelled, shoving Brutus away with all my strength and turned to face the other minions. "I didn't want to do this, but you guys left me no choice."

Moving as fast as I could, I whipped my staff around, jabbing it right into the heart of one of the cloaked men then yanking it out and going after the woman who was leaping at me like a pissed off cat. Whatever she was, turning her hands into claws was also one of her tricks but I slashed upwards, slicing open her chest, causing her to drop to the floor in a heap.

"Ah, so the gallant knight has a taste for blood," a voice purred behind me.

The chills that ran down my spine and the demonic energy that came off him told me before I even turned, this was Mozog. Turning on my heel, staff at the ready, I came face to face with a man dressed in a suit but what really threw me off were his eyes. They looked like that of a lizard, bright yellow with a black slit running down the middle that seemed to dilate when he was looking at me. He grinned at me and his teeth were sharp and pointed, like that of a shark, or something equally terrifying.

"I can sense your fear," he said, sniffing the air. "It's delicious."

He slowly walked around me, his hands clasped behind his back. Unwilling to give him my back, I turned with him, knowing the others wouldn't move unless he told them too. I was banking on the fact Mozog would want to get some information out of me before I was killed.

"You've come for this woman, haven't you," Mozog asked as he stopped behind Phoebe caressing her face. "She is very lovely and perfectly suited to being used as a conduit for our plans. You know about those, I assume, from your Lady Synergy." At that, the door to the room burst open and another black robed person walked in, holding Lailah to his chest with a knife to her throat. "It would seem your plan isn't working out as well as you planned, but you see, mine is going perfectly."

I frowned after hearing that. "Wait, you wanted us to come here?"

"But of course, did you really think the Dark Lord would let Synergy out of his grasp once he had a taste of her? She is bound to him by blood and ritual as much as she is to you knights," Mozog explained. "The serum wasn't strong enough to overpower her angelic blessing, but we have been working on that and testing it on many subjects all over the world. Imagine my surprise when it was discovered that you were here in my section. That barrier you put up sent out a signal across quite a distance, alerting us to your presence."

"That means the barrier is too strong for you to get

through, so you needed to lure us out of our safety zone," Lailah interjected, once she was set on her feet.

Looking at the pair of them, I knew she put up a good fight, the man had a black eye and a fat lip to show for his efforts. Lailah also had a black eye that bloomed out closer to her temple, making me guess that's how he got her so unbalanced or knocked her out even.

"That, dear lady, was something of dumb luck," Mozog answered. "We were making plans to do that exact thing, but you decided to come to us, allowing me to collect both of you. This is a good day for us indeed. Oh, and as for the others that are lurking around the building, they will be dealt with shortly, can't have more of them for you to feed off of, Lady Synergy."

Lailah's face became a mask of rage at that statement, elbowing the cloaked man in the gut, giving her enough room to spin and knee him in the balls. The man dropped like a rock but then Brutus was on her, wrapping a hand around her neck and picking her up until her feet could just barely touch. "Come on Synergy, show me what you've got, I love a woman who fights back."

Now it was my turn to rage at what was happening to Lailah. "Get your fucking hands off her."

Charging at Brutus, I dropped to my knees, sliding across the tile floor slicing at the back of his legs, while Lailah kicked out at him while clawing at his hold on her throat. My attack hit home, getting him right at the knees chopping them off at the joint, toppling him over and releasing Lailah at the same time. She rolled out of his reach and got to her feet coughing as I swung my staff and chopped off his head, watching as it rolled away from his body. The oddest part of this whole thing was there was no blood at all coming from the body. This just confirmed that the Higher-level demon had rotted the body from the inside out, until it was no longer human.

"No!" Lailah screamed, reaching out to something behind me.

Turning I found Phoebe in Mozog's arms, his hand holding her by the hair, neck exposed, with his mouth open as if he was going to tear out her throat. Terror flooded my body at the thought of seeing Phoebe killed before my very eyes and unable to do anything about it. Mozog met my gaze and slowly closed his mouth, pulling back from her skin. "Oh my, could it be that you have feelings for this woman as well? I suppose it would make sense for the man who is gifted with the element of heart to love more than one person at a time."

"Don't listen to him Lailah, he's a demon he'll say anything to make you doubt me," I growled.

Lailah edged closer to me in a show of solidarity. "You don't have to warn me about that, I can feel his malice filling the room."

"So tell me...would you let this woman die to save your Lady Synergy?" Mozog taunted. "If you have no love for her, then leave her with me and I'll let the two of you leave right now, along with the other two we've captured."

"We are not going to make any deals with you," Lailah snapped. "We are all leaving here alive, including Phoebe."

Mozog gave Lailah a toothy smile that set me on edge, as the two remaining cloaked people stood behind him. "Is that so? What would you do if told you that you were too late and we already performed the ritual on her?"

"There's no way, it hasn't been long enough and I would have felt that much demonic energy going around this place," Lailah countered. "You're stalling for some reason, which makes me think you don't have the other two of my men and you're trying to find them."

"I can see why the Dark Lord is so focused on you," Mozog commented as he handed Phoebe off to the two minions. "Too bad that I don't agree with him that you'll be the perfect person for the Mother of All to live in. This woman here would be a much better fit, you see, she has a darkness in her heart that the Mother would appreciate and be drawn to. Yes, you are powerful, Lady Synergy, but there isn't an ounce of evil in you that we haven't put there ourselves."

Both of us glanced at each other when we understood that Mozog had decided to use Phoebe for Lilith's host, going against the Dark Lord's plans. Now there was no doubt in my mind that we had to get Phoebe out of here and to safety. "We won't let you do this," I announced.

"Yes, I had a feeling *you* would feel that way about this. So, it seems that we will have to remove you while this happens."

With a snap of his fingers, the room was filled with more possessed people with weapons. But not the kind of guards we ran into earlier. That alone made me think that Lailah was right about them not having caught the others and they needed the guards to look for them. It also might be a ploy to keep us from killing them, seeing as they were normal looking people. Seeing the guns in some of their hands, I was very glad that we tested the fact that Lailah's shields could also block bullets. Otherwise, we would have zero chances of making it out of this alive. I felt that warm comforting feeling of Lailah drawing on my power as she placed an individual shield around each of us and she manifested her sword and shield. Grim determination to survive this filled me, along with the small hope that the others would find us in time to help.

Stepping closer to Lailah, I whispered, "let me deal with this, do what you can to stop them from doing the ritual."

"Parker, there is no way that you'll be able to handle all these people by yourself," she argued.

"You know we won't survive this without killing some of them, I can't let you suffer like that."

She looked at me, her crystal blue eyes hard. "How would having you suffer instead be any better? These people are lost and there is nothing we can do for them right now. It's better to let them pass on then to live as a puppet to a demon, causing them to do heinous things to others."

That was the last chance we had to discuss anything because they charged us. The sound of guns going off in the room was deafening, along with the screaming of the woman rushing at us with knives and claws. Lailah body checked a man coming at her with her shield, knocking him back into another, giving her some space as she dealt with another woman and her dagger. The battle was of the likes I've never experienced before, other than in a video game, and that didn't come close to this. The floor was getting slick with blood, making me realize that some of these people might not have been possessed long enough for their body to start deteriorating. A large man tackled me, causing my feet to slide out from under me so I slammed onto the floor with a grunt.

"Parker!" Lailah yelled, seeing me go down.

I slammed my staff into the man's face, breaking his nose and stunning him long enough to roll him off of me. "I'm fine." I called out so she didn't try to help me.

Taking a second, I looked around the room and saw that

we were holding our own but the fact that more people poured into the room didn't bode well for us. I was getting tired and I knew Lailah must be as well. She'd come a long way, but four months of training didn't prepare you for something like this. Then I heard it, outside in the hall was the unmistakable roar that Micah used as he fought. We finally had help coming!

"Parker," Phoebe and Lailah both screamed.

Whipping my head around, I tried to see who was where, then I spotted Phoebe thrashing on the stone altar. Mozog was straddling her with a slice in his arm bleeding over her everywhere, as he chanted god knows what. Without hesitation, I used my staff to shove everyone around me out of the way and charged towards the altar, tackling Mozog so we both toppled off the altar and onto the floor. Using my powers now that I had a hold of him, I filled the human brain with the fact that he was in the worst pain of his life, making him scream like he was being murdered which, in a way, he was. The human mind can only handle so much pain before it shuts down and you pass out to protect yourself, which is exactly what happened after a few moments. When I was sure he was out for the count, I crawled back to the altar and pulled Phoebe off it until she was curled up in my arms, sobbing.

"It's alright I've got you," I murmured as I stroked her hair. "I won't let them take you from me, I promise."

Another scream filled the room that I knew was Lailah's and in the next moment I too was in mind numbing pain. It felt like my heart was being ripped out of my chest and then an audible crack, like a lightning bolt hitting the room, sounded. I hadn't realized that I blacked out until I opened my eyes to see Phoebe looming over me grinning and laughing at me. Her eyes were completely black and the blood that covered her face gave her a maniacal look.

"Look who just saved the Mother of All demons over the woman he swore to protect and love above all others. Do you know what you just did, oh gallant knight?" She purred as she stroked my face with a bloody hand, then leaned down so her lips brushed my ear as she spoke.

"You. Broke. Your. Oath."

CHAPTER 20

LAILAH

When the room filled with possessed people, I knew that Mozog was trying to play to my humanity. The problem was, he also put Parker and Phoebe in danger which triggered my protective instincts, which overruled my need to preserve life. These people would never be free of demons, even if you knew how to save them from the demon inhabiting them now, because once it was out another could take it spot. The kindest thing I could do was to let these people be free and to die at peace, knowing they wouldn't be taken over again. Bullets bounced off our shields and I was even more grateful that we decided to test that theory out during training. Once they realized that it did them no good, they moved on to using other weapons.

Jay had been ruthless in his training with me, which helped as my body automatically did what it needed to. Keeping space clear around myself with my shield, I could then deal with one person at a time. Out of the corner of my eye I saw Parker get taken down by a massive man, making me falter in my own battle as I called out to him. "Parker!"

It took a few moments for him to respond, but when he

did I got right back to what I was doing. A gap opened up in the battle and I grinned at the fact we were holding our own, but I couldn't do it for much longer. My arms were getting heavy and sluggish as I blocked, swung, and stabbed those around me. Then I caught sight of Mozog with Phoebe at the altar, and I tried to get to her, knowing that if he performed the ritual to allow Lilith into her, she would never have a chance at coming back, antidote or not. I shoved forward, only to have someone behind me grab onto my ponytail and drag me back, slamming me to the floor. The air whooshed out of my lungs and the world around me went black as I felt hands grabbing at me, claws digging into my flesh so I did the only thing I could think of once I got my breath back.

"*Parker.*"

On instinct, I pulled on my connection to all the men and found that they were all here in the building, much closer than I anticipated. Micah and Brayden were in the hall fighting to get to us, while Hudson and Jay were on the roof making their way to the skylight. I felt them pouring into me, filling me with their strength, reassuring me that they were here for me. Then I felt Parker's connection and as I grasped it, I watched in my mind's eye as it shattered, splintering into a thousand pieces. Pain unlike anything I'd ever encountered before wrecked my body down to a soul level, making me scream as I was unable to hold it all inside. The people around me got blasted across the room and I was in a bubble of protection, sobbing as the realization of what just happened dawned on me.

The Oath—a solemn promise witnessed by the angels of heaven, had been broken.

Devastation filled me, as it felt like someone just cut off my right hand, leaving me crippled and vulnerable. I couldn't move or speak, other than to scream and cry as I curled up into a ball. The building around me started to shake as I continued to pull power from the others, needing to feel them, to know I hadn't been abandoned by them all.

"The building is going to collapse." Someone bellowed.

What did I care—let the building fall. Maybe then I wouldn't have to wake up from this nightmare, knowing that one of my men, who claimed to love me, had turned his back on me. I'd read the journals Aiden left behind, I knew exactly what it would take to break the Oath. To choose evil over good, abandoning your calling, was the only action that could possibly be grounds for the angels to revoke the promise he made to me.

"Lailah, you have to let down the shield so we can get to you," Brayden called out to me. "Please, let us in."

Through our Bond, I could feel his concern and pain, as he didn't understand what was going on. Hudson, as well as Micah, were trying to reach out to me any way that they could, trying desperately not to freak out. I allowed them into my space, along with Jay's steady stalwart presence, and the pain began to ease slightly as they reached out to touch me. Feeling them here with me, as I had this gaping hole in my chest where Parker used to be, gave me enough courage to open my eyes. The room was now in shambles, my powers having blown out the windows, walls, and crushed anything else that got in its way. The ground was littered with people, their bodies broken and dead eyes staring glassy eyed into the void as now all that remained was an empty husk.

Then my eyes landed on Parker.

He stood there staring at me, tears running down his face, making clean streaks where his skin was covered in blood and other debris. That one look told me he knew what happened as well as I did. Anger tore through me as I let the guys help me get to my feet. The building had stopped trembling, but now it started up again as my fury whipped out around me like a snake going for the kill.

"Why the fuck are you crying?" I screamed. "You did this! Get out of my sight. I can't stand to look at filth like you."

Parker flinched, as if my words really did hit him the way I wanted them too.

"I should have known, when you warned me you were processing everything after seeing Phoebe again, that this would happen. I defended you, I made them trust in the fact that you changed. What a fool I am to believe a man whore like you could ever truly love one person for the rest of your life. Thank god you didn't *really* bond with me or you would've been stuck with me your whole goddamn life. Now you can go freely be with Phoebe, or any other slut you want, because you sure as hell won't be mine!" I snarled, fighting against Brayden's hold on me.

Parker took a step closer to me, but a wall of fire shot up halting him in his steps to get to me. "Trouble—"

"Don't you *dare*," I screamed, collapsing to my knees on the ground. "Leave...just go...I can't, I can't deal with this."

Sobs wracked my body, as Jay picked me up and cradled me in his arms. He rested his head on mine and spoke into my ear softly. "Beautiful, I need you to pull back on your powers so we can get out of this place safely. Once we get outside, where it's safe, you can burn the whole thing down for all I care, but you need to be safe first."

In my head, I knew he was right, but it took a few tries for me to collect myself enough to stop drawing from them and feeding it into my own power. Once I did that, the oppression in the air seemed to lift, the wind stopped, and the ground stopped shaking. I peeked over his shoulder and found that the altar was indeed shattered into dust, so that no one else could use it. The others remained silent as we picked our way out of the room and down the hall to the stairs. Not wanting to deal with anything right now, I hid my face in Jay's neck as he held me together in his arms. Soon enough, we were outside and the sun was still high in the sky shining brightly, as if my whole world hadn't just come crashing down.

"Lailah," Dylan's voice called out.

Lifting my head, I saw him along with Kyle and Cami, running over to me. When they saw me though, they came to a screeching halt, eyes wide with horror.

"Lala...what happened?" Cami gasped.

"We need to get her to North Western, where the Elementi hub is," Hudson explained. "They will have doctors there that can look over her and assist, without having to deal with awkward questions about how she got hurt."

"Why are you so calm? Where is Phoebe and why is Lailah covered in blood and look like she's been tortured?" Dylan growled. "I'm not letting you take my sister anywhere until you give me some answers."

"Phoebe's gone," Parker stated his voice cold.

Dylan let out a strangled sound as he dropped to the ground. "She's dead?"

"In a manner of speaking. She's the conduit to Lilith, the Mother of All Demons," Parker announced. "She disappeared with another conduit by the name of Mozog when Lailah's power started lashing out."

"Care to share why that was, fuckface?" Micah demanded getting right up in Parker's space.

"I don't have to tell you shit," Parker snarled, grabbing the front of Micah's shirt.

Hudson stepped up and grabbed Parker's hand, stopping him from decking Micah in the face. "You were the only one there, Parker. We need to know what happened before we got there."

Parker shook off Hudson and shoved Micah away from him as hard as he could, almost knocking him to the ground. "I fucked up, alright! Is that what you all want to hear? It finally happened, Parker the idiot, the frat boy man whore, finally lived up to your expectations."

"You're not making any sense," Brayden interjected.

Parker turned to me, holding my gaze as he told them all. "I broke my Oath when I chose to save Phoebe over Lailah."

I thought I'd seen Micah mad before, but the wrath I saw on his face was almost as terrifying as the Dark Lord's expression when the ritual didn't work. "I'll fucking kill you!"

Micah tackled Parker and started to beat the shit out of him, pummeling him in the face while Parker did nothing to stop him—nor did the others. Hudson's face was hard as he watched what was happening and Brayden came to stand in front of me, so my view of what was going on was blocked. Parker had dug his own grave and the others were going to let him lay in it. Brayden reached out and brushed some hair out of my face, tucking it behind my ear, giving me a soft sad smile.

"I'm not going to ask you how you feel, because I know it's not good, but do you have any injuries we need to look after right away?" Brayden asked gently.

Reaching out, I grasped his hand. "I don't know, right now all I feel is numb. The pain of the Oath shattering was the worst thing I've ever experienced, even surpassing what the Dark Lord did to me. Can we just go home? I don't want to go to the Elementi hub, I just want to go back home, crawl into bed and never come out again."

"Okay, we can go home," Brayden answered as he looked up at Jay.

"He's not coming with us," Jay announced. "I don't care where he goes but it won't be back to the house."

Brayden just nodded his head and looked over his shoulder. "Micah, leave him, Lailah wants to go home."

The sound of fist hitting flesh stopped as a pitiful groan came from Parker. "Fucker's lucky all he gets is a broken face for now, since we need him alive long enough to end this shit with the Dark Lord."

"Wait, you're just going to leave him here?" Kyle called out after us. "Sis, where are you going?"

I couldn't face my little brother right now. I was too hurt to be anything but selfish. Wrapping my arms around Jay's neck, I let the tears fall as he held me tightly, he didn't even try to get me to let go as he climbed into the car with me. He put us in the very back of the SUV and let me cry, stroking my back soothingly as we drove back home. As much as I wished that I could just pass out, with how tired and drained I was, all I kept doing was running through the whole thing in my mind.

When had Phoebe been turned into a conduit? Had we been too late from the very beginning? Was she Lilith the whole time and I just couldn't sense her for some reason? No, there was no way that could be the case. It had to have happened today at some point. When I was in Hell, with the Dark Lord, he'd told me that she was being punished for trying to free all her children. How is it that she is awake already, or is it more of an echo, since Phoebe is connected to her? Fuck, I mean she's the Mother of All demons, why put it past her to have been storing up energy herself to get free? What if the Dark Lord fell into her trap, but how does Mozog fit into all of this? Who is he a conduit for?

"Lailah, I can feel your mind working like crazy trying to reason out what happened," Jay whispered. "No matter what you think, you have to know it's not your fault. Parker is the one responsible for what happened back there, it was his choices that broke the Oath, not yours."

Oddly enough I didn't feel any of this was my fault. Jay was right, Parker is the one who fucked up, making a blatant choice of Phoebe over me. "I agree."

Even if Phoebe hadn't been connected to Lilith, this still would have been a huge red flag to me that Parker was not ready to commit to me. I never wanted to rush any of them into the Bond, which is why I only accepted his Oath. I believe we both knew he was nervous about being connected to someone forever, and even though I trusted him with many things, I don't know that I really did trust him with my heart yet. If seeing his ex-girlfriend threw him so badly, then I don't really trust that he loved me the way he thought he did.

So where did that leave us now...?

That problem would just have to wait for another day, because I didn't have a flying fuck to care right now.

CHAPTER 21
LAILAH

The moment we got home, Cami led me right up to my bedroom and started the shower, helping me peel off my stiff blood-soaked clothes. Thankfully, we found that the wounds I did have were nothing too major. A few might need a couple of stitches, but I knew Jay could do them for me. The feeling of the water pelting against my sensitive skin, as I watched the water run red with the blood that covered my body and hair, was a surreal moment. The moment my mind tried to wander to the fact that I'd just killed so many people today, I shut it down and focused on one of the exercises my therapist used with me.

Fact: I did what I had to do to survive, and no one holds that against me but myself.

Fact: Those people were no longer people anymore, but puppets for demons, so what I did was the only way to set them free.

Fact: I did not harm these people in cold blood or enjoyment, which proves that I'm not a murderer.

I'd worked so hard to overcome everything that happened over New Year's, that I couldn't let myself fall down that rabbit hole again. Lailah Mackenzie was a survivor, and Knight of the Elementi, blessed by the angels with the gift of Synergy. I'd been given the gift of being the secret weapon that can turn the tables on evil to win this war and keep the world safe. Was I hurt, knocked down, and heartbroken? Yes, I absolutely would acknowledge those feelings and accept them to be true for myself right now. Was I broken beyond repair? Not in this fucking life-time, but I was going to allow myself to feel this pain and not hide it where it could be used against me. The Dark Lord had shown me more than once, anything hidden could be found and turned into a weapon. Lilith already used Parker's feelings for Phoebe to ruin him, but I wasn't going to let that happen to me.

When I finally felt like I was ready to be around the others, I toweled off, carefully dabbing at my skin in areas that were tender, before I slipped on a tank top and undies. Jay would need to take a look at everything before he decided how to deal with things, so no sense in putting on more clothes than I needed to. The room was empty, which surprised me since I expected Jay or Micah to be ready to pounce on me the moment I came out. Panic filled my chest as I worried that they left me too, once they saw what a mess I was. Did they judge me for killing all those people? Could I have been wrong about everything all along?

"Sunshine," Hudson's voice called softly through the bedroom door. "I can feel your panic, can I come in?"

"Yes," I squeaked out, as I fought against the panic that was trying to take over.

Hudson opened the door and headed right for me, pulling me against his warm body. He pressed my head against his chest, where I could hear his heartbeat and took in a deep breath, then let it out nice and slow. We'd done this so many times that words weren't needed, I knew to follow along and lose myself in the steady thump of his heart. People who didn't know this amazing man might call him cold or stiff, but it was only because he felt things so much deeper than anyone else I knew. His love was unconditional, his patience never ending, and his anger for whoever was unfortunate to witness it was swift and absolute. He was a man I completely trusted my heart with, no matter what my fear said, because I knew that I had his as well.

"What I wouldn't give to share this burden with you, my light, my soul, my Sunshine," Hudson murmured, as he placed soft kisses on each of my eyes where my tears leaked out, then finally my lips. There was no pressure for something more, just the simple comfort of touch. "Don't hide from us, let us in, we are strong enough to hold you up through this. Let us prove that we won't leave you, no matter what lies behind that wall you've built to protect yourself right now."

"How can I ask that of you?" I sobbed. "Then you won't want me once you see how truly broken I am. I was just managing to put myself back together, Hudson, and he destroyed it all in the blink of an eye. The ultimate weapon you've been waiting for is nothing more than a shattered girl with a broken heart."

"Lailah," Hudson pulled back from me so he could see my face. "I don't give a shit about saving the world right now, not if it means making you suffer more than you already are. What matters to me right now, in this moment, is that the love of my life is in pain, and I can't do much to help you except to just be there for you, however I can. Broken things can be made into something new, something better, and I'm not afraid of what you're truly feeling, nor will the others. Don't take my word for it, let us show you."

I nodded, tears rolling down my cheeks at his words, but still feeling numb in my heart. One of the strongest muscles in your body and yet so fragile when it gets stomped on. I let Hudson wrap me in a robe and lead me down into the kitchen, where everyone was sitting around the table looking as if someone died. In a way, I suppose they too felt the loss of Parker, having been friends with him for so many years and connected though being one of the knights. After centuries of the Elementi being in existence, something like this happening was unheard of. Even Cami looked as if she'd been crying, and made me wonder if she'd had to report what happened with HQ back at Ryevick. The moment they saw me, the guys all stood and walked over to me, each needing to touch me or hug me. Jay led me over to a stool near the counter, where his medical supplies were all laid out, and helped me out of the robe.

"You're lucky, this could have been much worse," Jay stated as he took in every scratch and bruise on my body.

"Thank God I had good teachers who always pushed me, knowing it would one day save my life," I answered, catching his gaze. "Thank you."

Jay reached out and stroked my cheek with the back of his knuckles. "I shouldn't have let you go there without all of us."

"No," I said, grasping his hand. "We are not going to play that game, Jay. Each of us made choices based on the information we had at the time. Some of them were wrong and others could have been handled better, but no one person is at fault for everything that went down. I shouldn't have jumped into dealing with that situation with only the two of us. I was just so worried about Phoebe going through what I did, and that made me rash, trying to compensate for my own fears."

Jay's stoic mask fell away, showing me just how much he cared for me and how the events of today had hit him deeper than he'd ever let on. "I could have lost you today, Lailah, that's twice now that I haven't been there."

"What do you guys keep telling me? Blaming doesn't change what happened, we need to learn from it instead," I reasoned. "I can't have you guys falling apart too, who will keep us going if we all crumble?"

"Oh, don't you worry about that Lala," Cami announced. "I'm not leaving until you lot convince me that you can be trusted on your own again."

I frowned at that, letting go of Jay's hand so he could start work on my injuries. "Wait, what about Maggs?"

"Trust me, when I explained to her and Beth what was going on, they both agreed that you needed me to stick around," Cami shared, confirming my suspicions. "There needs to be someone with estrogen, and not dating you, to keep a clear head about things—wouldn't you agree?"

"As selfish as it is, I'm glad you're going to stick around longer than two weeks," I answered, giving her a smile that I knew didn't reach my eyes.

"Beautiful, I need to put in a few stitches, but I don't have anything to dull the pain locally. What I can do is give you a pain killer that will make you sleep so I can deal with these," Jay informed me.

Glancing at the clock, I saw it was only four p.m. but I was more than ready to be done with this day. "I'll take the pain killer, might be the only way I get sleep right now."

"You know they make your nightmares worse," Jay cautioned.

"I'll have them regardless, but there's a chance that I

can have a solid few hours before they start this way," I countered.

Jay nodded and pulled out a pill bottle from his pack, handing me the pill along with a can of root beer. The gesture of making even taking a pill less awful, by having my favorite drink ready assured me that even if I couldn't see it now, I might just be able to rebuild my heart with these men. "It takes about thirty minutes to kick in, let's get you to eat something light and watch a show, hmm?"

Nodding, I let him prepare whatever he had in mind for me as I pulled up the robe and headed for the living room. The guys all joined me and carefully maneuvered me so I was touching them all in one way or another as we flipped through the channels. I'd just barely finished my bowl of soup before I started to fade, zoning in and out to the sounds of Bob's Burgers playing on the television, then I was out.

"Little Synergy, how nice of you to come back to see me," the Dark Lord purred. "I was beginning to think you actually believed you could be free of me."

Panic surged through me, as I realized that I wasn't just in the blissful darkness of sleep, no I was in the in between space that was nowhere really at all. The Dark Lord and I have had many encounters here since the time I started school at Ryevick. Of course, back then he didn't have as much of a foothold into my mind as he did now, but he managed to frighten me just fine then as much as now.

"Did you know Mozog's plan?" I asked, deciding to take charge of the conversation instead of him this time.

I could feel the air vibrate with tension at the mention

of his name. "That woman isn't strong enough to handle being the conduit to Lilith. There is a reason it had to be you, and not just any pathetic human woman."

"Are you saying the connection will kill her?"

"She won't last more than a week before her body decays and Lilith's connection will be cut off. Mozog will have to do the ritual continuously with a new woman if he plans to revive her that way. My plan was perfect!"

This made me think that is exactly what Mozog has been doing for her behind the Dark Lords back. "Is he one of her children?"

"Her favorite, the first born of the angel Samael." The Dark Lord shared. "Enough about him. He is a fool to think his plan will work better, flooding the world with useless puppets from the work I've done. You need to take him out."

"Excuse me?!" I blurted. "Did you just tell me to kill him? Why the hell would I do you any favors?"

"Haven't you heard the saying, the enemy of my enemy is my friend? Do you want him infecting and killing innocent women every week, just to try and free Lilith?"

"You're trying to do the same thing—with me!" I argued.

"Yes, but I don't want you dead, you serve me no purpose dead. We both need him dead, and I can't do it while he is on Earth, so you have to do it."

I just started to laugh at the whole situation. "I have to be stoned or something because there is no way the Dark Lord is coming to me right now and asking me to kill off one of Lilith's children—her first born I might add. Nope, this has to be the drugs talking, I need to tell Jay I'm never taking that again."

Faster than a blink of an eye, I could no longer breathe. I

clawed at my throat, trying to grab hold of whatever was constricting my airflow but there was nothing there. Terror flooded my body, making everything all that much worse as I gasped for air, but none would fill my lungs.

"You dare to laugh at me?!" The Dark Lord raged. "Do not mistake my attempt at reasoning with you to be seen as a weakness. I need you alive Little Synergy, but that doesn't mean anyone else should remain that way. You've had one of your lovers stripped from you in the blink of an eye, what would happen if I took the others? Maybe I've been going about this the wrong way, perhaps I should turn them into puppets?"

Just when I was on the verge of passing out, he released me and I gulped down air, coughing as my throat burned from being constricted. My body shook with terror as I tried to calm myself enough to take even breaths, but my heart was racing too fast to manage.

"Kill Mozog, or I will take them from you one by one until it's done."

With that, he released me and thrust me back into my body, where I felt someone pounding on my chest.

"Is she still not breathing?!" Micah demanded.

Another thump slammed directly over my heart, and I gasped, rolling onto my side curling up into a ball, coughing. My eyes were watering but I was able to blink them clear enough to notice I was in my room in bed.

"What the fuck just happened?" Brayden yelled.

"The Dark Lord doesn't like to be laughed at."

CHAPTER 22

LAILAH

The guys yelling had the others come running in and flipping on the lights, to reveal a frantic Micah and Brayden on his knees beside me, with his head in his hands.

"What the hell is going on here? We only left ten minutes ago," Hudson exclaimed.

Jay climbed up right on the bed, only dressed in his sleep pants, and pulled my hand away from my throat. A growl slipped out as he took in the sight of what I'm sure was bruised skin. The Dark Lord would want to be sure the others knew what he'd done to me, so I would have to tell them what he threatened.

"What did he want this time?" Jay bit out between clenched teeth.

"He wants us to kill Mozog for him," I rasped.

They all froze, but when I started to cough again, Hudson headed off to the bathroom and came back with a glass of water. "This should help."

"Why the fuck would he want us to kill one of his minions?" Micah demanded as he ran his hands through his hair. "That makes absolutely no fucking sense at all."

Shaking my head, I reached out resting a hand on his knee. "Mozog is Lilith's oldest child. Apparently, the Dark Lord and Mozog aren't on the same page for how to bring Lilith back. According to what he said, Lilith is too powerful for a normal human to serve as her conduit, which is why he needed—needs—me to do the job. Using a human means that the body will decay in a week's time, or less, depending on the person."

Jay narrowed his eyes as he searched my face. "What aren't you saying?"

"Of course I told him no, the whole thing was too absurd for me to even take seriously, so I laughed at him," I answered, then paused thinking over the whole interaction. "For a moment there, I thought I was just out of my mind off whatever Jay gave me for the pain, but the Dark Lord chose to show me the error of my ways. He reminded me that he needed me alive but that it didn't apply to anyone else in my life. Of course, those that I'm fully bonded with have to stay alive, but technically speaking, a puppet is still alive."

"So, he is now changing tactics after he saw what losing Parker did to you," Brayden mused. "The situation is a no-brainer though. We have to deal with Mozog regardless of what the Dark Lord wants, but then we'll also be giving him an advantage as well."

"Perhaps it's not as cut and dry as you initially thought," Hudson pointed out. "I think this is a cause for some deliberation into this matter. There needs to be another reason we go after Mozog that has nothing to do with the Dark Lord's agenda."

"Hold up guys," Micah interjected, drawing our attention. "Can we go back to the part where you laughed at the

Dark Lord, because that right there needs to be talked about for just a moment."

Seeing him grin at me with pride in his eyes, I couldn't help but reciprocate the action. I'd actually laughed at the boogie man that haunted my dreams for almost a year now. Sure, I'd gotten choked out for it, but still it was empowering to have done it at all.

"I might need to change your nickname to little badass, instead of Cookie Monster," he teased.

The others chuckled at that, chasing away the lingering shadows that had been hanging over me after the whole interaction. Then an idea hit me. "What if we didn't kill Mozog?"

Micah gave me a quizzical brow. "Ah... I'm not following."

"Okay here me out, I might still be delusional from lack of oxygen, or the drug Jay gave me," I reasoned, waving off their doubt. "What if we captured Mozog and convinced him to help us take down the Dark Lord?"

"How would one propose to do that exactly?" Hudson inquired, sitting on the edge of the bed.

"We need to offer him someone who could be a conduit for Lilith that will last longer than a week and isn't me," I reasoned. "It would have to be someone connected to the Elementi in some way but isn't really part of it, so they won't be making us break our oath by getting them involved as bait to a crazed demon."

"I know the perfect person," Micah announced, clapping his hands and grinning like a cat who got the cream. "Think my aunt will do? She's from a line that has produced Elementi Warriors, plus she technically is filthy rich and rules a country. All things that both Lilith and Mozog would want."

"How exactly would you even get the two of them to agree?" Hudson countered. "Your aunt isn't just going to hop on a plane and come out here because you ask her to. Then how on earth are we going to get ahold of Mozog to share with him that we have this perfect candidate?"

All of Hudson's questions seemed to let all the air out of Micah's balloon, making him deflate.

"Why don't we take some time to think about it and get some sleep. I don't know about you, but I'm exhausted and really don't have the brain power to deal with all of this right now." I said, following it up with a yawn.

The guys all stood and looked at one another, as if unsure what to do with themselves so I decided to put them out of their misery. "Could all of you stay with me tonight? If you guys are comfortable with that?"

"We would be honored to all stay with you tonight," Hudson assured me. "If we're being honest, I think it would help us all get some sleep knowing we are here with you."

"I couldn't agree more," I stated as I snuggled under the covers and patted the bed. "Come on, hop in."

That was all the encouragement they needed to all pile on in and maneuver around to get comfortable. Micah pulled me against his chest, my ass tucked right up against him, with Brayden reclaiming his spot on the other side of me. Hudson opted for sleeping on the other side of Brayden, and Jay was down at my feet, a hand wrapped around my ankle. There was no chance of me feeling alone tonight, with all of them here and so close. It seemed they predicted this might happen since the bed fit all of us fairly comfortably. Taking a deep breath, I closed my eyes, praying that the Dark Lord was done with whatever he needed to say to me tonight. If I was going to be dealing with the mess my life was right now, I wasn't sure I could do that without some sort of sleep.

The following morning, I found that I wasn't the first one awake, but the last. The sun was shining in through the windows, filling the room with a soft glow, making Hudson look even more handsome than ever. I laid there, watching him reading in one of the armchairs in my room with his hair still disheveled and wearing his sleep clothes. It was simple moments like this, that I couldn't believe that I had not just one amazing man in my life but five...I mean four. Cami was the one who started the whole, I'm basically married when we completed our Bond, but the guys latched on to that and ran with it. Brayden and Hudson both loved to secretly call me their wife whenever they could, but I'd more so brushed it off as them keeping the joke alive. Yet as I look at Hudson in this intimate moment, I could honestly say that I did view him as my husband, along with Brayden. Micah and I were still learning what our Bond meant to each other, but I knew he definitely saw himself as my husband.

Then a thought struck me...even though I called Parker my fiancé, I don't think I thought of him that way in my heart. Don't get me wrong, I love that man, even after all he's done, which makes it all the more painful, but I don't think I trusted him to put me first like the others have. Even though Jay and I haven't completed our Bond, I already think of him as my husband. Even when the Oath happened between us, it wasn't the same as the others, it was perfect and exactly how it needed to happen. Now, it was high time to lock that man down before he ever had a chance to doubt my love or risk the chance of something happening where I might lose him as well.

"Sunshine...?"

My gaze flicked back to Hudson from where it had drifted to the trees outside. "Hmm?"

"What are you thinking about so hard? I can feel the roller coaster ride from over here," He questioned, closing his book, giving me his full attention.

Grabbing a pillow, I propped myself up a little more so I could see him better. "I was thinking about Parker."

"Ah." With that acknowledgement, he stood up and offered me his hand. Frowning, I grasped it and let him pull me from the bed. "This is a conversation to be had with the others, but first you need some tea."

I couldn't help but smile at him for knowing me as well as he does. Holding up my robe, he helped me slip it on and tied the belt around my waist as he pressed a kiss to my forehead. "Good morning my beautiful wife, did you sleep well?"

"Why yes, surprisingly I was able to sleep without any dreams at all," I answered. "And you, my loving husband, did you manage to sleep well with the others in the bed?"

Hudson didn't answer me right away, his eyes wide in surprise and delight, a grin pulling at his lips. "Husband... I love the sound of that coming off your lips."

"Then I guess I should use it more often," I mused, wrapping my arms around his waist. "I like to see my husbands happy."

"Whoa, how did you get her to say that so casually?" Brayden exclaimed, as he walked into the room.

I let go of Hudson to face my first husband. "You should have told me it meant so much to you for me to call you guys that."

"Angel, that's not how this works," Brayden murmured as he cupped my face and pressed a soft kiss to my lips. "You can't force someone to call you their husband if they aren't ready to. We all knew that it was going to take you just a little longer to be comfortable with our relationship. You show us every day how much we mean to you, in your own way. Never once have you hidden the fact we are together, quite the opposite actually. If I had to wait a while for you to call me your husband because you truly view me that way, I was fine with it."

It was moments like this that made what Parker did even worse, but showed me just how lucky I was to have these four men. "I love you," I blurted. "That's another thing that I don't say as often as I should either."

"I love you too, Angel," Brayden said, nuzzling his nose with mine. "Now, let's head down. I was just coming to get you, Cami made breakfast for us."

"She did? I don't smell any smoke or hear any screaming," I pointed out as I headed downstairs with them.

Brayden chuckled and glanced at me over his shoulder. "She had Jay watching over her shoulder the whole time to make sure it was safe enough for you to eat."

I could only imagine how this whole thing went down and was even more surprised that I slept through all of it. Did having them all there with me make that big of a difference? Guess I would have to talk them into doing it again to see, oh darn.

When we reached the kitchen, I was amazed to see the table set and the guys gathered around it except for Jay who was removing something from the oven, with Cami right at his elbow.

"Okay, I get that it's been in longer than it should, but does it *look* right?" Cami asked.

"It's an egg casserole, if it's cooked through then it will be fine," Jay answered, setting it on the counter and pulling out a knife.

"Yeah, but how do we know if it's cooked all the way through?" Cami countered.

Jay looked at her with a scowl and pointed for her to leave the kitchen. She opened her mouth to argue but then she spotted me and her face lit up. "Lala, you're awake!"

Racing over to me, she grabbed my hands and led me over to the table. "Sit, sit, sit, I've got everything covered this morning. What would you like to drink? We have orange, apple, or grapefruit juice, coffee—wait never mind you don't drink that. Oh, I could make you a cup of tea!"

"Tea would be lovely, whatever kind you want to surprise me with," I said, trying to hold back my laughter.

I absolutely appreciated what she was trying to do for me and I couldn't have asked for a better best friend to have right now.

"Got it. Okay, make some tea... you just need hot water and a tea bag, right?" Cami questioned, then held up her hands. "Never mind, I'll figure it out, I got this covered."

Leaning over to Micah who was sitting next to me I whispered. "What's up with her?"

"I think she's trying to coddle you after everything that happened yesterday and last night. The moment one of us was awake and out of the bedroom, she demanded answers about all the yelling and why none of us left," Micah explained. "Just humor her, you're the only best friend she has ever had and I think she's scared she might lose you." I blinked at him, shocked that he, of all people, would say something so insightful about emotional matters. "Don't look at me like that, Cookie. She's the sister I never wanted but got stuck with anyway, just because I act like a dick doesn't mean I don't care."

That is exactly what people thought of him, but I knew how wrong they were. "That is one thing I would never think about you, Micah. You act all tough but really you're just a burnt marshmallow, hard and crispy on the outside but soft and gooey on the inside."

Micah caught my chin with his hand and pulled me forward to him. "You ever tell anyone else that, and I will deny it till the day I die, but yes I would say that is fairly accurate." Before I could say anything more, he seared his lips to mine, making me hum with contentment.

"Okay, do you think we can keep the PDA to a minimum while we eat, it's unsettling for those of us not in this relationship," Cami interjected.

Micah pulled back and gave her a grin. "Jealous?"

Cami scoffed as she took her seat. "Please, if I wanted to make a move on Lala there's no way she could resist me. I'm just *that* good, so watch yourself or you might be gaining another member to your harem buddy boy."

"How would Maggs feel about that?" he shot back.

"Really, that's what you're going with? You think Maggs would really care if it was my dear sweet Lala who she is also good friends with? Hell, I'll just tell her we're in a true polymerous relationship," Cami declared.

"So, you would be fine if Maggs got another girlfriend or boyfriend if she wanted?" Brayden asked, his tone surprised.

Cami frowned at him. "Okay, when did this become about my love life? To answer your question, B-man, no I wouldn't have a problem with it *if* that is the relationship we both agreed to and we were open and honest about it. I told Lala this way back in the day when I was setting you guys up all sneaky like, but it's not fair to expect one person to fulfill all your needs. If that means adding in another person to the party, why the hell not?"

"That is very astute of you, Cami," Hudson commented. "Looks like everything is ready, shall we eat?"

Bless that man, taking the heat off my bestie. "I'm starving, Jay, load me up."

CHAPTER 23

LAILAH

Since Jay and Cami made breakfast, the rest of us pitched in to clean up, even though Cami argued the whole time. "Guys, this is not how this is supposed to work, I'm here to help out and take off some of the pressure."

"Cami, you did that when you made breakfast, we have a rule between all of us that whoever cooks doesn't clean," Brayden explained. "There are a lot of us and so it's really not that much of a burden."

"Yeah well, we don't have the idiot helping us this time so that helps," Micah commented, acid in his tone.

At the mention of Parker not being there, I was brought to an abrupt halt as my heart ached with his absence. Even though my brain was pissed at him and knew he didn't deserve to be here with us right now, it didn't do a damn thing for my heart, who missed him terribly. "Has anyone heard from him?" I whispered, half hoping no one would hear me, but I wasn't that lucky.

"Dylan texted me, letting me know they took him to your parents for the night," Jay answered. "Dylan also said that everyone wanted to come over to check on you, but I also think it's because he has questions."

Unable to deal with the simple task of putting the left-overs in a container, I shoved it away and splayed my hands on the counter. "How can I tell him there's no hope for Phoebe? No matter what plan we come up with, it will always end in Phoebe dying."

"Angel," Brayden ventured, reaching out to me.

I didn't want to be comforted. I wanted to be left to feel angry about the situation. "Don't, please." I snapped as I stepped away from him. "I'm going to get some clothes on and call my parents."

"Alright, we'll be around if you need us," Brayden said, assuring me he wasn't upset with me.

I just nodded and headed upstairs, feeling all their eyes on me as I walked away. In the refuge of my own room, I slid down the door and crumpled to the floor as the pain I'd been pushing off gutted me full force.

He left me—no it was worse than that. Parker, my grinning, goofball of a boyfriend, betrayed me and left not even putting up a fight. He just let Micah beat him to a pulp and let me leave, without trying to stop me! So what if I told him to fuck off, if he really wanted me he should have said something... right?

Tears streamed down my face as my body shook with the effort to keep my sobs quiet so the guys wouldn't come up here. They were going through their own emotions over this, but they didn't know what it felt like to have a piece of your soul ripped out of you, while at the same time you weren't sure you were going to live.

Could someone even come back from a fuck up as big as this? Would the angels allow us to form another Bond if he broke his Oath to me and them? Why?! Why the fuck was I the one who had to deal with all of this? Hadn't I suffered enough for this goddamn calling? If I was supposed to be some mythical weapon to end the hold the darkness had on this world, it would mother fucking help if they didn't keep kicking me while I was down. Letting out a growl, I pulled myself to my feet and wiped my sleeve across my face to dry my tears, before tossing it off. Yanking open one of the drawers that held my work out clothes, I pulled out what I needed and slammed it shut. I made quick work getting ready, tossed my hair up and out of the way, snagged my headphones, and jogged down the stairs.

"Lailah," Jay called out to me as I brushed past him out the front door. "Do not ignore me."

The tone he used made me pause long enough to look him in the eyes and toss out what he wanted to know. "I'm going for a run. No, I don't want company."

"We are not the enemy, and I don't appreciate being treated as such," he barked, making me flinch.

Whirling on my heel, I turned to face him. "That's what you think this is?"

"How would I know differently when you won't take the time to speak to me?" Jay reasoned, his arms crossed, face unreadable. "You only run from those you don't want to be around."

Something about the way he said that made me snap. "I can't think with all of you constantly listening in on my emotions and trying to make things alright when it's not, Jay! Nothing is okay right now, I'm broken, pissed, and in pain. A pain that no one understands but me, and everything is so fucked up I can't process anything, so I need to go for a run. That okay with you, or do you plan to stop me because the world is too dangerous out there to be trusted on my own?"

"Don't pick a fight you can't win, Beautiful," Jay warned

but he relaxed slightly after my outburst. "Go have your run, all I ask is that you take your phone with you."

I opened my mouth to say something sassy, but he was right. I was trying to pick a fight. So I just nodded my head and showed him my phone attached to my arm. "I will... and thanks."

In true Jay fashion he didn't say anything, just turned and walked back into the house. Guilt compounded on my other mix of emotions, making me need this run all that much more. I walked to the end of the drive and took a moment to stretch against a tree so I didn't do more harm than good. Thankfully, the stitches didn't pull that bad as I started at a light easy jog, following the beat of my running playlist set up just for this purpose. It surprised me that I was in even better shape now than I had been running track all through high school. I was up to my old times and distance, even being able to outdo them with a little effort. That wasn't what today's run was about though, I needed to clear my head and this is how I always did that best. The slap of my feet on the asphalt, the music in my ears, and the breath moving in and out of my lungs was all I focused on, bringing me back to center.

Having no idea where I was running or the layout of the community, I just decided to stay within the gates and GPS my way back if I needed to. Although I had a feeling if I took too long, Jay would be showing up at some point. He would let me have my space but that didn't mean I wasn't being tracked by him, either through my phone or some other way he found to keep an eye on me. Either way, I would take the illusion of being on my own for now and deal with that when it happened. Now that I was good and warmed up, I put some real effort into my run feeling the need to push myself, to feel the burn of my muscles getting used, the stress of things slipping away with each droplet of sweat.

Interestingly enough, my thoughts drifted to Micah's idea about using his aunt as the bait for Mozog. What if I approached the Dark Lord and used him just as he was using me to get the job done? He of course, would expect us to kill Mozog but we would capture him instead, in the hope we could gain some knowledge about the Dark Lord, or even what Mozog's own plans were. The whole situation would be a gray area in following the rules, but I believed that to get this mission done we would need to walk that edge of the knife as best we could without falling.

I was responsible for killing many innocent people, regardless of the fact they had been possessed by demons and infected with the serum. Everything about this whole situation was a blurred line depending on how you looked at it. The only things I refused to do was become callused to the suffering of those being used and their lives lost. If I felt for a second I no longer felt guilt or remorse over the things I'd done, I would end it all in a heartbeat, because that was not who I was. Lost deep in thought, I didn't notice the car until it was moments away from hitting me. Diving out of the way, I landed in the bushes that bordered someone's front yard with the car sounding a long and excessive honk as they kept driving.

"What the hell?" I swore, picking myself up off the ground and pulling the branches out of my hair trying to get my heart rate to calm down.

"This is exactly why I never understood why Synergy was going to be a human, you're just so fragile," a voice said from behind me on the other side of the bushes.

I froze as my brain registered that it was Phoebe's voice

who'd spoken. Slowly turning, I came face to face with none other than Lilith, Mother of All, using Phoebe's body.

Lilith pouted when I met her all-black eyes. "You don't look very happy to see me, Synergy... or should I call you Lailah? Just a few months ago, you were destined to be my conduit so I could stop using these filthy human flesh sacks. "

"What are you doing here?" I demanded, finally getting over my shock.

"I would think that would be obvious, I'm here to steal your body of course," Lilith laughed, tossing her hair over her shoulder. "While this one does have a deliciously dark heart, I'm just too powerful for her body to contain. If it makes you feel any better, she absolutely planned on crushing your brother's heart and stealing Parker from you. How could I resist helping her and you for that matter. I exposed the bastard for the man he truly is."

"Don't you dare say his name," I snarled, my power pulsing around me in anger. "You manipulated and used him for your own sick and twisted enjoyment."

Lilith looked down at her nails, feigning boredom as I spoke. "Blah, blah, blah, like I haven't heard it all before. Babe, my own children locked me away, drained all my power, throwing away the key because they feared and hated me... what makes you think you're a threat at all? God, it's like you're a mouse squeaking away at the lion who's playing with you."

"Well, if I'm not a threat to you then I guess I'll just have to kill Mozog instead. Someone told me he was your favorite child, born of an angel, if the rumors are true," I threatened.

A grin spread across Lilith's face at my words. "Would you look at that, an Elementi who knows how to play the game. I warn you though, it's not wise to threaten something that you also could be hurt by in retaliation. See, everyone's got a favorite to lose, but you have far more of them than I do, little warrior. We'll have to do this again another time, seems we are about to be interrupted." Bopping me on the nose, Lilith stepped back and in a cloud of smoke she disappeared.

"Could my day get any worse?" I muttered as I tried to shake off that encounter and picked off the rest of the bush from my clothes. Then I heard footsteps approaching, but didn't bother to look up having a good guess as to who it was. "Jay, I haven't even been gone long enough for you to need to come looking for me."

"Trouble—"

My head snapped up and there was Parker, standing a foot away from me. He looked awful, black eye, split lip, bruise on his chin, and his clothes rumpled like he slept in them. "What are you doing here?"

"I wanted to talk to you... alone, without the others breathing down my neck. Not that I blame them for wanting to keep you away from me after what I did," Parker answered, rubbing the back of his neck nervously. "I don't even know where to begin to tell you how sorry I am, or that I know I fucked up big time."

"You fucked up? That's what you think you did?" I demanded, taking a step towards him. "Are you under the impression that I'm just going to brush this off, forgive you and move on like you didn't shatter my heart into a billion pieces? I fucking loved you, Parker."

His face paled at my words, making his bruising stand out even more. "You said loved... like past tense."

"Well, I'm glad to see your hearing wasn't affected by Micah's pounding," I said, baiting him. "Yes Parker—*loved*

— I don't know how I feel about you right now, but I know it isn't love."

"Lailah, I deserve all your rage and pain for what I did to you. I also know that I have a lot of work ahead of me to prove that I do love you and want to earn your trust back," Parker explained. "The question is, are you going to give me a chance?"

Oh hell no, he is not going to make this my problem I wasn't the one who fucked up!

"Parker, I told you from the moment you told me about Phoebe that you were the one in control about whether things would cause problems or not." Seeing that he still wasn't getting it, I decided to spell it out for him. "I. Did. Nothing. Wrong. You did. And now, it's your problem to figure out how to solve it."

"Are you telling me there is no hope?" Parker pressed.

I covered my face with my hands, unable to deal with this situation, then dropped them to meet his gaze once again. "Before I knew about the Elementi, or the fact that I was Synergy, you were one of my best friends. We've been more than friends for five months and you still can't seem to understand me. How is there any hope for us to be more, when you won't even risk trying? I'm not the person to ask how to fix this, because at the moment I don't want to give you a chance, for fear you'll do it again or something worse. With everything we have been through, I used to think I trusted you with my life, but I don't think that's true anymore since you abandoned me for you ex-girlfriend, who was already a host to the Mother of All demons." Unable to continue this conversation I turned and started walking away.

A hand shot out and grabbed my wrist, pulling me against their chest. I knew it was Parker, the feel of his body against mine was familiar and comforting, no matter how badly he betrayed me. "Please don't walk away from me, Trouble. I can't lose you, it will destroy me if there is no chance to fix things between us."

My heart and mind were at war with each other on how to handle him, but I was saved when Jay rolled up in the Audi. Putting the car in park he got out and walked over to us, his eyes locked on mine, ignoring Parker completely. "Your parents are here, along with your brothers, it seems they decided you were taking too long to talk to them." Reaching out a hand, he gave me an out if I wanted it and I took it.

"Lailah, please," Parker begged. "Tell me there is even the slightest glimmer of hope I can fix this."

Jay wrapped his arm around my waist as I looked at Parker. "It won't be easy, and I have no idea how long it will take, if it ever will, but you can try. All I ask right now is time apart so I can heal from the damage you've done already. If you can't respect that simple request, then I guess I'll have all the information I need to know that we will never work."

"How much time?"

"I don't know," I answered honestly. "Guess you'll have to decide if you're willing to wait."

Parker nodded, his hands balling into fists. "I'll wait for as long as it takes, Lailah, I refuse to lose you forever, if there's a chance."

Jay opened the car door for me and helped me in before shutting it. He said something to Parker who nodded, not taking his gaze off of me until we drove off, leaving him there in the road.

CHAPTER 24

JAY

"Your stuff is sitting in the driveway, don't even try to come in the house," I warned Parker in a voice low enough that Lailah wouldn't hear me.

Even though I didn't have the connection yet to feel her emotions, it was written all over her face as I got into the car. This situation had been even more traumatic to her than we had first suspected. Without a doubt, we knew this had broken her heart and set her back from the progress that she'd made getting herself back to some sense of normal, but what I'd just witnessed told me it was more than that. Part of me actually worried for the first time that she might do something she could never come back from if we weren't careful.

The car was silent as she sat next to me, her hands clasped tightly together in her lap, as if she was trying to hold herself together with everything she had. I'd see that same look on my mother's face when my father came to take me from her when I was old enough to start training with him. Having me with her was the only connection she had to my father, who for some reason I still don't understand, she loved. Reaching over, I covered her hands with mine and squeezed, trying to tell her that I was there for her. When I went to pull my hand away, she clutched it as if it was a lifeline to her, so I let her have it, willing to do whatever it took to help her through this. If picking a fight with me like she did earlier was going to help, then I would go toe to toe, or if it simply was the need to not feel alone, then that's what I would do.

Lailah had no clue what she truly meant to me and that was partially my fault, I wasn't good at sharing emotions after being punished for so long when I did express them. My father saw them as a weakness and used any chance he could to cut them out of me, after he took me from Mother. Since Lailah came into the picture, I've spent less time with my father doing missions for him now that my true team was complete... or had been. I knew the others had seen a difference in me as Lailah worked her spell on me, pulling me out of my emotionless shell. After seeing how fragile this connection I had to her right now is, I *needed* to find a way to finish this between us because I was never going to take the chance of losing her. She was my life, my soul, my perfect partner to spend the rest of my life watching over and protecting her from everything I could.

"I thought we were going back to the house," Lailah questioned as she seemed to realize where she was.

I didn't answer her right away as I parked on the side of the road that had a gravel pull off. I'd discovered this trail when I'd been running the other day and when I saw where it led to, I knew I needed to bring Lailah here. "I thought you might want a little time to process talking with Parker before you spoke to your parents."

She nodded as her eyes started to shimmer with unshed tears. Gently, I pulled my hand out of hers, turned the car off and got out to open her door. "Can I show you something?"

Blinking, she looked up at me surprised by my question. "Ah...sure."

Holding out a hand to her, I pulled her out of the low car, giving her a tender smile that seemed to catch her off guard. "Follow me."

Without releasing her hand, I intertwined our fingers and led her down the narrow path deeper into the woods. It took us about ten minutes to get there, but the path was easy and our silence was comfortable, as we took in the nature around us. Back at Ryevick, we'd spent much of our alone time on trails like this running or hiking, just enjoying each other's company and I wouldn't trade it for the world. We'd all adjusted to sharing Lailah amongst ourselves for the most part, but we all craved our time alone with her, getting her full attention even for an hour or two. None of us ever felt neglected, but when you loved someone the way I did Lailah, you craved being their entire focus even for a moment.

Lailah paused when she heard the tell-tale sound of running water, which made me smile as a flicker of interest appeared in her eyes. "Where are we going, Jay?"

Turning to face her, I took both hands in mine. "Do you trust me?"

"With my life," she said without hesitation.

"What about your heart?"

That one took her a moment to answer as she searched my face, almost trying to see into my soul. I dropped my guard and let her in completely, no longer wanting to hide anything from her. Lailah's eyes widened in surprise, taking an unconscious step closer, pulling a hand from me to rest it on my cheek. Then the brightest smile I'd ever seen on her face, bloomed into existence as a tear slipped down her cheek.

"There you are, I knew you were lurking under there somewhere," she whispered as she stroked her thumb along my skin. "Jay, I trust you with my everything, without question or reservation. Time and time again you have proven to me your love and loyalty, but just now you showed me you trusted me with your heart. Who could ask for more?"

Using my free hand, I pulled her to me by the back of her neck and kissed her, infusing it with everything I'd been too afraid to show her before. We were both taking the risk to bare our souls to each other and it was the closest thing I could think of souls intertwining. Pulling back, I lifted her hand and kissed the back of it before I took a few more steps backward, not willing to take my eyes off her as she saw what was behind me through the break in the trees. Her soft gasp as she took in everything was just what I'd hoped it would be. Stepping to the side, I pulled her in front of me and held her against my chest as we took in the sight of the river with it's swiftly moving current over the small six foot waterfall and rapids below curling around the boulders and fallen tree below. The trail took you to the base of the waterfall, but you could easily climb up to the top portion as well.

"Jay, how did you find this?" Lailah asked in awe.

"Dumb luck," I answered grinning with how pleased I was.

"This reminds me of that first trail run you and I did together."

I hummed my agreement, having thought the same thing. Even though this was smaller, it had the same magical feeling to it, being secluded deep in the woods with just the sounds of nature around us. I tugged her over to a soft patch of moss that I'd used the last time I was here to enjoy the atmosphere, setting her in between my legs so she leaned against me as I was propped up against a boulder.

"Can we stay here a while?" Lailah murmured.

"We can stay as long as you like, Beautiful, the others know you're with me," I assured her.

When her parents arrived and told us that they brought Parker with them, Micah lost his shit, but Brayden was able to hold him back. Not understanding the reaction, Hudson tried to calm things down with them. I was glad he was someone we could count on to be the rational out of us in that moment while I left to go find Lailah. I knew if Parker found her on her run that she wouldn't be able to make it back to the house on her own after. I made sure to send them all a text letting them know I would be back with her when she was ready and not before. The last thing she needed was high emotions, blunt logic, or pandering, even if it was meant to be supportive.

Having her here in my arms, completely relaxed as she watched the water, was exactly what I'd hoped would happen. Using my power, I picked up the breeze near the waterfall causing the water spray to float through the air into the sunshine where it turned into a shimmering rainbow of colors. Lailah took a sharp intake of breath as she gripped my leg, which brought my dick to full attention as she wiggled between my legs. Trying to keep my mind off her perfect ass rubbing against my dick, I performed a few more tricks, making her giggle with excitement.

"I had no idea you could do things like that."

Leaning down, I kissed the back of her neck before I

whispered in her ear. "It's not often I get the chance to show off."

A shiver ran through her body at my words, which led me to kiss her behind her ear. In an act of complete trust, she tilted her head to the side exposing her neck to me more with a sigh of pleasure. Bringing my hands up, I let them skim down her arms as I started to kiss along her neck, nipping every so often, getting a moan of pleasure each time I did. This wasn't what I had in mind at all bringing her out here, but if she asked me to continue, I wasn't a strong enough man to say no when I craved her so completely.

"Jay," she sighed, leaning her head back against my shoulder bringing her hand up to pull me down to her lips.

My hands slipped under her shirt and didn't stop until I had them on her breasts, kneading them over her sports bra. Devouring her moans as she arched into my hands was the sweetest nectar you've ever had, driving me to pull more from her. Breaking our kiss, I pulled her t-shirt up and off, setting it beside me before returning to shove her bra up, freeing her so I could attend to them better. Pinching at her erect nipples, I pulled them slightly making her cry out.

"Oh god, *yes* Jay."

With a growl, I grabbed her by the hips, lifting and spinning her around so she was facing me as I latched on to one of her breasts. She clutched my head to her as I feasted on her soft flesh, rolling the tight bud with my tongue as I massaged the other. Her hips ground against my pelvis, trying to gain any kind of friction.

"I need to feel you, Jay," Lailah murmured as she started to pull at the back of my shirt. Leaning forward, I held her securely as she yanked it over my head and tossed it behind her, then started to paw at my pants.

I grabbed her hands in one of mine, halting her attack on me with a grin, kissing her softly. "There is no rush, Beautiful, we have all the time we need."

Slowly, I laid her down on her back in the moss before I worked on getting my pants off. In an almost methodical movement, I rested my hands on her hips and slid my fingers in her waistband so she knew what I was going to do. I felt her tense but then relax, giving me a nod to keep going. Peeling off her leggings was like unwrapping the best gift I could have been given in life, she wasn't even wearing any underwear, so the moment I got them over her hips, I was greeted with the sight of her perfect pussy. It was already glistening with her need, making me all but purr with my need to taste it. Somehow, I managed to get her pants off before I spread them wide and kissed up her leg, making it clear what my intentions were.

Her breath came in pants, as she anticipated what was about to happen. I kept a watchful eye in case it ever became too much. Being on her back had been one of her triggers, but from what I gathered that was getting better. When I finally got to my prize, I almost didn't want to cross that line right now with how vulnerable she was, because the moment I started this, it wouldn't end until I was finishing inside her claiming her as mine for the rest of our lives together.

"Please, I need you, Jay. I know you said our time will happen when it's right, but I don't want to wait any longer. I need you to be mine forever," she pleaded, and that was all I needed to make my choice.

My lips skirted her inner thigh before I nipped at it with my teeth. Finally, I made it to her center, it was the most beautiful sight I had ever seen, making me want to lick it until my tongue fell off. Her taste was even better than her smell. I licked up her slit before I buried my tongue inside her, discovering the sweetest most perfect taste in the world. I never wanted to stop but I knew my cock needed to be inside her just as badly.

I used my hands to spread her lower lips so I could lick her more easily. I started to use my fingers inside her as well, the extra stimulation making her writhe beneath me. I knew she was close, but I focused on getting her ready for me. I slid my hand down to her ass and lifted her up so I could get even deeper inside her. I put all my focus on making her cum, on my face making her come for me. I was rewarded with her juices coating my lips as she came, almost causing me to drown in her cum. I kept at it though, sucking her sensitive clit into my mouth and lightly grazing it with my teeth, before I gave it a lick to take the sting away.

"That was amazing, Jay. I can't wait to feel you inside me," she moaned, and I knew I couldn't wait anymore either. My dick was aching for her. I gave her a few last licks before I got up and gave her a bigger kiss. She tasted herself on my lips and tongue and I could see the desire in her eyes.

"Are you okay if I try to do this with you under me?" I asked as I slowly moved, kissing up her body until I reached her mouth. "I need to watch your face as we do this for the first time, I want the image of you becoming mine, forever ingrained in my mind for eternity."

"How could a girl turn down a request like that?" she answered, smiling up at me. "I told you, Jay, I trust you in every way, you'll never hurt me."

Cupping her face with my hands I devoured her, overwhelmed with the trust and love that was shining in her eyes as I slipped into her. She groaned into my mouth as my cock filled her to the point I reached the end of her. She was tight and hot, the most exquisite feeling I'd ever known. We stayed like that for a few moments, not moving, just feeling as we became one.

Pulling out just as slowly as I'd slipped into her, I watched as her eyes opened and her pupils dilated as she looked at me.

"Are you ok?" I asked, pausing before I thrust back into her with a nod of her head. Her breath caught and I felt her muscles contract around me. This was going to be one hell of a ride.

I fucked her like there was no tomorrow, pounding into her over and over again, and she took it and then some. She was tight and wet and her pussy muscles were milking me as I thrust harder and deeper. I felt her body tighten as she came and as I felt her clench down on my cock I came, too. I felt my cum as it pulsed out of my cock into her, then I pulled out, flipping her over so she was on her knees and I could slide back into her.

Power crashed around us as I entered her again, wrapping us in its heady grasp as our Bond snapped into place, but I wasn't done with her yet. I'd waited too long for this moment between us and I was going to enjoy every moment of it.

This new angle was fantastic, allowing me to slide deeper into her than before, as I grabbed her hips and fucked her hard. Wrapping an arm around her waist, my thumb slid across her clit as I rubbed it. I slid in and out of her, watching where we were connected, filling my need to own her body, marking it as mine. The sight of her naked, out in the open air, her firm round ass thrust back, her pussy wet wrapping around my dick, and crying out for me was almost too much to take.

I came again, my balls tightening as I filled her up. Then

I collapsed onto her back, my arms still wrapped around her. I could feel her body trembling beneath mine as I kissed her neck, then her back and then her ass as I pulled out.

"I love you." I heard her whisper, as I rolled to the side and curled her into my arms.

"I love you, too." I replied as I stroked her hair. "You, Lailah, are my very soul which I cannot live without. I will always be here to protect you, even if you resent me for it sometimes. Just know I can't bear the thought of losing you, Beautiful."

CHAPTER 25

LAILAH

Jay and I stayed at the river for a little longer, just holding each other, taking time to enjoy the feeling of our new Bond. Out of all the Bonds, I was most excited to be able to get a glimpse inside Jay's brain since he was the hardest to read. To say that I was stunned at the intensity of his love for me was an understatement. It was borderline obsessive, but made me understand his need to keep me safe and healthy all the time. This didn't mean that I was going to let him control everything in my life just to make him feel better, but it helped me see his point of view. We walked back to the car hand in hand, not wanting to let anything come between us, even getting into the car with that fleeting moment when he had to get in on the other side was too much. I wasn't sure if it was his need or mine that was driving the clinginess but neither one of us wanted to fight it.

In a way, it was odd that I'd been so comfortable and adamant about him sealing our Bond after what I just went through with Parker, but now I knew he couldn't ever leave me. Knowing that I now had four of them tied to me for the rest of my life curbed some of the fear that I would be abandoned by them all, as irrational as that fear was. This is one of those moments where the heart and the head didn't agree with each other right away—not that it mattered, since the deed was done. We arrived back at the house where I paused at the front door, knowing the moment I walked in there I was going to have to face all the problems I'd left behind.

"Beautiful..." Jay murmured, wrapping his arms around my waist. "You're not alone in this, we will help you figure this out."

"They're my parents though, how do I tell them that I let my brother's girlfriend get taken and turned into a body for one of the most evil female demons?" I countered leaning into him.

"First of all, you didn't *do* any of this," Jay stated. "Secondly, they are our family now too, and I know any of us would be happy to explain things if you don't want to."

Taking a deep breath, I let it out slowly before squaring my shoulders and giving Jay a nod to let him know I was ready. Together, we walked in to find everyone seated in the living room with tense, worried expressions on their faces. No one was speaking, just sitting in uncomfortable silence taking coffee from Cami as she handed them out to everyone. Hearing us enter, all their heads snapped in our direction and Mom was half out of her seat before Dad took her hand to stop her. She looked down at him then returned to her spot, clutching the coffee mug in her hand and waiting for me to join them.

"I was just getting everyone something warm to drink, did either of you want coffee or tea?" Cami asked, breaking the tension as she walked up to us.

Without letting go of Jay I hugged Cami with my free

arm. "Thank you for looking after them, Cami. What would I do without you?"

Cami gave me a warm smile. "Well, you need someone to keep a level head around here when all your men lose their shit without you around. How you manage them being all moody, I'll never know." With a wink she headed back to the kitchen to do who knows what.

Jay and I took one of the remaining open armchairs, him pulling me onto his lap and resting his head on my shoulder.

"Did we all look *that* whipped after we Bonded?" Micah asked, grinning at us.

"You have no room to tease, mister. I remember someone being very needy about spending quality time with me after it happened," I shot back.

Brayden snorted at that. "No one was as bad as Hudson though—he was a total goner."

"Says the man who got her all to himself for two months," Hudson countered, looking down his nose at Brayden.

My father cleared his throat, drawing all of us back to the reason that they were even here. "Lailah, I know this is going to be difficult for you with what Parker's told us, but we have so many questions and he felt it was better to talk to you about them."

I tensed hearing this. "What *did* Parker tell you?"

"Well...he explained how you two are no longer together because of something he did, that also resulted in Phoebe going missing," Dad explained. "It didn't really make sense to us at all, and then Dylan was saying something about demons at the powerplant."

My gaze shifted to Dylan, and he looked just how I felt about the whole situation. Both of us lost someone that we thought we loved, in ways we never expected. My heart ached for both of us, but I knew there was nothing I could do to fix things for him, especially after I talked with Lilith.

"Dylan," I started drawing his attention. "What can I do to help you?"

"You can get her back," he bit out his eyes stormy with anger. "But not until you kill the bastard who did this to her."

Standing up, I walked over to Dylan and knelt down in front of him. "I will bring her back to you just like I promised I would, but you have to understand that she won't be the same. Even if I can bring her back to you alive, which I can't guarantee, the Phoebe you know is gone forever. As for your second request...it would be my honor to avenge her death for you, because I will take them all down—every last one of them. I won't leave here until I destroy whatever hold they have here and then I'll move on to the one who started this war."

"How did this happen Lailah? I just don't understand it, why Phoebe?" Dylan pressed tears welling up in his eyes. "She was a good person."

My thoughts went back to my talk with Lilith and I knew I couldn't trust her to say anything truthful, but I was sure that some of what she said was true. "The demons look for people they can manipulate in some way shape or form. Good or bad, everyone has a weakness, whether it's money, power, fame, it's the crack they can use to get their foothold in. This demon could grant Phoebe's wish, and manipulation is the strongest weapon they have. I've experienced it myself, the reason that I have these markings is because they tried to do the same thing to me they did to Phoebe. They threatened to kill everyone I cared about, and a group of innocents, if I didn't comply. I decided that it was better to give up my own life than to let you all suffer at their hands."

"Why can't you save Phoebe if you got away?"

"It would seem that being an Elementi Warrior, and blessed with Synergy, made me somewhat resistant to their efforts. If I hadn't been bonded to these men I would have been lost, but since they hold a part of my soul it couldn't be taken from me the same way. I suffered in many other ways, but it gave us hope that my blood might give us a chance to save those who are lost. They just haven't been able to find the right combination yet to make it work," I shared. "Please trust me to do everything I can to save her and if I can't, I won't let them use her for something evil, I'll set her free in another way." Dylan looked at me, numbly nodding his head, turning his gaze away from me. "I need all of you to be careful, they have already started to threaten to hurt you to get to me if I don't fall in line. I would ask that you guys stay here for now, we have a protective barrier around our home they can't get through, so I know you'll be safe. The rest of us need to head into Chicago to meet up with the Elementi team that is there."

"We can't just stop living our lives to hide here!" Kyle blurted. "Doesn't that show them they've won?"

"Kyle these are demons—pure evil. They don't give a damn about playing by the rules; all they care about is how they can get me to do what they want. They can't win this war without me being on their side. The biggest weakness I have is you guys and they know that. If I'm going to be of any use to anyone, I *need* to know you are here safe so I can do everything in my power to end this while keeping you all alive."

"Why is this all on you? Why don't the others help?" Mom demanded as she frowned at the guys behind me.

Looking over my shoulder at them, I gave them a soft smile. "Don't worry, they will be right by my side the whole time, keeping me safe." Turning back to Mom I took her hand. "The five of us are a team and we are our best when we all work together to get this done."

"What about Parker?"

"That's hard to explain Mom, but Parker made me a promise that was witnessed by the angels, and he broke that promise, along with my heart," I answered, trying my best to keep my voice steady as the words were like a dagger into my heart. "Time will tell what will happen with that, but right now I can't rely on him."

"Alright so we stay here, but for how long?" Dad questioned. "How do we keep in contact with you through this, because I'm not just going to let my baby girl put herself in danger and not be able to reach you."

"I'll stay here to guard you guys and keep in contact with the Elementi base of operations. As Lala's bodyguard, it's my honor to keep her family safe while she can't." Cami announced. "That way, you don't have to worry about a human servant coming to get them or manipulate them into leaving the safe zone."

"Thank you Cami, that will lift a huge burden off my shoulders," I agreed.

Dad snorted as he looked Cami up and down. "I don't mean any offence, but what can a small thing like you do to protect us?"

"I'm so glad you asked," Cami answered with a grin. "I've been trained since I was a small child for this type of job. You could say that I'm the equivalent of a Navy Seal special ops soldier in our organization. I might not be able to kill a demon if one showed up, but other than that, I've got you covered."

My parents looked at her with shock and amazement.

"If you think this is what's best, then we'll trust your judgement in this, Ladybug," Mom said, leaning into Dad as he wrapped an arm around her shoulders.

"What your mother said. We don't want to make this harder for you, but watching one of your children put themselves in harm's way to keep us safe is just hard to swallow," Dad explained.

Mom patted Dad's leg, giving him an understanding smile before she turned back to me. "When are you heading to Chicago?"

"In the next hour or so, there are too many moving parts and not enough information for us to make the moves we need. Dylan, what is the name of the lawyer that Phoebe was working under?"

"That would be Mr. Lewis, he's one of the founding partners. Why do you need to know that?" Dylan inquired, brows scrunched in a frown.

"Nothing you need to worry about," I assured him, not wanting to even hint at our plan, no matter how rough it was. "If you need anything from the house, two of the guys can go with you while I get cleaned up after my run. I would plan for a few days just to be safe, hopefully we can get this cleared up quickly, but I honestly don't have a clue what we are walking into yet."

"Brayden and I will take them over," Micah volunteered.

I reached out to him to pull me to my feet, then gave him a quick kiss. "Thank you, I'll see you guys when you get back and we'll head out, alright?"

"You're the boss," Micah teased, trying to get a smile out of me, which worked.

"I'll clear out a few of the bedrooms and move everything into the master so that you guys have rooms," Hudson offered, heading off to do as he said.

This is when Mom started to fret. "Oh, I don't want to put you out or make more work for you to have us here."

"Mom, two or more of them stay in my room most nights as it is. Believe me when I say, this is not an inconvenience to them." The blush that appeared on my mother's cheeks upon hearing that made me realize what she assumed. I mean, she wasn't wrong but shared activities were a new concept in our relationship but I wasn't going to explain that part of our lives now, if ever. Some things a mother just doesn't need to know.

LAILAH

Jay followed me up to the bathroom, and joined me in the shower, since we both needed to clean up from our adventure in the woods. He kept his hands to himself for the most part, since he could clearly read that I was more focused on our next steps.

"Do you want to tell me why you really wanted the name of the lawyer?" he asked eventually, as we dried off.

Pausing I took a moment to consider whether I should tell him or not since it wasn't my story to tell, I said, "If we want to go with the plan to get Micah's aunt here to the states, I feel that he will be useful to us with other information I know. I'm not purposefully trying to be cryptic, I just don't want to say more than I should without his permission."

"I understand and respect that," Jay said as he headed into the bedroom where his duffle bag now was. "You keep secrets for all of us in one way or another, but I trust you to tell me if it was something I needed to know."

I wrapped my arms around his waist and leaned my head against his still bare chest as he held me tightly to him. "Tell me we can really do this, that we can end this, and I won't have to keep losing parts of myself for nothing."

At the feeling of another person walking up behind me, I tensed but then I felt Hudson reach out to me through our connection, setting me at ease. He kissed the back of my neck as he pressed against me, so I was cocooned between them. "Sunshine, I know that at the end of all of this we will come out on top. Everything we have all suffered through will have been for a reason and we will finish this once and for all."

"How can you be so confident?" I questioned. "I have no idea how we're going to manage everything I promised to my brother. The more I look at things, the more lost I'm feeling; like my hands are tied behind my back with nowhere to go."

Jay pulled back enough to lift my chin, so I was looking him in the eye. "Fear is nothing more than a weapon to keep us from doing what we must. It blinds us to things that could be staring us right in the face because we are already accepting the fact we'll fail. It takes true courage to throw off that fear and take a step forward, even if you can't see the way out."

"Together, with all our minds and skills, we will find the answer," Hudson agreed.

"Can we do this with one of us missing?" I challenged, knowing that without Parker we were vulnerable.

Hudson rested his head on my shoulder, pressing his lips to my skin in comfort before he spoke. "Even if we had Parker with us right now, he wouldn't be of any use to us. This is something he needs to work through and learn about himself, no matter how we wish we could help him. If he can't trust himself, then how can he expect you to?"

"I know that is super logical and smart Hudson, but it

doesn't make it any easier," I huffed as I pulled out of their arms to get dressed.

"Trust me, Sunshine, I know," he sighed. "Because he'll have to prove to us, as well as you, that he won't do something that fucked up again."

That was the part of this that I hadn't really thought through much. Parker broke their trust as much as mine by doing what he did and putting me in danger—the one thing they might not be able to forgive. Pushing aside that problem, I focused on what we needed to do now.

"Jay, do you mind reaching out to the Chicago hub and letting them know we're coming?" I asked. "It might be smart for us to pack a few things to take as well. I won't return back here and look my family in the eye unless we've finished this."

"Of course, Beautiful I can do that," Jay answered.

"Want me to help you pack some things for the other two?" Hudson offered. "It might be just as easy to do it now than wait for when they come back."

"Guys only need a clean pair of boxers and a shirt right?" I teased grinning over at him where he was digging through his own luggage.

"That might work for some, but I prefer to have a whole new set of clean clothes to change into, otherwise I just feel dirty," Hudson shared, setting a few sets of clothes to the side.

Walking over to him I kissed him on the cheek. "Why doesn't that shock me? Did you grab things out of the other two bathrooms?"

Shocking the hell out of me, Hudson smacked me on the ass, making me yelp as I headed to the door. "Not yet, while you're at it you should switch out the towels—wouldn't want to have the in-laws using dirty ones."

"What a considerate husband you are, even if you like to play dangerously at times," I commented, narrowing my gaze at him while rubbing my butt cheek that smarted.

He just smiled and gave me a wink, before turning back to continue what he was doing. Rolling my eyes, I headed to the bathroom in the hall that Parker and Jay had been using, only to find Parker's things had been cleared out. Rationally, I knew the others wouldn't let him back in the house and I told him to give me space, but this was irrefutable evidence that he was well and truly removed from this home. Shaking myself out of the darkness I was spiraling towards, I collected Jay's thing and headed for the other bathroom Micah and Brayden used that was shared between the two rooms they had claimed when we first got here. Cami had the second master bedroom that had its own bathroom, which worked out perfectly.

Tossing everything I gathered into the bag that Hudson was packing, I paused when I caught them both watching me with cautious expressions. "What?"

"We know you noticed Parker's things are gone," Hudson ventured. "More so, that it upset you... should we not have made him leave?"

Shaking my head and letting my shoulders slump, I sat on the bed. "Seeing as I told him to give me time and leave me alone, it was the only option. There is no way that he could have stayed here. It would have hurt too much to see him every day, just seeing him now was almost too much. Especially after talking with Lilith, it caught me off guard."

"What the fuck!" Jay roared, marching over to me. "You're just telling us this now?"

Flopping back onto the bed I groaned, rubbing my face with my hands. "I'm sorry, I wasn't trying to hide it, I prom-ise. Everything just happened all at once. She showed up to basically threaten me directly about the same thing the Dark Lord wants, then Parker showed up, and we went for our walk in the woods which led to Bonding. Where was I supposed to fit that in?"

Clearly not happy with my answer, Jay decided to straddle me so we were face to face. "Lailah, that is the first thing that should have come out of your mouth when I picked you up," Jay growled. "I took us to a secluded place and made us both vulnerable. What if she had attacked us and stolen you away from me?"

"Obviously, I wasn't thinking," I snapped back at him, pissed that I knew he had every right to be mad. "I just wanted to forget everything that happened and enjoy a moment with you—is that so wrong?"

"Yes, when it puts you in danger," Jay stated. I could feel his panic at the thought of me being taken from him and the turmoil that was churning through his emotions. "Lailah, you can't keep doing this to me. I know you're hurting and avoidance seems the perfect answer, but not at the cost of your own life. It would ruin us, all of us, if we lost you. Don't you get it?"

Hudson walked up behind Jay and placed a hand on his back, causing him to sit up and roll off me, allowing Hudson to sit on the other side of me. "What else happened?"

"That's the odd part, she left when Parker showed up, not willing to be seen by him or anyone else," I answered, sitting up and crossing my legs. "She did say that she thought Phoebe would last less than a week, even if she was perfect in every other way. I took a chance and threatened Mozog, but she just laughed it off telling me that it wasn't wise to threaten something I too could lose."

"It would seem she wasn't supposed to be approaching you on her own, makes me wonder how weak she really is in a normal human," Hudson mused. "Her threat seems to be more of an eye for an eye situation so I can understand why you want them here when both Lilith and the Dark Lord are after them."

The sound of people returning clued us into the fact that everyone was back.

"Can we talk about this more in the car? We do have a two hour drive to get to Chicago," I requested.

They both nodded in agreement and they left the room. Jay grabbed the bag with all our stuff in it, caught my hand, and quickly followed the others. Gathering once more in the living room, I gave each of my family members a hug and held them as tightly as I could.

"This house is yours to use as you like. Food is stocked, there's a movie room upstairs, bathrooms have been cleared out, oh and all the rooms but mine and Cami's are open to use," I explained. "I don't know how long we'll be gone but I'll make sure that Cami is kept in the loop if we can't update you ourselves. I love you guys and I'm doing everything I can to end this as quickly as I can."

"We love you too, Ladybug, be safe and come back to us as quickly as you can," Mom said, giving me one more hug and a kiss on the forehead.

Then Dad grabbed my shoulders and looked me right in the eye. "You give 'em hell, you hear me?"

"Oh I will," I assured him. "Be safe Dad, promise me you won't leave here until I tell you it's safe to do so."

"All right baby girl, we'll stay here in your cushy mansion safe and sound," Dad promised.

Brayden came up and took my hand, leading me out of

the house, knowing it would be too hard for me to do it on my own. Out of all the men in my life, he understood my connection to my family the best but I was learning that each of them had a special connection to me, in one way or another, that the others didn't. We all piled into the car and headed out for Chicago, where the Elementi hub was waiting for us with all the various reports and things that Jay rattled off to them.

"Do you want to stop for food?" Brayden asked me.

"Am I allowed to say no?" I asked in a teasing tone.

"No," Jay and Micah both said at the same time.

That got a chuckle out of me. "Yeah, I didn't think so, if you guys want to stop along the way I'm fine, otherwise we can eat in Evanston."

"I think it would be better for us to get closer to the hub than to risk stopping out here in the open," Jay reasoned.

"Are we worried about getting caught in the open?" Micah asked, turning to look at me from the front seat.

The bastard set me up with that comment so I would have to tell them about Lilith. "I might have had a visit from the Mother of All."

"What the actual fuck," Micah exclaimed, almost leaping out of his seat to shake me. "How are we just hearing about this now?"

Letting out a heavy sigh, I leaned back in my seat staring up at the roof of the car preparing to repeat myself. "All she wanted was to talk and taunt me in Phoebe's body. She took great delight in telling me that Phoebe was evil and even then, wouldn't last her a week with how weak she was, being a human. She wanted to follow the Dark Lord's plan and use me as her human suit."

"And what, she just let you walk away?" Micah sneered.

Sitting up, I opened my mouth to yell at him, but

instead I just screamed at a massive truck that came around a blind corner slamming into the front of the SUV sending us rolling into a corn field. The world was a blur of yelling, crunching metal, glass shattering, and getting slammed into the side of the car so hard I was knocked out cold.

CHAPTER 27

LAILAH

"She better not be fucking damaged, I told you not to hit them going that fast," an angry voice snapped.

"Fuck off, Bill," another grumbled. "We had to make sure the rest of them were taken out so we didn't have to fight them all. It worked and all of them are alive, just like we were ordered to make sure happened. Now, if you're done being a little bitch, could you help me get them in the truck?"

I felt myself being lifted and I groaned at the movement. My head was pounding, and everything felt sore-- almost like I was hit by a truck. As much as I wanted to stay conscious to figure out what was going on or if the others were okay, that was dashed when they chucked me into the back of the truck. I landed with a thud on the hard metal surface, then was shoved deeper until I thudded into something solid and unmoving making me whimper.

"You trying to get yourself killed?"

"Look she made a noise, it's fine, she'll live. Now we need to tie up these assholes so they can't use their magical weapons to get free."

"If we get in trouble just know I am completely fine throwing you under the bus. That Lilith bitch is fucking crazy. I'm not going to be one of her punching bags when things don't go her way."

"Pussy."

"Yeah--but still alive."

The sound of another body getting tossed in and shoved should have warned me what was coming but I didn't have the ability to move, let alone protect myself. When the body slammed into me, I had the glimmer of a thought that it was Brayden and he was alive, before I was lost to the world again.

As my senses started returning, hearing was the first to arrive, having been drawn out by the talking that was happening around me.

"Tell me, when I said that I needed her alive and unharmed was I not clear enough?" a female voice purred dangerously. "Because it seems that she is alive—just barely, which was not the agreement!"

"Listen bitch, I don't know who you think you are, but we did the job for you, now give us the rest of the money you owe us," one of the male voices from before snarled.

A maniacal laugh seemed to burst out from the woman. "You think I'm going to pay you after you failed to do the job? Oh, you poor foolish human, no I have something better in mind for you."

I finally got the energy to attempt to open my eyes, only to be greeted by the sight of Lilith cutting off a man's head with her claws to have it roll over towards me. Lilith turned to face me, but I snapped my eyes closed so she still thought that I was unconscious, trying to figure out what the hell happened to us. It was clear that Lilith was behind this, but it didn't really explain why she attacked us the way she did. How had she known we left the house? Did they have someone watching? Why didn't she take the guys when they left with my parents?

"Come now Lailah, I know you're awake," Lilith chided me as a claw ran along the side of my face. "Thankfully, there is no lasting damage other than a concussion and some bruising. I did tell them to be gentle with you, I promise." Resigning myself to the situation, I opened my eyes to see her face right in front of mine. A smile bloomed across her face. "There you are, it's good to see there wasn't any brain damage."

Gripping my shoulders, she pulled me into a sitting position leaning me against the wall, so I didn't have to hold myself up. I took a moment to look around the space and found that we were in another type of factory, but this one looked like it's been abandoned for quite some time. Dust and cobwebs covered every flat surface and dust motes floated through the air on a breeze that was flowing through the space from some unknown source.

"The place isn't much to look at but, *someone,* was responsible for exposing our last base of operations to the Elementi," Lilith sighed, as she stood. "Now we're stuck in this shit hole."

Groaning as I lifted a hand to press to my pounding head, I searched for the guys. Something told me I knew they had been brought with us, but everything was so fuzzy I couldn't remember why I knew that. Nothing about the area I could see told me that I was correct in thinking that, seeing as the only other person around was the dead man whose detached head was staring at me. *Why wasn't that bothering me more? It's not normal to have zero reaction to a severed head with blood leaking out of it...right?*

"Where are they," I croaked out.

"Hmm?"

"The others. Where are they?"

A look of understanding appeared on her face as if she'd all but forgotten about them. "Oh them, they're alive."

"That's not what I asked. Where are they?"

Letting out a huff, Lilith put her hands on her hips. "Well, if I tell you that, then you'll go find them and I can't have you doing that. You're already fully Bonded to four of them, but thankfully I got the last one to break his Oath so there's still a chance I can make this work."

"You did that on purpose?" I snapped, anger coursing through my body.

Lilith clicked her tongue at me. "If you Bonded with all of them, then I wouldn't be able to use your body. Just because the Dark Lord was leaving you alone for the past few months, doesn't mean he wasn't keeping an eye on you. You hold a part of him inside you. It's like a GPS for him to find you wherever and whenever he wants to. His plan to turn you into my conduit didn't work, so I had to come up with one of my own once I knew who all the players were. The knight who is ruled by his heart was the easiest to go after, since throughout history they are known to be fickle."

"Mozog didn't seem to know who Phoebe was though, I heard him talking to the person who brought her to the power plant," I argued. "How could you have set this all up without his help?"

"God, you're kind of stupid aren't you," Lilith sniffed. "He has been supplying me bodies for months while I set this in motion. Some were more useful than others, but I worked with what I had to get the job done right. Phoebe got the internship and came out here, where she met your brother who was a total sucker for a woman with major daddy issues. It was easy enough to get them to fall for each other, with some influence on our part." Lilith tapped her chin as she thought about something. "Personally, I wanted the jaded fire knight to be the one to break your heart. I set up everything up, but I underestimated how much he really loved you."

"Micah, what does he have to do with this?"

"Did you really think his aunt was smart enough to pull a move like changing the one major thing required for him to take over the trust and other investments?" Lilith shot back.

I frowned at that.

"Oh my, did he not tell you that he had to be married? It used to be that he had to graduate college to get access to the full trust and ownership of the businesses, but someone changed things and got the board to vote. They felt that a wife would be better stability for Micah than an education and working his way up to the position of power. Little did they know, that dear sweet jaded Micah never wanted a wife or to be married, because it was just too painful for him if he ever lost another person he loved. Not to mention, the pain for said wife if he died on her." Now pacing, she chewed on her lip glancing at me and her watch. "I thought for sure it would be enough to send him running for the hills after seeing what a hot mess you were after what happened with the Dark Lord, but *nooo,* he had to go against the plan. Thank Satan I had backup plans for the other two you hadn't bonded with."

"You have a plan for Jay as well?"

Lilith rolled her eyes. "Come on girl keep up will you, I

know you smashed your brain, but really is it that hard to think like a demon?"

Other than myself, there wasn't much that Jay held with enough value to be swayed by... except for one other person. "What have you done with his mother?"

"See, it wasn't that hard to figure out," Lilith praised, clapping her hands. "His mother is lovely by the way, very sweet pure soul that one."

"Again, that doesn't tell me what you did to her."

"Can't you let me have a little fun with you? Once I take over your body, we won't get to talk like this, and for some odd reason I just find you fascinating." Glowering at her, she pouted and sighed. "Fine, be that way. Currently, she is spending some quality time with two of the Dark Lord's pet demons that he rules over. They can't really be trusted around large groups of humans. They tend to draw attention to themselves with how messy they slaughter them. On the other hand, they are the best at running the training camp preparing our new puppet soldiers to fight your Elementi forces. See once the Dark Lord and I join forces with my new body and powers, you'll give me then the world is ours!"

Over my dead body was that ever going to happen. Now that I knew her full agenda, I needed to come up with a plan to stop it from happening.

"Will you at least let me say goodbye to them?" I asked.

Lilith gave me a scathing look. "Don't try to play me, Lailah, we've already established you're not smart enough for that. Besides, there is no time. Mozog will be back with the last few things we need and then you'll become my personal puppet."

"How do you know this is going to work, when the Dark

Lord couldn't do it when we were next to your real body in Hell."

"That was the problem, he shouldn't have taken you to Hell to begin with," she stated. "But the biggest game changer is going to be that you'll invite me in all on your own."

"How do you figure?" I inquired, my heart rate picking up as dread filled my body.

Lilith flashed me a bright smile before squatting down before me. "Well, if you don't, then I'll just kill you all. If I can't get you to accept me, then I'm sure as hell not going to leave you alive to destroy us. This is the closest we've gotten to taking over the world and I'm not going to be locked away for another two thousand years."

While the Dark Lord was scary and gave me nightmares, Lilith was another level of unhinged, seeing absolutely no value in keeping things alive that didn't serve a purpose. Being her host was my purpose and if I couldn't do that, then better to be rid of me. The Dark Lord knew that I was worth more than just her puppet, was there a way that I could use that to my advantage? His blind love and obsession for Lilith was what drove this whole plot to take over the world in the first place. Would he listen to me if I told him he needed to lock her up again?

"How much time do I have?" I asked, catching her off guard.

"Oh about fifteen minutes or so... why?"

With a shrug of my shoulders, I leaned back to stare at the ceiling. "Just wrapping my head around not existing anymore."

"Dramatic much? You'll still know everything that's going on, you'll just be unable to do anything about it," Lilith explained. "As my puppet you're still intact, it's just the body that I destroy that kills them. For you though, it will be different since that won't happen, instead you'll just sit in the corner of your own mind and watch while I control everything."

Hearing this made me want to throw up. So not only would I be unable to stop the heinous acts she was going to use my body for, but I would be fully aware of it happening.

"Don't look so glum, once I get enough power, I'll give you back your body. It will be like your reward for helping us win the war."

"What happens to the guys during that time? You know if you kill them, you kill me, so are they going to be puppets as well?" I questioned.

"I'm leaving that up to the Dark Lord, he's in charge of the military, which is where they will be the most useful, of course. Although, I might keep them around to play with. It's been so long since I've had a good fuck and I can already tell your men have some talent."

Yup, I'm going to be ill if she keeps talking about that. Time to change the topic. "So, how is this going to work?"

"It's rather simple really, I just need you to hold Phoebe's hands and allow me to transfer my essence over to you. Since you'll be willing, already have the markings, and been exposed to the serum, it should be easy enough."

"Then what are we waiting on?" I pressed as an idea trickled into my brain.

"How much pain are you in? That can cloud the brain and make this worse for me when I enter your body. One of the downsides to being in a puppet is feeling unnecessary things like pain and other emotions. Mozog went to get drugs that would block those while we complete the process."

"The Mother of All is afraid of a little pain?" I challenged. "That doesn't seem right."

That seemed to do the trick. With strength that I knew Phoebe didn't possess, she picked me up by my throat and slammed me against the concrete wall. "Don't think you can get out of this by trying to make me kill you, Lailah. I might not have the same morals you do but you still serve a greater purpose."

"Well, if I wasn't in pain before, this sure isn't helping," I sassed, now that I'd gotten under her skin. "Seems like you might need to wait for the drugs after all, but I would make sure you give it the full thirty minutes to kick in. Wouldn't want you to be uncomfortable in your new body."

Snarling, she got right up in my face. "Stop talking or I'll rip out your tongue."

"Oh, can you grow it back? Seems like it would be hard to take over the world if you couldn't speak..."

Her hand whipped out and smacked me across the face, making me groan at the pain. "Do you want your life to end so quickly you'll force my hand? Let us not forget I have your lovers here and as long as they don't die, I can do whatever I want."

"So that means they're in the building then," I commented. "I hope you have some good guards watching them, because when they wake up and I'm not there, they will be out for your blood."

"Not if I control you first, they would never harm their precious Lailah."

"Sounds like maybe you should just get it over with then, the longer you wait the more time it gives them to get to me. With our Bond they can find me wherever I am, guess you could call it a failsafe for situations like this. We've already proved that the puppets you have around you aren't strong enough to handle us-- only Mozog is." I taunted, seeing the furry in her eyes as I kept pushing her.

Then something shifted as she came to her decision, letting me go so I dropped to my feet, only to crumble to the floor. Lilith dropped to her knees in front of me, cupping my face with both her hands before resting her forehead against mine.

"Once I have you under my control, the war is already lost and there's nothing you can do about it."

With that final statement, she thrust her power into me, making me gasp for air as my heart stopped beating and my lungs no longer drew air. This wasn't at all what she'd described, but I should have known better than to believe the devil in female form.

CHAPTER 28
BRAYDEN

"Brayden, come on man you need to wake up," Micah whispered harshly as he moved my arm.

Pain shot through my body at his touch making me sit up, eyes snapping open as I started to scream. Jay, who was behind me, wrapped a hand around my mouth to muffle the sound.

"I'm sorry man but you have to stay quiet," Micah cautioned, from where I could see him kneeling in front of me. "You dislocated your shoulder in the accident and we have to get it back in place. This is gonna hurt like a son of a bitch, but you need to keep it together man."

Accident? What accident is he talking about? Then in a series of flashes, I remembered the massive box truck that came out of nowhere and hit us. The image of Lailah screaming as she saw it coming at us, then everything became fuzzy until I got tossed into the back of the box truck with the others.

"Is everyone else alright? How's Lailah?" I asked as they started to work on getting my arm in the right position to put back in.

Micah looked at Jay over my shoulder and gave a slight shake of his head no. Then Micah made his move and the sickening sound of my bone popping back into my shoulder socket filled the space. Clenching my jaw at the pain, I was thankful that Jay was still behind me, because I wasn't sure if I was going to pass out or not.

"You were the last one to wake up, the rest of us started to get worried," Micah shared.

Glaring at him as he tied a ghetto sling around my wrist and neck to keep my arm somewhat stable, "So your solution was to put me in pain?"

"If we plan to get out of this fucking cell to get to our girl, then yeah—I'll do whatever needs to be done."

My hand shot out, grabbing Micah's shoulder before I truly registered what he said. "What the fuck did you just say?"

"Lilith has Lailah," Jay answered, making me whip my head around, which was not my best move since it made me light headed.

Groaning, I pulled my hand from Micah to try and stop the pounding in my skull. "Fucking hell, why did they have to hit us with a truck?"

Micah, being the asshole that he is, chuckled. "I mean it wasn't all that bad of a plan, seeing that it worked."

Slowly, I dropped my hand and looked around the dimly lit room we were in. Sure enough, it looked like a cell with a steel door, no windows, and only a single light bulb in the ceiling to shed light on us. Carefully, I scooched back to lean against the wall, taking in Jay's appearance with half his face covered in blood from cuts on his face. True to Jay's nature, he didn't even act like it bothered him in the slightest. Micah seemed to be fine, until I noticed that he wasn't bending his left leg at all. Then I spotted Hudson in the corner, shirtless with a nasty gash on his chest that he was trying to staunch with his shirt.

"We're lucky to be alive, you know that right?" I question Micah, not really sure he understood how bad this was.

Parker and Lailah had been able to handle things for a little while when they were attacked, but they were in good shape. Currently, we looked like we already lost the war and we had no idea what was happening to Lailah. When I reached for her, I didn't feel much other than she was in pain but with how I felt I wasn't surprised.

"Trust me when I say that we will continue to stay alive, because they want Lailah. Remember, if one of us dies it could take her down too, let alone all four of us," Micah argued. "I have a feeling someone will come to check on us soon, which is when we make our move."

"Right, solid plan there bro," I sassed. "Hudson's bleeding everywhere, I don't have use of my right arm, and you busted something in your leg. Tell me, how are we going to overpower anyone, let alone a whole demon army?"

Micah rolled his eyes at me as he sighed. "I forgot that pain makes you act like a bastard."

I opened my mouth to share my thoughts on that retort, when Hudson cut me off. "Would you two shut the fuck up? I refuse to sit here and play the victim when we need to get to Lailah." I shut my mouth so hard my teeth clicked, knowing he was right. "I think I have the bleeding stopped enough if you can do the rest Micah."

"You sure? I've never tried to do something like this before," Micah warned as he pulled himself over to Hudson.

"If there is any chance that I'm going to be useful, then you need to do it, or at least try," Hudson pointed out.

The moment Micah put his hand on Hudson's chest, I

knew what he was being asked to do. My stomach clenched at the thought of how much pain he was going to be in if this actually worked, and I had to admit he was a bigger man than me. There is no way I would have even thought of the idea of having Micah cauterize my wound for me.

"Wait," Jay called out, getting up and removing his black leather belt. "You might want to bite down on this, the last thing you need is to crack your teeth or hurt your jaw."

I gaped at Jay, envious of how calm he was about this whole situation, as Hudson took the belt and bit down on it and laid down on the floor, nodding for Micah to go ahead. I knew the moment it started to work as he screamed, his whole body going rigid as he did everything in his power to keep still and let Micah work. Now that it wasn't covered by a shirt, I could see how large the gash was, starting from his collarbone arching down to his ribs. Micah moved as quickly as he could, using two fingers to glide over the blood-slicked skin, sealing it up, filling the air with the smell of burning flesh. Not soon enough, Hudson passed out from the pain, as Micah finished up the last part of the wound. When he was done, he looked it over and touched up a few spots that were still bleeding but it had done the job—crude but effective. The room was silent as we listened to Hudson's even breathing, wanting to make sure he wasn't in too much distress. Just as we started to even consider relaxing, my whole body filled with mind numbing pain that I remembered from when Lailah was being tortured by the Dark Lord.

"Holy *fuck*," Micah roared in pain. "What the fucking hell is happening to us?"

"Lailah," I grunted. "They're trying to take her again."

"Brayden, what are the chances you can use your

powers to knock one of these walls down without crushing the rest of us?" Jay asked through gritted teeth. "I can use my wind to keep some of it at bay but if we can make the walls unstable it might work."

"Hell, I could melt the door," Micah offered.

"That will take too much time, this is faster," Jay countered.

I closed my eyes, trying to focus on my center where my powers slept, but the echo of Lailah's pain was too distracting. I needed to override it somehow. Turning to Jay, I looked him dead in the eye and made my request. "Punch me in the shoulder."

Without hesitation, Jay landed a solid hit right on my busted shoulder, shocking my body with enough pain for me to center myself in my own body. Using that pain, I thrust it into the ground on the side the door was farthest away from us. The ground started to rumble as I gripped it and yanked like I was ripping it from the earth, creating a fissure in the floor that the wall and door fell into. Knowing that we wouldn't be able to jump the gap with Micah's leg, I slammed it back together, causing the whole building to shudder and cracks to appear in the ceiling.

"We've got to move now, I don't know how long the ceiling will hold," I yelled, grabbing Micah's arm and pulling him up so he leaned on my good side and off his bad leg.

Jay grabbed Hudson, tossing him over his shoulder, and we moved as quickly as we could out of the room, moments before the whole thing caved in on itself. The fallen section opened up to the outside, letting me know that we weren't underground, which I was very thankful for, so we weren't buried alive. People came running from both ends of the hallway we were now in, but Micah tossed up a wall of fire, keeping them out of the way. This gave us the chance to climb through the rubble into the outside world, where we discovered we were in a section of a large factory.

"Don't stop, we need to get to Lailah," Jay barked charging forward. "She's in the main part of the building. I can feel it."

"What the hell are we going to do once we get there?" I demanded as I pulled Micah along as fast as we could.

Jay tossed me a look over his shoulder. "Kill the bitch and get our girl back, of course."

"Oh sure, it's that simple," I muttered following him.

"Don't be a little bitch, Brayden, you just busted us out of jail without killing us. I'd say our chances of getting out of this alive are way higher now," Micah pointed out.

Grunting my acknowledgement, I sped up even more to try and keep up with Jay, making Micah swear under his breath. "Don't be so dramatic, Micah."

"Very funny prick, I'll remember this the next time you ask someone to punch you."

"Let's hope we get through this so there is a next time," I grumbled, as Jay kicked in a door, leading us into the main part of the factory. "Into the lion's den we go."

CHAPTER 29

LAILAH

As the pain became my only existence, I instinctively reached out through my Bonds to the guys. In a small part of my brain, I knew this would hurt them as well, but once I grasped onto them I couldn't let go. Lilith's energy was like claws digging through my brain, trying to climb inside. I was taking the biggest risk of my life, but I knew deep in my soul that it would work not because I was Synergy-- no it had everything to do for the men I knew were trying to do everything within their power to get to me. Without them or my family, then there was nothing left in this world to save, but right now I was the only one who could do this and we wouldn't get another chance.

A gust of calming wind swirled around me like a warm hug and I knew Jay was trying to tell me to hold on. He was going to be so mad when he figured out what I was doing, but the way he felt about me was exactly how I felt about all of them. There was no way I would let them get turned into puppets to be used against this world we've been struggling to protect. No, I was going to take Lilith down, but to do it she had to let down her guard and having her within my body was as perfect a moment as I could ask for.

"Stop fighting me, Lailah," Lilith panted. "It's hard enough to get past all the Bonds you already have without you putting up a wall too."

Clinging to that feeling Jay sent me I tried to relax, open up my mind, and draw her in.

"Yes, that's it. Welcome me with open arms, Lailah, we will become one and do great things together," Lilith purred.

In an effort to calm my mind, I let my body sag against hers, wrapping my arms around her waist and letting her hold me up. Doing this, I could feel Phoebe's heart slowing much like my own was ,until they started to beat in sync. Lilith's power flooded me, but this time it felt more like slippery oil trying to sneak in every crack it could, trying to blanket me so nothing remained that she didn't cover. Finally, I was able to take a deep breath and that's when I felt her leave Phoebe completely, but she hadn't fully transferred to me.

Now was my chance.

I delved deeply and grabbed hold of my powers and yanked it free to flood my body, encasing Lilith's power in my own, then layered over it with each of my Bonded lovers. It was just like we'd done with the barrier around the house, only I used my own powers as the foundation instead of all of us, knowing it would be far stronger since it was coming from the source. I could hear her screaming in my head as she fought against my hold, but I held on tightly with an iron fist.

"Mother, I have returned."

Hearing Mozog's voice, Lilith thrashed within me like the snake she was, trying to get even a tendril of power free to contact her first born. It didn't matter, I'd locked the chains in place, keeping her well and truly trapped. Slowly, I opened my eyes and found Phoebe's lifeless body laying in my lap. Everything in me wanted to weep for her, to show how sad I felt about the whole situation, even if she'd meant to hurt my brother and Parker. The poor woman had been a victim as much as any of us, costing her life at the end of it all. Now she was free, never to be used again and I only hoped that she would find peace.

Languidly, I looked up from where I was on the floor to Mozog, once again dressed smartly in a suit. I reached a hand out to him and he dropped the bags he was holding to help me to my feet. "You're late."

"I'm sorry Mother, the knights seem to have caused a disturbance in the other section of the factory. With how wounded they are, it shouldn't be too much trouble to get them back under lock and key," he explained, watching me with a critical eye. "You were supposed to wait for me before you made the switch. It was reckless of you to make such a move without protection."

Even locked away, I could feel Lilith's anger at being scolded in such a way. If I was going to make sure Mozog believed I was being controlled by his Mother I needed to be convincing. Yanking my hand out of his, I slapped him in the face and without meaning to, I drew on her powers turning my nails into claws. Three deep slashes showed up on his cheek, making him hiss jerking back from me.

"You dare to speak to me that way?! I am the one who knows what is best with my own body and the puppet I choose to rule," I snapped. Kicking out at Phoebe's body, I sneered. "She was failing faster and you were *late,* do not make this my problem, Mozog."

Clutching his cheek, he dropped his head in submission. "I'm sorry, Mother, I didn't mean to question you, but we knew there was a chance she would fight you. It won't happen again."

"See that it doesn't," I commanded, brushing the dirt off my body. "Did you get what I asked for? It seems those idiots that were sent to do the job damaged her more than we originally thought. You know how much I detest feeling things in these meat puppets."

Picking up one of the bags he dropped, he pulled out a pill bottle and a bottle of some sort of coffee drink. As much as I detested coffee, if it was her favorite thing in the world to drink, then I would be more than happy to guzzle it with a smile. Yet like anyone, we can't help but give a reaction to things we don't like.

"That better not be for me," I stated, looking at the bottle with disgust. "Don't you know anything? To think *you* were my first born."

"No Mother it was for me, I got you your favorite and it should help settle you in this body as well," Mozog said, pulling out a bottle of red wine.

Why couldn't it have been the coffee? Other than the few times I've gone out with Cami, I don't drink or handle my liquor well. "Lucky for me, I won't have to adjust to a new body ever again, soon we'll win the war and I'll have my own back."

"Speaking of which, I need to reach out to the Dark Lord and let him know that we no longer need the knight's mother. The less loose ends we have, the better."

It was an odd feeling to have Lilith's consciousness lurking in the back of my mind feeding me emotions and information. The more my power latched onto her it created a stronger bond with us as well, giving me clues. Then I found the perfect reason to have to drink the wine.

"Indeed," I mused. "I want to clean up and change before the wine, this girl had such a terrible sense of fashion. Before all that, we need to make sure that her boy toys have been dealt with. There's no way I could relax without knowing they are safe in a padded room, I can't lose this body."

The sound of a scuffle was coming from the other side of the large room we were in and when I checked my connection, I knew it was the boys.

"Seems they are coming to you," Mozog pointed out. "Once they see you own this body, I believe they will fall in line easily."

"Don't count on it, I doubt they're very bright... she wasn't."

Mozog let out a huff of laughter at that, as the doors to the room burst open and there stood my four boys. They were bloody, battered, and bruised but they were alive before my eyes. What more could I ask for?

"You're too late knights," Mozog called out to them. "Your Synergy has been taken from you and now serves Lilith as her conduit."

The look of fury on their faces as they hobbled their way over to us made my heart ache.

"Like we would believe a fucking demon," Micah growled. "How do we know you aren't lying to keep us from attacking?"

"Our connection to her is still strong, I can't even feel Lilith in her," Hudson added, talking more to Micah than either of us.

"Foolish knights, she isn't dead. Lilith has just taken over control and we need you alive because of that connection you have with her." Mozog said as he shoved his hand into his pockets, completely relaxed.

My plan had been to hold the ruse up long enough to find them so we could fight Mozog together, but seeing them told me they wouldn't be strong enough. This left the matter to me. Lilith was more than able to take on her son, but I wanted to make sure the bastard couldn't come back in another body. He needed to be dead for good, just like Dantalion was now.

Demon puppets poured into the room ready to capture my men, but I thrust out with Lilith's power and knocked them all away. "Don't touch them!" I snarled. "If you kill one of them you risk my safety, we will deal with this, since you clearly can't handle the simplest of tasks."

Lilith tried to use that moment to wriggle free from my hold, but I drew from the guys slamming another chain around her prison. When this happened, they all snapped their heads to look at me, eyes wide with confusion and fear. They believed that now Lilith could use their powers just like I could, causing Brayden to lose that glimmer of hope he'd had in his gaze. *Oh, I was going to be in so much trouble when this was over.*

"Mother you need to trust they won't let them get killed or you'll never be able to use them in the war," Mozog cautioned as the lesser demons left the room.

"It hasn't even been a half hour since I took over her body, don't you think you could give me a little time to adjust? I've been waiting for this since you and your brothers locked me away all those years ago. Forgive a mother having some caution," I snapped.

Mozog actually looked pained about the fact he'd locked his mother up. "You know I didn't help them, I tried to warn you, but you didn't listen."

"Enough," I said, tossing up a hand. "Let's not fight in front of the mortals."

Then a thought came to me from Lilith that I wasn't expecting. "Did you find the fifth one?"

"He got away, I don't know how he found us to begin with, but he's proved to be quite irritating," Mozog grumbled.

Turning to him giving the guys my back, I let out a heavy sigh. "Must I do everything myself?" With my back turned I gave them all a thumbs up and the okay hand gesture, hoping they would understand what it meant. "Remind me why I keep you around?"

"I suppose now that you have a permanent body, I will have to find a new purpose along with supplying bodies for the army."

Reaching out I placed my hand on his shoulder and ran my hand along it as I walked around behind him. "Yes... a new purpose."

Grabbing his head, I pulled on Lilith's power and snapped his neck, dropping him to the ground as I manifested my Sai and stabbed him in the heart, pouring my power into him. Now that I was Bonded to four of the five, my level of power had quadrupled so it didn't take as much out of me to send it right into the heart of the demon he was a conduit for. Even though the human part of him was dead, his eyes flew open and he grabbed my wrist, trying to pull the weapon out of his chest.

"How?" he gasped looking at me, realizing that the real me was in charge, not Lilith.

Leaning down, I whispered right in his ear. "I'm mother fucking Synergy and you attacked my family, for that you are not allowed to live in this word or any other."

With a final surge of power, I felt the connection sever as the demon died wherever he was in the depths of Hell. Lilith screamed in my head, fighting with everything she had to get free of my prison and rule over my body. She had every intention of killing my men in revenge, which would in turn kill me ,but her rage was so blinding she didn't care. A strong blow tossed me onto my back, gasping as I desperately kept my hold in her chains but without all five of them it might not be enough.

Then as if I was dreaming, Parker's handsome face appeared over me, fear bright in his eyes. "What do you need? How can I help?"

Unable to speak, I lifted a hand up hoping he would know what to do. Right away, he clasped mine with both of his and bent his head over it as if he was praying. Since we didn't have a connection any longer, touch made it far easier to draw on his power, giving me the upper hand on sealing Lilith away. Calling the guys through our Bonds, I soon felt them all touching me in some way, allowing me the ability to delve inside myself to deal with Lilith once and for all. This time, I was the one who pulled her into the darkness of the in-between, where the Dark Lord and I talked when he needed me.

———

"So, Lailah's not so dumb after all," Lilith mused from where she stood, bound in chains made from our combined powers. "What do you plan to do now, use me like I planned to use you?"

I can't deny the thought crossed my mind when I felt the connection I had with her in my own mind, but I also knew she would fight me forever. She'd waited thousands of years to get out. Dealing with me would be a piece of cake and I couldn't risk her taking me over.

"No Lil, I plan to end you for good," I announced.

Lilith tossed back her head and cackled like I'd told her the best joke she'd ever heard. "Oh, really now? How do you plan to do that? You aren't strong enough without your bond to Parker to manage killing the Dark Lord, let alone me."

"See I don't plan on killing you," I corrected. Reaching to her powers, I brought us right down into Hell where we stood next to the altar and where her body lay. "Now, the only good part about sharing a brain with you has been the fact that I could pick up on a few things. See, the Dark Lord is actually one of the Princes of hell and you're right, I don't have the power to kill him or you, but you know who does? The other Princes of hell, and they warned you that if you pulled shit like this again you would be killed, as an example of trying to overthrow them."

"You won't survive an encounter with the Princes of Hell," Lilith sneered.

"Which is why I'm going to sever our connection and leave you here with a lovely beacon of the pure power of Synergy. Nothing gets their attention faster than that of an angel, and I'm the closest thing to an angel as you can get in the bowels of Hell," I explained as I drew a ball of my power to place over her.

It was at this moment that Lilith started to panic. "Wait, we can come to some sort of deal, I know we can. See how useful I've been to you? Think of all we could do together."

"If our time together has taught me anything, it's to never trust the word of a demon... they always lie." With that, I tossed my ball of energy right in her face, severing the connection she had with me in my mind.

"This isn't the end, Synergy, I will find a way to take everything you have from you. The Dark Lord won't let this slide, with me gone there is no more use for you to him, I was the reason he kept you alive!" She screamed as I grabbed my Bonds and yanked myself back to the world of the living, leaving her trapped to face the consequences of her choices.

Karma's a bitch, and even the mother of demons has to pay for what she's done in the world.

CHAPTER 30

LAILAH

My eyes blinked open to the sight of all five of my knights leaning over me with worried expressions. Tugging on whoever's hand I was holding, which turned out to be Parker, I sat up with a groan. My body was beat to hell and back—literally. "She's gone."

All of them seemed to release a breath they'd been holding, as their shoulders sagged and they relaxed slightly.

"Now, we just need to find a way to get out of this shit hole," I muttered.

Parker cleared his throat, drawing our attention. "I have a car hidden not too far from here."

"That's great dick-munch, but what are we going to do with all the demons lurking around on the property?" Micah demanded.

As tired as I was from everything that's happened so far, I knew the answer. "We have to send the demons back."

"That will kill everyone." Brayden argued.

"I know..." I whispered, covering my face with my hands.

"She's right though," Jay spoke up. "If we fought our

way out of here it would kill them, maybe not all of them, but most. Then what? We just leave them to their own devices until the Elementi comes to kill them?"

Brayden opened his mouth to speak, but then thought about what Jay said and closed his mouth, hanging his head in defeat.

"If I can make a barrier like the one back home, it will force out any demons inside its walls. It will be painless for the human and who knows, they might not die," I hedged.

"We don't really have a choice, they will die one way or another. Better to have us do it and know it was done as humanly as we can," Hudson concluded.

Shifting so I was on my knees, I took a deep breath and closed my eyes. "Alright I'm gonna need all of you to touch me for this to work with how tired I am."

"Even *him*," Micah growled.

"Yes, it's harder to do this with no connection at all," I sighed.

Once they were all in contact with me again, I started the process, but I did it the same way I did for Lilith and put my power as the foundation. The layers went smoother than it had back home, but it might be because I've now done it and the second time is easier. Only when I got to the last layer using Parker's energy, did I have trouble working with it. Each time I held onto it and tried to pull it over the others it seemed to rip, leaving holes that I needed to go back and patch up, almost as if it was a representation of our personal struggles. Finally, I managed to get it how I needed it before I thrust it into the ground, putting my intention behind it and shaking the whole building around us in a much more visual example of what we did before. Then the air started to fill with screaming, as demons were ejected out of the humans they were living in. It was as if the gates of Hell opened wide, ready to receive them hurtled out of this existence back where they came from. Unlike the barrier at home, I wasn't leaving it permanently, this was only to exist for as long as I held it, which was getting harder and harder with how maxed out I was.

"Lailah, you need to let go," Parker demanded. "Your nose is bleeding and you're pale as a ghost, please Trouble, let the barrier go."

Gritting my teeth, I held on for a few moments longer, until I felt the last demon getting thrown from its host. The second I released it, I collapsed panting and sweating like I'd run a marathon.

"Don't touch her," Hudson snapped as I felt an arm wrap around my shoulders.

"You guys are beat to hell. Would you trust yourself to carry her two miles back to where my car is?" Parker challenged as he slipped another arm under my legs. "Yeah, I didn't think so. Micah needs more than Brayden to help him and Hudson, it's a miracle that you're even conscious right now with how much blood you probably lost with a gash like that."

"Please, can we just get out of here?" I begged, really wanting to take a shower to wash off all the death that I'd just experienced, in an effort to keep from having a mental breakdown about it.

The guys all scowled at me in Parker's arms but didn't say anything more.

The way back to where Parker hid the car was much farther than two miles, but we managed. Thankfully, it was a Suburban and we could all fit in it and by the looks of it he'd been planning to sleep in the back of it. It reminded me of what Mozog said about Parker showing up here and causing trouble for them. Had he been planning on dealing with all this himself? Quickly, I shook myself out of worrying about it, not having the energy to process it all. We did discover that the factory was a food processing plant just outside of Madison, that got shut down when the company went under. The drive took about an hour to get back home but it was over in the blink of an eye, since Hudson and I snuggled up and fell right to sleep.

"Angel, we're home," Brayden called softly, running his hand up and down my arm.

Groaning in irritation for being woken up, I cracked an eye and looked out the windows just to be sure. Seeing that we were indeed home, I let Jay pull me up out of Hudson's arms and out of the SUV. Hudson took his time, but he managed to get out on his own, wearing a purple shirt that Parker had given him. My gaze shifted to where Parker still sat behind the wheel making no move to stay, even going so far as to keep the engine running.

"Thank you for being there," I said when he looked back at me through the rearview mirror.

Turning to face me so I could see his whole face, he responded. "Words are fleeting but actions are permanent. I know I still have a lot of work to do to fix this, but I will do everything in my power to try, until you tell me there is no hope for us."

Unable to say anything, I just nodded and let Jay pull me away from him to head into the house as he pulled out of the drive.

"While you were sleeping, I called the Elementi and they are going to the plant now to retrieve all the bodies so that their families can be notified. They are going to say it was a cult that performed mass suicide to prove some political point," Jay shared. "This way the families will have closure and can bury their loved ones."

Hearing him say that made me realize something. "Jay."

Stopping, he looked at me with a questioning brow. "There is a lot that I learned from sharing a brain with Lilith, things that I will be more than happy to share with you all later. But there's something we have to deal with right away."

"Beautiful, I'm sure it can wait until we get in the house at least."

"No Jay, it can't," I demanded. "The demons have your Mother..."

The end!
Rescuing Air coming 2022

ABOUT THE AUTHOR

International Best Seller Elizabeth Knight, has been writing and telling stories as a hobby for years, but wasn't sure it would make a living. After her other job was shut down due to the pandemic she was encouraged to take her writing more seriously. So she published her first reverse harem Discovering Synergy April 2020. Since then Elizabeth has written prolifically and is constantly exploring new genres and ideas, putting her own twist on things. It's incredibly hard work, but she's never been happier than when she sits down at her desk with new imaginary best friends to share with us all.

If you'd like to stay in the know, then sign up for her newsletter:

Sign Up Here
https://geni.us/EKLinks

ALSO BY

Omegaverse

Knot All Is

Knot All Is Lost Duet - Complete

Knot All Is Ruined Duet - Complete

Sunshine & Rainbows Omegaverse

Bailey-Rose duet:

Clouds & Daydreams + Petals & Promises

Lyra/Eli duet:

Knot Now Knot Ever + Yes Now Yes Forever

Mafia Royalty Shared World

Caprioni Queen

Glitter & Guns

Blood & Heartache

Revenge & Truth

Love & Power

Gun Runner Princess

One For The Money

Two For The Show

Complete Series

<u>Hidden Empire Series</u>

Two Tricks

Three Tricks

Four Tricks

More Tricks

Our Tricks

<u>Hidden Empire Novel</u>

Harper's Renegades

[Read after Four Tricks for best series context]

Omega Assassin

Dual Nature

Hidden Nature

Perfect Nature

-

<u>Hope Series</u>

Hidden Hope

Claiming Hope

Defending Hope

Obtaining Hope

-

Standalones

Nicolette - MC Feline Shifter Story

Lying Lainey - Dark Omegaverse

Books Not in Kindle Unlimited

<u>Elementi Series</u>

Discovering Synergy

Refining Earth

Liberating Water

Taming Fire

Rescuing Air

<u>Mercenary Queen Series</u>

Birthright

Dragon Queen

Forgotten Throne

The Final Battle

www.ingramcontent.com/pod-product-compliance
Lightning Source LLC
Chambersburg PA
CBHW060259310726
48976CB00007B/2135